Hiking Sticks, Hawks, and Homicide

A Riley Creek Mystery

Mary Lucal

This is a work of fiction. Similarities to real people, places, or events are entirely coincidental.

HIKING STICKS, HAWKS, AND HOMICIDE

First edition. October 1, 2022.

Copyright © 2022 Mary Lucal.

Written by Mary Lucal.

Chapter One

As Martha Sloane emerged from her well-worn Subaru station wagon, she quickly took in the piles of leaves dotting the roadside and blowing in swirls around the side yard of Aunt Lorna's cottage. Glancing up at the familiar wraparound porch, Martha felt a sense of relief tinged with melancholy. She was relieved to finally have arrived at the closest place to home she'd ever known, yet full of sadness because the person that made it home was no longer there to greet her. Aunt Lorna, just seventy years old, had died from a massive heart attack and been found face down in her flowerbeds five days ago. Martha was here to say goodbye to her, goodbye to Riley Creek, and return to Boston as soon as possible.

Martha had left the city around lunchtime the previous day, but now that she'd arrived, the whole drive was nothing but a blur. You had to pay attention to get to Riley Creek, but as usual her muscle memory had steered her home. Nestled in the Paris Mountains, it was a rugged area in southern Tennessee that was hard enough to get to that it escaped the throngs of tourists that flocked to the Great Smoky Mountains National Park. Martha always knew she was close to Riley Creek when her spotty cell service became nearly non-existent.

Martha had carefully calculated how many days she would need to settle affairs here and be back at work at Berry College; she'd estimated seven.

Clock starts now, she told herself with a deep breath and a quick glance at the time on her iPhone.

Martha had been leaning on the doorframe of the car and contemplating where to start, but was brought back to the moment by the slow unwinding of the little dog on the passenger seat. The salt-and-pepper miniature schnauzer gingerly stepped over the stick shift and onto the indentation in the driver's seat. As she moved, she stretched each back leg as if she'd just awoken from her winter hibernation rather than a nap that stretched only as far back as the most recent rest area.

"Good afternoon, Penny," Martha said, letting her hand rest on the dog's head. "We finally made it." Martha leaned over to take the keys out of the ignition and Penny cautiously climbed down and out and headed to the green grass of the front yard. They had been traveling for over fifteen hours, stopping overnight at a Red Roof in Scranton, Pennsylvania. The night had not been too restful, with a thunderstorm buzzing the hotel's old metal window frames and too few blankets to make for a comfortable sleep. Instead of the buzzing hotel windows, Martha could now make out the din of the Little Pigeon River that flowed down from the Great Smoky Mountains and past the back of the cottage.

Just as Martha was contemplating whether it was more efficient to unload her car first and then open the front door or vice versa, she heard a distant, "Martha? Is that you?" in the slightly quaky voice of an older woman. At the sound of the voice, Penny took off like a much younger version of herself.

"Penny! Come back here!" Martha yelled as the dog ran down the street like a shooting black star. She ran straight into the arms of the voice's owner, who picked her up and stood outside her fenced yard and next to her mailbox about a half block down the street.

Martha jogged over as quickly as her clogs could carry her. "Mrs. Ritzenwaller! I'm so sorry. I should have put her on a leash."

"Don't be silly, child. Why put a dog on a leash on a beautiful fall day like this? And you know to call me Delores." Delores moved to pull Penny's muzzle away, halting the wet and beardy kisses Penny was planting on her. She leaned over and gently placed the little dog inside the fence and on the pathway up to her cottage, and Penny quickly went to work catching up on all of the doggie news of the day.

"Oh, my girl," said Delores, pulling off her work gloves and taking Martha into her arms for a long and heartfelt embrace. "I am sorrier than I can say. I don't know what we're going to do without her." They parted and Martha could see tears in Delores's eyes, which was enough to break the dam in her own heart. Tears began to fall in earnest now, and Martha did her best to soak them up into her shirtsleeves as Delores held each of her hands in hers.

Delores lived in a beautiful A-frame cottage, slightly larger than Aunt Lorna's, a small brown hip-high picket fence lining an eye-catching yard that featured sturdy Virginia pines, massive tulip trees, and naked but healthy redbuds, as well as artistically laid-out beds of native plants. The canvas tarp, rake and wheelbarrow that lay just to the side of the cottage made plain what Delores had been doing this cool October day.

Delores was as Martha always thought of her: eighty-something, sturdy and practical, yet elegant and well put together. She wore sensible tan work pants, a denim shirt that looked soft and lived-in, and a corduroy barn jacket with felted elbow patches, and had her gray hair done in a single long braid that disappeared down her back. Her only nod to whimsy was the bright purple gardening clogs covered in clusters of white daisies.

Delores, the town librarian when Martha was small and had spent her summers there, was as much a fixture in Riley Creek as Martha's Aunt Lorna had been. Many a day had Martha run down the steps of Aunt Lorna's front porch in her swimsuit and towel, heading the three blocks to the library to get a pile of books and sneak in a visit to Mrs. Ritzenwaller on the way to splash in the river. To this day, Martha had a hard time thinking of her as Delores.

It had been over eighteen months since Martha had visited Riley Creek. It had always been home, more than her own home with her parents in northern Ohio. Each time she'd visited in more recent years as an adult, it had been hard to head back to Boston. Now fifty-one years old, she'd lived and worked in Boston for almost thirty years, yet she hadn't ever really found it a place of true comfort as she had Riley Creek. The impersonal hustle and bustle of big city life—making work acquaintances who, it turned out, were only passing through on the way to their real lives—had made it difficult for Martha to establish roots. Losing Aunt Lorna made the ground shift beneath Martha's feet as she wondered what the future held. Now that Aunt Lorna was gone, where was home? Did she even have one?

She shook the thought from her mind. This was not the time for emotions. It was time to accomplish what she needed to do and get back.

Just as her mind became lost in a swell of emotions, Penny's high-pitched barking brought Martha back to the moment.

From around the back of the house came Mr. Ritzenwaller, as always walking perfectly erect and wearing a warm wool cap with the ear flaps folded up, wide-wale loden-green cords, a tan chamois shirt with a white turtleneck beneath, and comfortable-looking work boots. Walking close to him was Fritz, the couple's sturdy caramel-and-black German Shepherd, his ears pointing forward and on high alert. Penny, whose temperament was nowhere near as aloof, ran straight for Mr. Ritzenwaller, and then flopped down onto her back, eager for tummy rubs and to show Fritz that she was definitely *not* the boss. Mr. Ritzenwaller bent down and gave Penny some vigorous snuggles as Fritz heeled and watched, but once the tall man stood back up and uttered a low, "Free dog," Fritz and Penny immediately ran off in a jumping, snarling, happy dog reunion.

"Those two," Mr. Ritzenwaller muttered, shaking his head as he approached Martha with his hand outstretched.

Martha took his hand and gave it a firm squeeze. "Hello, Jimmy," she said, feeling no less relieved to see this old friend, even if he held his emotions closer than did his wife Delores. Martha knew the emotional expanse that lay under his reserved exterior, having spent many childhood days with him fishing at Audra Lake, learning to whittle, and even smoking a pipe once (that was still their secret). It bothered her not one bit that he preferred a shaken hand over a bear hug.

"Hello there, Martha. Wondered what time you'd roll in today."

"Well, I wanted to get here earlier, but I had so many work things to rearrange, this was the fastest I could manage. And I wanted to drive, so..." She let her voice trail off, unsure how to explain the need for her own car this trip when so many other times she'd flown into Knoxville and rented a car to enjoy the winding roads to Riley Creek. No Uber driver was going to take her to the secluded little village that was no more than a dot on most published maps.

Jimmy nodded in understanding. "I was just going to walk down to the shop to check on things if you want to join me," he said.

"I'd love to, but Penny probably needs a good stretch," Martha said regretfully. "Perhaps another time?"

"Penny is fine with me. I'll be out in the yard trying to corral these leaves for another hour at least," said Delores. "You two go on." She took out her gloves and slid them on. Martha eyed her, trying to gauge if she really wanted to have the little dog around or not. "*Go on*," stressed Delores. "It's no bother to have Penny around. It's good for Fritz. Reminds him he's actually a dog."

"Coffee should be ready. Shall we take some along?" Jimmy said, stiffening his shoulders at the nip in the air. Then he winked. "It's from the shop so it's the good stuff."

"Well... sure. I wouldn't expect you to drink anything else," said Martha. A cup of coffee might clear her head after the long day on the road. *Not to mention needing a clear head for all that I'm going to have to think through.*

"Give me half a sec," Jimmy said, and disappeared up the porch and into the house. The screen door slammed before the thick wooden door clunked behind him.

"He's as upset as I've ever seen him," said Delores, her voice lower. "Finding Lorna took a few years off of him, I'm fairly sure." She stared after her husband, shaking her head slightly, her brow furrowing with concern.

"Delores, I'm not totally clear on what happened when," said Martha. She wanted to know more about Aunt Lorna's death than the little that had been told to her over the phone four days ago, but wasn't sure how to ask or if she *could* ask without starting the tears streaming again. Everything since that day had been a blur, but now that she was in Riley Creek, she wanted to know every detail.

"You know Jimmy. He'll tell you what you want to know when you want to know it," Delores said quietly. "Only, please go easy on the asking. He may not show it, but he was very attached to your aunt and is heartbroken at losing her. We'd been neighbors for over thirty years and came to be close."

Before Martha's tears could start streaming again, the screen door slammed and Jimmy came down the front steps, a to-go cup in each hand. Martha's read "Reading is For the Birds" and featured a bluebird kicked back in a recliner, reading Shakespeare. Jimmy's light blue one read "Gone to the Dogz" and was covered in tiny paw prints of various shapes and sizes.

"C'mon," he said. Martha took a small sip as they turned to go, the coffee's powerful richness hitting her bloodstream like liquid lightning.

"Whoa," she said, shaking her head to help her taste buds recover.

"Italian Roost," Jimmy said simply, and Martha recalled that being the blend Aunt Lorna had sworn by when a jumpstart was needed. *There's a coffee for every occasion*, Aunt Lorna always said. Martha had never been a big coffee drinker, but this steamy brew hit the spot indeed.

The two walked along the roadside path toward the downtown of Riley Creek, though "downtown" might have been an overstatement. The outskirts of the village had started to grow (there was now a full-size Kroger's about a twenty-minute drive away, something that hadn't existed when Martha was a kid), but the main square of Riley Creek was still home to just the basics: the hardware shop, the bank and post office, Toad in a Hole Bookshop owned by crazy old Mr. Bennett, the market and various other small businesses that provided for the foothills community and the seasonal influx of tourists. Only one new storefront caught Martha's eye; Fins to Fur, from the looks of it a pet shop that had not been there the last time she'd visited.

Looking across the square, Martha spotted the familiar flapping yard flags that proudly—and loudly—announced Aunt Lorna's coffee and birding shop, Birds 'n' Beans, nestled between Silent Sisters antique shop and Threaded Needle needlework store. It was distinguished by the visually frantic activity going on in the front. In addition to around fifteen bird-themed house flags hanging from the top of the awning, birdhouses and birdfeeders dangled from its sides and swirled in the breeze. Three quaint bistro tables huddled together under it, as if trying to shelter from the wind, and a small wrought-iron fence enclosed the entire scene. Where the adjoining shops were austere and genteel, Lorna's shop was colorful, loud and bombastic. Martha reflected that everything looked normal, except for the darkened windows and what looked like a bunch of wilted daisies lying on the "Dirty Shoes Are For the Birds" mat just outside the front door.

As they made their way across the square, Jimmy gently guided Martha by the elbow to a bench with worn wooden slats that was oriented with a view toward Birds 'n' Beans.

"Sit down a minute?" he asked. Martha only had time to glimpse the *Charlton Riley, Father of Riley Creek 1918–1950* etched onto a brass plate before she eased down onto the memorial bench. "I know you probably need a moment before we go into the shop. Just to catch your breath."

Martha sat and admired the lovely fall baskets hanging from each light pole that encircled the square. Potato vine that had long since seen its best summer days and various shades of purple and green coleus tumbled down around the sphagnum moss that cradled each huge basket.

"And I'll tell you as much as you want to know," Jimmy said softly.

"Tell me everything," she said, taking a sip from her sturdy cup as if bracing herself with a shot of whiskey.

"OK," he said, in doing so honoring the no-nonsense way of coping with the world around them that they both shared. "I was walking Fritz down to Toad in a Hole around eight to get my usual newspaper, and it was Fritz who alerted me. He looked over toward Lorna's house and whined, which he rarely does. I glanced over and there she was, lying across the coneflowers out front. I recognized her gardening dungarees and ran as fast as I could, but she was already gone.

"It had to have been fast. I can tell you that her face registered no pain, and Delores and I stayed with her until the ambulance took her. They were very respectful with Lorna every step of the way."

The idea that Lorna had died in her front garden had felt somehow peaceful to Martha. *At least Jimmy and Delores were with her,* she thought. *What was I doing at that moment?* She knew the answer instantly; she had been working. Aunt Lorna had not even been on her mind at the time.

The tears came again and Martha was slightly embarrassed. Her relationship with Jimmy was one part familiarity, another part companionable silence. Crying didn't usually feature in the equation. But she had no choice; the tears had a mind of their own and kept on flowing.

"I can't take it in," Martha said, trying to keep her voice calm even as she wept. "She was strong as an ox and I had no sign she was unwell. She didn't say anything to me and I talked to her every Sunday!"

Well, almost every Sunday.

"Well, Martha, at my age, with as many friends and relatives as Delores and I have had pass away, you get used to things just happening. Sometimes because someone is ill, and sometimes because their time has come. Doesn't make it any easier, it just is. Why, half of the folks that were at our wedding are no longer around." Jimmy shook his head.

Martha sniffed. "She's all the family I had left. This all feels... surreal." On the edge of her mind was the similarly disorienting loss of her parents in a car accident the summer before her freshman year in college. It was Lorna who had comforted her and encouraged her to put one foot in front of the other.

"*My girl*," she'd always say, "*there's only one thing to do. You gotta keep on keepin' on.*"

And keep on Martha did. After the funeral, she had taken a semester's leave from college, and she and Lorna had stayed in Ohio for a few months to handle the sale of her parents' real estate holdings. Lorna, as executor of the estate, had eventually sent Martha back to stay in Riley Creek while she arranged the sale. When she returned to Riley Creek, Lorna had been driving a U-Haul truck with all the things from the house that Martha had wanted to keep.

The following weeks were spent setting up "her" room in Lorna's house. Lorna insisted on Martha arranging it however she liked so that she'd always have a comfortable place to come home to on college breaks. Martha had pushed to skip college and stay in Riley Creek; it had been Lorna who'd *insisted* through her own tears that Martha follow her dream of becoming a writer.

The money from the sale of her parents' house and rental properties was more than enough to cover the cost of college, but by then, Martha's dream had dissipated. The sparkle and promise that higher education had held for her was gone. Instead of studying to become a writer, she decided she needed to become more practical, to prepare for a life that could drop a boulder of disappointment and grief on her head at any moment. It was time to grow up and put her feet on the ground. She focused her writing talents on a degree in Communication Studies, accomplished in record time.

All through college, Martha confided to Lorna her every achievement, disappointment, and anything in between. Even though they'd been close during Martha's childhood, their bond grew unbreakable through those years. Having helped her fight through her grief and persist to graduation, Lorna later persuaded her to go on to graduate school. She had sent care package after care package while Martha finished her thesis and finally graduated with her Master's in Business Communications.

And it was Lorna who helped her pick up the pieces years later, after Brian.

Fast forward and she was now the Director of Communications for Berry College, a small school on the outskirts of Boston. Moving through a succession of progressively more responsible roles after graduating with her Master's, Martha perfected her no-nonsense approach. She was a keen listener, and by keeping an ear out, picked up on each organization's internal squabbles. She became adept at learning what made people tick, and used that knowledge to coax her various bosses toward business strategies that addressed the internal issues and created external success.

As she'd climbed the proverbial ladder, Aunt Lorna had been the single part of her life that connected Martha to her past, to a carefree time when all things were possible. And now she was gone.

Coming back to herself, sitting next to Jimmy, Martha realized that Lorna had also made sure she would never be completely alone. Jimmy and Delores had been constant fixtures at the dinner table; on the porch in the evenings; waiting with open arms every time Martha returned home from Boston. Though they were not blood relations, they had watched her grow up through her visits to Riley Creek as a child, and then as a young woman, and shared with her a love for Lorna. Those shared memories now became a shared grief.

"Now, now," said Jimmy, clearly not knowing the right words to ease her sense of loss. "You know Delores and I are here, and there are so many others that loved Lorna and are ready to help you with anything you need." Jimmy cleared his throat. "Do you want to go check the shop with me or would you rather wait for me here? Plenty of time for you to go in later. PJ and Helen thought it best to close for a few days, but I told them I'd keep an eye on things and pop around for the mail."

"I think I'll wait. I'm tired from the drive and don't think I can handle going in right now. Do you mind?"

"Sure. I'll be just a sec."

Martha watched Jimmy walk the few hundred yards to the storefront, stoop to pick up the flowers, and put the key in the door, all in one fluid up-and-down motion. He disappeared into the darkened store, and she could vaguely see his shape moving around in the light that streamed in through the picture windows that ran the length of the back wall.

Though Jimmy had almost three decades on her, Martha could easily see what might have drawn Delores to him. Not only was he quietly thoughtful and tall, but he still had a full head of hair, now moving nicely from dark brown into thick salt and pepper. He had been an aerospace engineer and had traveled a good deal during much of his and Delores's marriage, which could be why they had never had children. Martha briefly wondered at the motherly figure Delores had been to the many young readers in town, slipping snacks to those who looked hungry or giving a stern look to those who needed one.

In about five minutes, Jimmy was back out, with a handful of mail tucked under his arm. He locked the deadbolt in the glass front door and came strolling across the green to the bench where Martha sat, feeling the fall sun on her swollen face.

They walked in companionable silence the three blocks to the cottages, Jimmy offering to go get Penny and bring her back to Lorna's. While he headed up the small road, Martha opened the hatchback of her wagon and pulled out her Osprey backpack that doubled as a suitcase, an overstuffed canvas briefcase, and

Penny's pillows, water bowls, leash, and toys. It occurred to her, not for the first time, that Penny traveled with more accessories than *she* did.

She had just got everything in through the front door when Penny came bounding up the steps and pushed right past her into the house.

"Thanks, Jimmy," Martha said, turning to see him standing at the bottom of the steps. "I'll see you at the funeral." She'd been able to make most of the arrangements with Floyd Funeral Home over the phone. Her aunt had wanted to be buried in a plain pine box that would eventually decompose and, as the consummate gardener always said, *become one nice pile of compost.*

"We'd like to ride over with you if you'll have us," said Jimmy.

"I'd really appreciate the company," Martha said solemnly. With a nod, Jimmy turned and made his way home.

Turning into the cool, dark cottage, Martha immediately took in the familiar scent of Lorna's homeplace. It was some unknowable combination of pine (possibly from the white pine flooring original to the house's 1919 construction) and patchouli that Martha always teased her about.

"Guess it can't hurt to smell like a hippie," Lorna had said on more than one occasion. "After all, I did enjoy the sixties!" With this, she would pinch her thumb and index together in front of her mouth, pretending to inhale something less than legal. Martha doubted her sweet aunt had actually ever smoked marijuana (she never even drank alcohol to Martha's knowledge), but the gesture always left them giggling.

While Penny hurried all around, smelling each nook and cranny like it was her first time there, Martha moved her things into her old bedroom and returned to the back of the house to look out the huge sliding glass window down over the back yard and onto the river. The empty tripod for Aunt Lorna's precious Swarovski bird-spotting scope stood just inside the back door, a *Basics of Backyard Birding* book on the pine table nearby. Martha wondered briefly where the lightweight scope had gone. Perhaps her fastidious aunt had taken it down to have it cleaned. Lorna had been so good with birds, she could tell you not only that you were looking at a hawk, but what kind of hawk. The high-end scope had just helped her a bit.

The view from Aunt Lorna's French windows never failed to calm Martha. The wide expanse of un-manicured yard sloped gently before dipping down to the river. To the left of the yard, a huge weeping willow towered and swayed over a wooden porch swing hanging from its solid A-frame stand. Martha and her Aunt Lorna had spent many an evening swaying back and forth until it got so dark, the fireflies were dancing through the trees at the base of the mountains. When Martha had been little, Aunt Lorna sat alone on the bench, watching her splash in the river—when she wasn't in the water herself, teaching Martha to catch crayfish with a couple of plastic cups.

On the right side of the yard, at the top of the rise and nearer the cottage, clusters of small trees huddled: redbud, medium-sized maples, and the ubiquitous dogwoods that were native to this area and dotted the surrounding ridges. In the foreground was Aunt Lorna's pride and joy: her Bird Paradise. When Martha was small, a laundry line had hung here, stretched between two old iron Ts. But some time ago—perhaps in Martha's teens—Aunt Lorna had replaced this with a homemade wooden structure. It was nothing so fancy as a pergola, more of a structure made of eight-foot landscaping timbers stuck in the ground:

two in front, two behind and two stretching across the top. This had just been the beginning.

Aunt Lorna had planted a series of decorative grasses and butterfly bushes behind and around the structure, sprinkled three birdbaths of varying heights at the front and sides, and over the years had hung every conceivable style of birdfeeder from it. There was a large and colorful Rock City feeder with its familiar red sides and black roof; there were regular tube feeders of various colors and lengths (most covered in squirrel-proof wire to keep out these furry friends) and hummingbird feeders with their telltale red bases and glass bulb tops. Square green suet feeders were affixed haphazardly to the posts themselves. Martha smiled when she read the splintered and faded hand-painted wooden sign tacked to the top: *Every Birdie Welcome.*

Aunt Lorna had been an equal-opportunity wildlife feeder. To the left of Bird Paradise was what Martha imagined could be called Squirrel Paradise. While not as dramatic, the wrought iron corn plant, with an artistically rendered tassel adorning the top and realistic black iron leaves tipping down at the ends, featured perfectly straight spikes, angled up like the leaves. Impaled on each of these and running up and down the "plant" were husks of feed corn, long stripped of every kernel. At the base of the corn plant and leading out almost five feet in every direction were clumps of high daylilies, some the expected light orange and others fiery red and purple. Small paving stones made a tiny path between the plants so Lorna could refill the feeders and corn stand.

The entire scene of trees, grasses, flowers, and hardscape assembled over years and years with no apparent advance design was incredibly artistic. Resplendent with layers of color, shape, height, material and purpose, a perfectly serene whole blended each single element together. The only thing that was missing was food. Most of the feeders were empty and swinging in the breeze, having been unattended since Lorna's death days ago.

Martha slid open the glass door and walked to the spot where Aunt Lorna kept her stash of food hidden from view behind a wall of thick fountain grasses and butterfly bushes. Unlocking the front doors of the waist-high storage shed where her aunt's garden clutter was kept, she located around eight bags of different bird food, each food combination mixed for a particular species. Martha went back to Bird Paradise, pulled down each feeder and filled them accordingly: nyjer for finches, sunflower for nuthatches and cardinals, suet for chickadees and woodpeckers, and so on.

Closing up the shed after having hung the refilled feeders, she spotted next to it an industrial-sized clear plastic bag labeled "Ear Corn." Nearly empty, the bag was angled over on its side and almost tipping into a pile of leaves Aunt Lorna must have raked the week before. Leaning over, Martha pulled the bag open and toward her, and reached in to pull out some fresh cobs. As she yanked out a handful, her eye caught five white circles pressed against the outside of the bottom of the bag.

Her brain not computing what she was seeing, she pulled the bag clear of the leaves. The fresh scent of the fall day was quickly replaced by something far less pleasing. A bloated human hand peeked lazily out of the leaf pile, fingers cupped as if ready to receive a baby bird.

Chapter Two

The next several hours were a blur. Somehow, Martha had stumbled back into the house, called 911, then run with Penny to Jimmy and Delores's.

Jimmy barely took a moment before he'd said in a low voice to Fritz, "*Come.*" The dog immediately sensed the seriousness of his master's demeanor and was at the door and ready, while Penny wriggled in Delores's arms, clearly unhappy at being left out of the reconnaissance mission. Walking back to Lorna's house, Martha, Jimmy and a hyper-alert Fritz waited no more than two minutes before a siren drew near.

A white Crown Vic with forest-green *Riley Creek Police* scripted on the sides pulled into the gravel berm in front of the house. Expecting a tall, lanky officer, Martha was slightly taken aback when a short yet solidly built woman who looked to be in her mid-forties emerged. If she'd had another six inches in height, she would have been what Martha's father had called a "big-boned gal." Her most striking feature was her dark red hair, cut short and spiked up on top. She strode forward, one hand on her utility belt and the other outstretched in greeting.

"Mr. Ritzenwaller," she said, nodding in the tall man's direction. Looking slightly down at the German Shepherd who'd remained perfectly still with his big ears cocked forward, the officer said in a softer tone, "Hello, Fritz." Fritz shifted on his paws from one to the other, his big mouth salivating with pride at being included in the conversation.

"Officer Tomlinson," Jimmy replied. "This is Martha Sloane, Lorna's niece from Boston."

"Hello, Ms. Sloane. I'd heard you were in town. I'm very sorry for your loss." Officer Tomlinson extended her hand. Martha put out hers and was momentarily surprised by the tight grip of the shorter woman's handshake.

"Call me Martha. But I found a body..."

"Yes, that's what dispatch told me," said Officer Tomlinson, as if responding to a small child whom she was trying to focus. "Why don't you show me?"

They all rounded the house to the back and Martha stopped short, pointing beyond Bird Paradise.

"It's behind there and next to the shed. Under the leaves by the corn." Martha hated that adrenalin was making her babble.

"No need for either of you to come. Just stay here for a moment, please," said the sturdy officer, her voice deep and reassuring. Resting the palm of her right hand on the butt of her Glock sidearm, Officer Tomlinson clicked on a small Maglite with her left as she walked toward the shed. The fur on the ridge of Fritz's back stood straight up as he scented the air, detecting something not quite right. Night birds sounded as Officer Tomlinson disappeared behind the tall screen of grasses.

In a few minutes she emerged, her right hand stretched up to release the radio handset that was clipped to her shoulder, her expression serious. As Officer Tomlinson issued a few brusque commands, Martha felt a rush of lightheadedness and pulled on Jimmy's arm.

"Jimmy, why don't you take Ms. Sloane—Martha—into the cottage?" Officer Tomlinson suggested. "I've got backup coming and there's no need for her to stay out here."

Over the next several hours, police cars came and went, then an ambulance. At some point, Delores arrived to make coffee and shuttle cups to and fro to the many officers and technicians teeming around the front and back of the house. Though Martha couldn't have said when, Fritz had been taken home to entertain Penny.

Somewhere around midnight, the second to last police car rolled away. Officer Tomlinson came to Martha who was sitting on the couch with Delores.

"How are you doing?" she asked.

"I'm not sure," Martha replied. "I've never seen a body before."

"Well, as it's late, I've talked them into putting off your official statement for a day or two. The body has been removed and we're all done here for the time being. We've secured the scene in back, and there's no reason you can't stay here tonight. That is, if you feel up to it."

"Oh, Allison, thank you," said Delores, exhaustion sounding in her voice. "It's been a long day for Martha and she needs to rest."

Nodding in understanding, the officer said, "I'll get going, but I'd suggest some aspirin and a hot shower before bed. These kinds of things make sleep pretty hard to come by for most folks." Giving Delores a knowing look, she strode out the door, still as confident as she had been hours ago, but showing her own exhaustion through slightly stooped shoulders. Shortly afterwards, Delores and Martha heard her police car pull away.

A few moments later, Jimmy strode in with Penny under his arm. The moment her paws hit the wood floor, she was across the room and in Martha's lap. Martha had to admit it felt good to have the familiar terrier with her. Though the shock had worn off several cups of coffee ago, she felt completely depleted.

Delores rose and said, "Are you sure you won't stay with us? Or that you don't want me staying with you for tonight?"

"Honestly, Delores, I would say if I did, but right now, I just want to take Officer Tomlinson's advice and shower and go to bed. I'm as tired as I've ever been. I'll come and see you tomorrow, I promise. Thank you so much for staying with me through all of this."

Martha already felt bad that the elderly couple had had to stay up so late to support her. While she was not exactly at ease with the idea of her and Penny being alone in the house, she was darned if she was going to ask them to do any more for her this night. Bizarrely, all Martha could think about was climbing into bed with the Frances Fyfield mystery she was currently reading.

After a bit more tut-tutting, Delores was successfully led out the door by Jimmy, who always seemed to read Martha's state of mind without the need for any words. Martha scooped up Penny and headed up the stairs to her room. Forgoing the shower, she rummaged around to find her toothbrush, and was under the heavy quilts with her book in no time. Penny jumped up and made herself a little circle of warmth behind Martha's legs.

They both were asleep in minutes, the mystery lying barely touched atop the blankets.

The next morning found Martha refreshed, albeit groggy from the previous evening's events. Dressed in hoodie and sweatpants, she made her way to the first floor, Penny's nails clicking along beside her on the wooden stairs. She slid open one of the large glass doors onto the back deck to let the dog out, noting the police tape marking off a large square that encompassed Bird Paradise and the shed. The local birds did not seem to respect the instructions to stay away, and jays and starlings were gorging themselves on the platform feeder. She was going to call Penny away from the area, but didn't have the energy to try and corral the little ball of unexpended energy. Instead, she slid the door closed and turned her attention to the morning's first priority: coffee.

Compared to her Aunt Lorna, Martha knew precious little about coffee, but after rifling around in the kitchen, she found what she'd hoped for; a carafe left over from the night before. She knew Aunt Lorna would cringe at this, but hey! It was dark, it had caffeine, and it was already made. She warmed a full mug in the microwave until it was piping hot, found some creamer in the fridge that was still fresh, and stood sipping the brew.

The doors of the stainless-steel refrigerator were sprinkled with magnets commemorating various birding festivals, aged photographs of Martha herself as a freckled kid and, later, graduation pictures. There was also a list of about fifteen or so crossed-out names, some of which she recognized: *Margaret, Octavius, Carl, Helen, PJ—nice try, Me.* The last two were not crossed out. Probably a list of people Lorna was planning to have at some event or other. But what did the "PJ—nice try" mean?

Martha sat down at the thick and weathered wooden dining table to think. Before she'd gotten very far, Penny was lightly clawing the window to be let in. Martha had to find the dog kibble. *Heaven forbid she actually have to wait!* she thought wryly. Since Penny was a semi-frequent visitor to Aunt Lorna's, there was a sealed plastic tub of food for her under the sink, and Martha poured out a half cup into the white ceramic bowl announcing in cursive letters that it was "Penny's Bowl." The dog food was over a year old, but Martha figured she could get a fresh bag when she was out and about.

Aunt Lorna had spoiled Penny as much as she had spoiled Martha while she was growing up. A fleeting memory of Saturday mornings on the couch under an afghan, watching cartoons with pancakes on a TV tray, flashed through her mind.

"Those were the days," she mumbled, thinking on the new troubles that faced her since discovering the body last night. She planned to stay only long enough to provide a proper burial for Aunt Lorna and wrap up whatever needed wrapping up. To others, this might make her seem cold, but losing her parents had made her understand early on that there was nothing to be gained by giving in to grief. You had to push forward. Lorna had taught her that. And now that she only had herself to rely on, there was simply no time to lose herself to emotion. Time to keep on keepin' on.

Snapping herself back to the present, she took a sip of her coffee and registered that she was ravenous. She didn't expect there to be much in the house, but she was able to find some juice and granola; not quite her preferred breakfast of oatmeal and fresh berries, but it would have to do. She made a mental note to pop into the market later, jotting *dog food, oatmeal, milk* and *berries* into her iPhone.

As she scrounged around the kitchen, she noticed layers of dust coating shelves, expired food in the fridge, and sticky spots on the counters. The sun just peeking in the picture window over the farmhouse sink revealed streaks and splatters, she was surprised to see. This was very unlike Aunt Lorna, who typically liked "a place for everything and everything in its place." It was a saying that drove Martha crazy when she was a kid, but it had become such a habit to her that she now kept both her office and apartment as neat as pins. Her colleagues teased her about her OCD, but Martha knew that her orderliness was born right here in this cottage, handed down by a woman who had watched her share of Julia Child and took seriously the concept of *mise en place*, in her kitchen and in her life.

Now that Martha was more alert and observant than she had been the night before, her eyes took in the graying throw rugs, the dusty side tables, the dirt in the corners of the wooden floor. This was not Aunt Lorna's typical spick 'n' span housecleaning. What had gone on here? Had Aunt Lorna been sick and not told Martha?

Feeling puzzled and a tinge of guilt, Martha climbed the stairs to the bathroom. She couldn't really take everything in just now, so decided to shower and head down to the shop. Throwing on some jeans, turtleneck and a comfy fleece vest, Martha donned her clogs and settled Penny onto her pillow by the fireplace. At least for this first trip to the shop, she figured it might be easier to check things out without Miss Nosey Pants in tow. Penny turned on her side and let her head flop over the edge of the pillow, indicating that she was ready to be left behind just this once.

The morning air was nippy—Martha was glad she'd chosen a turtleneck—but the cold was bracing and restorative, kick-starting her brain as the coffee hadn't quite been able to do. It was only 8 a.m. and most homes were just waking up. A few had smoke coming from the chimneys, which gave the morning a cozy feel.

Maybe she'd make a fire tonight with the wood she'd spotted on the front porch log rack. There were no newspapers waiting for residents in robes to come retrieve them; Riley Creek was too far up in the mountains to be included on any delivery route. Even so, and with all that filled Martha's heart and brain, she was not immune to the promise of a new day this secluded mountain village provided.

Walking into the square, she glanced around, taking more time than she had yesterday to look over the familiar scene. All around, tall oaks and tulip trees rained down their rusty leaves, reminding Martha of the beautiful opening fall scene in the movie *Halloween*.

I may have found a body, but I'm no knife-wielding Jamie Lee Curtis, she thought.

The square resembled a hundred others in Small Town USA. While it didn't quite reach the perfection of a New England village scene, it was uniquely Riley Creek. Over time, the town had adapted to suit its residents' needs. A perfect example was Toad in a Hole, a compact bank with beautiful limestone columns converted into the village's own indie bookshop. The old Woolworth's was home to the town thrift shop. And, of course, there was the soda fountain that Aunt Lorna had converted into the "Beans" part of Birds 'n' Beans. The village seemed to know what its people needed and simply sprouted a new equally useful limb in place of the old.

Before she knew it, Martha had strolled along the left side of the square and come to Birds 'n' Beans. Instead of the darkness she had watched Jimmy Ritzenwaller go into yesterday, light came streaming out of the large glass windows and recorded birdsong sounded through small speakers set into the upper corners of the brick storefront. Taking a deep breath and pushing out a long exhale, Martha opened the door and went in.

Chapter Three

The first thing that assailed Martha was the rich, deep aroma of coffee. It was as spicy as a Moroccan bazaar and as warm as a bowl of chocolate pudding, and nearly made her weak at the knees. The second was PJ, who came flying out from behind the coffee counter, frilly apron around ample waist and owl-covered dishcloth over his shoulder.

"Oh, my dear. My poor dear. Come and sit. We've been waiting for you!" His commanding words softened by his empathetic eyes, PJ led her past the "Birds" part of the shop that took up the right-hand wall and consisted of pallets of seed, an entire wall of feeders, rows of books, and a display case of birding binoculars. As they made their way to the back of the store, Martha saw the eight tables with mismatched chairs that comprised the seating area for the "Beans" part of the business.

When Martha had asked Lorna once why she didn't just buy matching tables with chairs, her aunt replied, "People want to come in here and relax, feel like they're home without actually being home. Mismatched tables and chairs feel like home, but people don't have to think about the thousand little things they have to do. They can just drink coffee and watch the birds."

They certainly could. The tables were spread out in front of a solid glass wall, a feature that allowed customers to view the many different types of feeders on offer inside the store. Martha briefly took in the massive platform feeder that was the centerpiece of the whole display, set among tiny trees and herbaceous borders tumbling wildly around all four sides of the square enclosure. Benches sat in each corner. The overall effect was of a symmetrical yet free-spirited garden for the birds.

A few other shops backed onto this hidden garden, but Lorna's fellow shopkeepers had been more than happy to let Lorna tend what had formerly been an overgrown weed patch. Currently, the artfully placed feeders hosted a flicker or two: a female cardinal and some house finches were bustling around on the platform, making seed pieces fly in all directions onto the ground where grateful mourning doves tended to them.

A few familiar faces were coming over and filling the two tables that PJ had pushed together, but Martha was grateful PJ had been the first person to spot her. She was, in some ways, as much the heart of the shop as Aunt Lorna had been. The two had started the store together, with Aunt Lorna as owner in charge of the business end and PJ the warm hearth firing the spirit of the operation.

PJ was a study in contrasts. He (though he took no offense if referred to as "she") was short yet solid, with broad shoulders and a torso that best resembled a barrel. He wore a burgundy velour tracksuit and running shoes, accessorizing with rings on both hands: a simple thick gold band on his left ring finger; a delicate women's signet ring on the other hand's pinky; a silver ring with inset turquoise pieces on his index finger. His Apple watch sported a light-pink band, chosen no doubt to complement his tracksuit. PJ wore his curly dark-brown hair as he always did, tied in a long ponytail that went halfway down his back. Today, he had applied eyeliner and just a spot of rouge. That eyeliner was threatening to smudge as he tearily put a strong arm around Martha and saw her into a chair.

"Oh, child," he took one of the other chairs and reached out for Martha's hand, "I barely know the words to say, but it is just so *good* to have you here. How are you? What in the world happened yesterday? I mean, we heard through the grapevine, but what in the *world*?" He looked at her, brow wrinkled in concern.

"I'm not sure," said Martha, speaking honestly. "I'm not even sure I really understand what happened to Aunt Lorna, and now there's a dead body under the leaves in her backyard." It felt uncomfortable to share so much personal information with someone who was much more Lorna's friend than hers, but she held PJ's gaze.

"A body under the eaves? Oh dear!" This was delivered in a squeaky voice. Martha turned in her chair to see an elderly woman in a black dress and equally dark knitted wrap sitting at the next table, a white tea cup grasped in both hands just above the keyboard of her laptop.

"Under a pile of leaves, honey, not under the eaves," said PJ, his smile softening the edge of irritation in his voice.

"Oh..." The woman's voice trailed off, a troubled look moving her thick-lensed kitty-cat glasses a tad lower on the bridge of her nose. Martha didn't mind the eavesdropping; after all, this was Margaret Goodman, a fixture in the shop since its opening years ago. Aunt Lorna had always made sure to have the peppermint tea on hand that the retired high-school English teacher loved. Margaret was a kind lady, but seemed afraid of her own shadow.

Martha's brain registered the contrast between Margaret's glasses and her sleek MacBook Air. Right now, she was peeking at Martha from behind the screen of the laptop, wiggling her fingers in a shy greeting.

Wonder what she's working on? Martha thought randomly, recalling she wouldn't be here long enough to find out. *Grief and exhaustion do weird things to the brain.*

"Crank up your darn hearing aid, Marg. This is no time for everyone to have to repeat themselves. And it's no time to be a Pollyanna." Ethel Jean Sizemore, another of Lorna's friends, but one whose soft side was often hard to detect, flopped down into a seat at the table. The older woman nodded a sober greeting to Martha, who smiled tentatively in return.

"Girls, girls," said PJ sweetly. "Now is not the time to be snappy, either, Ethel Jean. And Margaret, I know that Lorna's death and yesterday's events are unsettling to all of us, but we need to be here for Martha right now. Martha, what can we do?" he asked, his kind brown eyes awaiting her response.

"I don't know," said Martha. "I told my college I would need a week down here to bury my aunt and sort out her affairs, but with finding a body in the backyard, I just don't know..."

"Yoo-hoo!" a voice sang from the open hallway connecting Birds 'n' Beans with Silent Sisters Antiques.

"Oh sheesh," grumbled Ethel Jean under her breath as she rolled her eyes skyward. "Here comes Miss Friggin' Sunshine."

"*There* you are, Martha!" exclaimed Mary Jane Noel, all six feet of her essentially oiled self flowing into a seat at the table with PJ and Martha—after she'd given Martha a quick squeeze around the shoulders. "How *are* you?"

"We were just asking Martha what we could do for her. I'm afraid that Lorna's death and the body in the backyard have thrown her for a complete loop."

Mary Jane pulled back and looked more closely at Martha. "Before we hear what happened, when did you last eat?"

"Oh, I had some granola earlier. And I think a sandwich last night, though I'm not totally sure."

"For heaven's sake, PJ, she's starving! Have you even had coffee this morning, Martha?"

"I warmed up the leftover carafe Mrs. Ritzenwaller made for the police and EMS guys last night." This brought a collective groan from those seated at the two tables. All of them—even mousy tea-drinking Margaret—knew that warmed-over coffee was sacrilege in this establishment, and certainly not sufficient for a cold post-dead-body morning.

"I've got just the thing," said PJ, bouncing up out of his chair and heading for the coffee bar. While he busied himself in the small kitchen area and cranked up the espresso machine, Mary Jane moved to sit next to Ethel Jean, who scooted over slightly as if not wanting to catch a dose of her sister's perpetual cheeriness.

"Do you know anything about the body in Lorna's backyard? My word, you poor thing. You actually found the person? The *dead* person?"

"I did, Mary Jane," Martha said sadly. "But I guess all I really saw was a dead person's hand in the leaf pile." A whimper came from Margaret's general direction. "And now I have to deal with a cottage that looks like it hasn't been cleaned in a month, my aunt's funeral tomorrow, and police who want to interview me." She put her head in her hands. This already heartbreaking trip to Riley Creek had gone from bad to worse. "And I have to be back at work in a week."

As if counting off the three challenges Martha had just listed, Mary Jane raised her index finger. "Well, I don't know what to say about the dead body, but we're surely all going to be at the funeral to support you"—here she raised her second finger—"and say goodbye to Lorna. And this ex-ER nurse"—finger three—"sure knows how to apply elbow grease. We'll help you clean up Lorna's cottage so it's spick 'n' span—right, team?"

She looked around. Margaret's head nodded enthusiastically on top of her skinny neck, her eyes wide. Ethel Jean's lips were pursed together, but she too nodded, albeit with a distinct lack of enthusiasm.

"And you can visit the police later," concluded Mary Jane.

"But who'll watch Silent Sisters tomorrow?" Martha asked, uncomfortable at these busy people doing so much for her. As if on cue, the shop's clock chimed a sharp *Birdy-Birdy-Birdy*, telling them all it was 10 a.m. Aunt Lorna had bought the clock when she first opened the store, and for years now, each hour had been announced by the call of one of twelve familiar species. Ten; northern cardinal.

"We can close for the day. We'll simply hang a sign that says *Closed for a Personal Matter*." Mary Jane glanced over at the doorway that led from the back of the coffee counter to her and Ethel Jean's antique shop. Ethel Jean looked up at the sky, as if willing a co-owner with an ounce of business sense to fall down from the heavens and into her lap. "And I know that Helen will want to help, too."

Helen Chelton, a part-time-employee-cum-gal-pal to Aunt Lorna, handled the "Birds" side of the business. She lived at the ranger station with her husband Don, a park ranger in Paris State Park about five miles deeper into the mountains than Riley Creek. Don and Helen led birding walks in the park, and fall was one of their busiest times, with leaf peepers coming through and birders wanting to get a peek at the area's many species.

Before Martha could respond, PJ arrived back at the table. "A Mexican mocha and a chocolate croissant. Just what the doctor ordered," he said. Martha stared down at the tall glass coffee mug in front of her and the whipped cream, chocolate shavings and cinnamon candies adorning the top of a delicious-smelling brew. "The pinch of cayenne in there and the double shot of espresso will perk you right up. It was one of Lorna's favorites and she used to treat herself to one after refilling all of the empty feeders in the winter."

That chore should get an award, thought Martha as she glanced out at the array of feeders. *There must be twenty-five out there*!

"Wow. After this, I'll need to take a run. Looks delish," she said, noticing Mary Jane eyeing the croissant and the tip of her tongue peeking out from between her lips.

"Oh, you're an athlete? I'm not sure Lorna ever mentioned that," said PJ.

"Oh sheesh, here we go," muttered Ethel Jean. A wide-eyed look from PJ sent out a clear message:

Stick a sock in it.

"I started running a few years ago, mostly on trails north of the city. I really don't do it much up in Boston unless I can get to the woods or the coast, which is rare these days with my job. Now that you mention it, I'm not even sure Aunt Lorna knew I'd taken it up." Martha felt another twinge as she realized that her calls home to Riley Creek of late had been brief. She'd been so wrapped up in her work, she had likely not shared as much with her aunt as she now wished she had.

She came back to the moment. "Right now, the most physical activity I get is with my bowling team." She waited for someone to laugh at the absurdity of a fifty-something woman with all the distractions of a big city spending her time at a bowling alley, waving her hand dismissively at the lack of response. "I know, I know. Imagine someone my age on a bowling team."

She looked up and noticed everyone gazing at PJ with their eyebrows slightly raised. PJ's eyes were twinkling as he twirled one of his gold rings.

"Martha, we sure wish you were staying around. I coach our co-ed any-age bowling team and we just lost a couple of players. We're short for this week's game." He looked down. Margaret crossed herself.

"Oh, you mean you LOST them, lost them?" asked Martha, a little too loudly for her own taste.

"Yes. Our team motto is '*It's Not How You Bowl, It's How You Roll.*' Anyone is welcome, no matter how old or young, as long as they want to have fun and get a little activity in. We do tend to have players cycle in and out for a variety of reasons. A few of our founding members passed away last year, and now we've lost Lorna..." Martha recalled Aunt Lorna mentioning going bowling once some time ago, but she hadn't realized she'd been a member of an actual team! Looked like Martha hadn't been the only one holding back information. "Anyway, we have a few slots to fill and would love to have you for as long as you're here."

"Maybe we oughta change our motto to '*Come On and Bowl Till You're in a Six Foot Hole*,'" Ethel Jean said snarkily. A few of the gang shot her a stinging glance, the only one causing Ethel Jean to retreat a bit being PJ's laser-like glare.

For a guy that wears makeup and a ring on every finger, he sure knows how to command a crowd, thought Martha. She reflected on how easy it would be to say yes, to escape for a while from the pressure cooker that awaited her back in Boston. She had worked hard to become Director of Communications at Berry College, and her boss, the President of the college, depended on her. Especially now, with the school facing a possible merger with a large nearby university, there was a lot on the line. She was here to bury her aunt, settle Lorna's bills, clean out the memory-filled cottage, put it on the market, and figure out how to sell Birds 'n' Beans. No more, no less. She had a job to go back to; an apartment, bills, a few friends; she had to stay focused on her life up north. A part of her cringed as she wondered if bills equaled a life, but she brushed those thoughts aside.

Focus, Martha, she thought. *It's about goals and execution, not bowling with a bunch of senior citizens.*

"I'd really love to, but I can't. I've got so much to do to get Aunt Lorna's affairs in order, then I've got to get back home." But again, that little voice in her head nagged.

Home? You call that home? You've never felt at home up there.

Martha felt more than heard their collective disappointment. "We understand, dear," PJ chimed. "You need to do what feels right to you—handle things here and move on. This place can't feel very good to you now, what with Lorna's passing and so many people asking questions about her..." PJ looked off into the distance, shaking his head slightly. As if on cue, the others took on similarly forlorn expressions.

Martha looked up. "Asking questions about Aunt Lorna? What do you mean?"

"Officer Tomlinson was in earlier today, asking about Lorna and whether she'd been acting out of character in the last while. And we all know she had," Ethel Jean stated brusquely as she reached into her cargo pants and pulled out a bandana. From the pocket of her fleece vest, she pulled out her cell phone and rubbed the screen vigorously with the bandana. "She hadn't been herself for a while, even saying no to walking the Talisman Trail with us to look for owls a couple weeks back."

That is *unusual*, thought Martha. The Talisman had been her aunt's favorite trail to walk for years. In fact, it was on the high part of this trail that Lorna had taught Martha to use a compass, and to identify countless wildflowers and birds and the tracks of various animals. Aunt Lorna *never* turned down a chance to walk Talisman.

"Let me read you a text I got from her a bit ago. That'll show you what I mean." Holding the phone up toward the window until she got decent reception, Ethel Jean scrolled through and found the exchange. "I asked her if she wanted to go find the barred owl that the Hot Spotters had seen the day before up on the high part of the trail. She texted no thanks. I said, are you OK? She said she just didn't feel like it. No explanation, no nothing. You know Lorna. Have you ever known her to say no to spotting an owl?" Ethel Jean shook her head.

"That *is* odd," said Martha. "We don't yet know what killed her; maybe she was sick and I didn't notice it. Like I said, her house isn't its usual spick 'n' span."

"Come to think of it, I noticed something myself." Margaret looked around the group, her eyes a little larger than usual. "It was my tea," she said tentatively. "Every Wednesday, I come in here to work for a few hours, and every Wednesday, Lorna would come and sit and chat with me. But the last couple of months, she gave me the wrong flavor of tea several times and never came to talk. I thought it odd, but I didn't want to pry. She just seemed... preoccupied."

As the group compared notes, it seemed that everyone could think of a recent unusual interaction with Lorna. Mary Jane even reminded PJ about Lorna forgetting to place some coffee bean orders for the store—something that was very un-Lorna.

"Martha, I don't want to upset you," said Mary Jane quietly. "You know Lorna was one of my dearest friends, but between her odd behavior, her passing, and now a dead body in her back-yard... well, it all seems a bit odd. We had to tell that to the police, and now they seem curious about Lorna's possible... connection to the dead body."

Quizzical, confused eyes stared all around Martha. Margaret hid behind her laptop, one eye peeping out from the edge of the open screen. Martha took all of this in, a deep sense of focus cutting through her shock.

"You know, I'm thinking about some of my last calls home. I'll admit that I was often preoccupied with my work, but Aunt Lorna didn't seem her happy-go-lucky self. I didn't think about it at the time; I suppose I chalked it up to leaf peeping season, which you all know always makes the shop extra busy. But when I put that together with what you are saying, and now a body in the backyard... something *was* up. There's no *way* my aunt had anything to do with that dead guy, but something was definitely going on. And I'm going to find out what. That's the *least* I can do for her. Oh, and count me in for that bowling game."

Martha drained the last sip of her spicy mocha, pushed back her chair, and marched defiantly to the door. As she glanced back, four sets of eyes were watching her. Then Ethel Jean settled her gaze on Mary Jane and spoke with a hint of a grin.

"Sister, I'd say that was a strike."

PJ's serious face broke into a twinkly smile. "My dears, I do believe that performance earned a spare."

Her heart warmed by her aunt's friends now extending their care and companionship to her, Martha let the door click shut behind her.

Chapter Four

The next morning, after staying in bed to read a chapter of her mystery, Martha stopped in the kitchen just long enough to brew some of the coffee PJ had handed her the day before in the familiar brown Birds 'n' Beans waxed bag, *Birder Blend—Medium roast—Medium body—Mild finish* written on it in his distinctive handwriting. Then she clipped on Penny's purple leash embroidered with the words "My Rescue Dog Saved Me" and set out to give the terrier a long walk as she'd hardly spent any time with her the day before.

Once they were ten or so minutes out of the village and heading into the woods, Martha unclipped the lead and let Penny investigate the many sights and smells of the hardwood forest floor. With the river on her left and the sun slanting through the towering oaks, ash and hickory trees, the chill of the morning easing off her worries, she pushed away a little of what today held in store for her: her beloved Aunt Lorna's funeral and her interview with the village police, and the start of her work in figuring out what was to become of all of her aunt's worldly possessions. She also had to figure out what had been preying on Aunt Lorna's mind before her death. What in the world was a body doing in the backyard of her cottage? But how could Martha, a college administrator only in town for a short time, solve a murder mystery?

Her to-go coffee tumbler drained, she whistled Penny back and smiled as the miniature schnauzer came running to her, leaf detritus in her beard and sticking to her wet nose.

"Silly girl," Martha said as she reattached the leash and they turned back toward home, coming up from the river's edge to the back porch. As they stepped onto the deck just outside the French doors to the dining area, she could hear the high whine of a vacuum cleaner.

Martha slid open one of the doors and unclipped Penny to enter, only to be confronted by a blast of magenta so bright, she thought for a split second that she'd walked into the wrong house. A short and slightly stooped woman with severe black hair pulled back in a bun was working the standup cleaner over the living room floor like she was trying out for the vacuum Olympics. With each stroke, she pushed the vacuum out in such a broad arc that she nearly fell forward with it. Her rose-colored leggings, sparkly pink tennis shoes and magenta hoodie sweatshirt matched (or at least lived in some first-cousin association on the color wheel) the slash of bright pink lipstick that covered her lips.

"Joanne?" said Martha. Nothing. "Jo*anne*?" she said again. At the same moment, Penny jumped her stubby front legs onto the back of the future Olympian.

"*Merde!*" the study in pink howled, throwing a hand to her chest as she turned around. Just then, a tall woman came trotting down the stairs, this one dressed as if she were off on a camping adventure in trail pants, low hiking shoes, and long-sleeve microfiber shirt rolled up to the elbows.

"Martha!" the women said simultaneously, engulfing her in hugs. Then the taller of the two leaned down and picked up little Penny, much to the terrier's slurpy delight.

"We heard from PJ and Mary Jane that the place needed a cleaning, and since I don't have to open the store till nine and Joanne doesn't teach till ten, we decided to tag team and get everything looking nice before the funeral. I hope you don't mind that we let ourselves in. Everyone knows Lorna leaves her doors unlocked."

"It's fine, Helen," said Martha reassuringly as the tall woman blushed. "More than fine! Aunt Lorna would have been so touched to see how you are all helping me with this." At the mention of Aunt Lorna, Martha was brought back to the reality of all that was ahead of her today. It felt like a ten-pound bag of birdseed had landed on her shoulders.

Margaret came creeping down the stairs, dressed from head to toe in her customary black.

"Powder room's done," she said in her small voice.

"Beds too!" boomed Ethel Jean right behind her, only a slight edge of crankiness detectable in her voice.

"My gosh, you all! I can't thank you enough." Martha knew Joanne Jablonski, the quirky French teacher and local IT expert, and Helen Chelton from her many visits over the years. But having them and Lorna's other friends here in her aunt's house, cleaning in preparation for Lorna's funeral, meant more than she could put into words.

Helen pulled a dust rag out of a cargo pants pocket and made for the low coffee table. The front door opened and in came Mary Jane, a bucket of cleaning supplies in tow. Joanne coiled the vacuum cord and Mary Jane got to work, opening the tan linen curtains and letting the morning sun flow in.

These ladies are a cleaning machine, Martha thought. *Thank heavens for them.* As she observed the group of friends go to work on dusting, polishing and straightening the downstairs, Martha gazed around the cottage, taking it in in a way she hadn't in some time. Natural materials abounded in the open-plan Arts and Crafts home, which featured beautiful wide-beam oak floors with tasteful floral rugs arranged carefully here and there. The furniture was mainly mission style, much of it collected in Amish country over the years as Lorna made visits north for the annual Wings on the Water festival in Ohio. Martha wondered what Helen must be thinking as she gently rubbed the side tables with a lemon-scented polish; Helen had accompanied Lorna on many of these birding jaunts, when they'd stopped on their way home to cram tables, lamps and other finds into Helen's camper van.

Martha's favorite part of the front room attracted her eye as Mary Jane carefully cleaned the windows. Geometric leaded stained glass topped each window facing the front of the house, every rectangle featuring straight-lined designs that collectively formed shafts of wheat containing parallel colors of green, orange, and yellow. Those colors were cast onto the floors when the sun caught them just so. The geometric designs matched those on the Tiffany lamps scattered here and there throughout the house; like all Lorna's items, they were fully functional. A throw blanket here, pillows there—everything was comfortable, but spoke of Aunt Lorna's no-frills approach to life.

As the gang of gals gave the cottage its finishing touches, Martha could swear she was beginning to feel warm again—the warmth of belonging she hadn't felt upon arriving at Aunt Lorna's this time. Everything had felt wrong, cold, off; but now, today—with her aunt's friends around her and the cottage brightening up—she felt a glimmer of the hominess that usually comforted her here.

Out of the corner of her eye, she saw Helen staring at some papers on Lorna's antique secretary.

"Helen, is everything all right?"

"Oh yes." Helen quickly flipped the large oaken door of the desk closed and turned the key in the top. "All good here. Just straightening up."

Joanne walked up to the three of them, gently sipping from a pottery mug in her hand.

"Fresh pot. Want some?" she asked, lowering her nose almost into the cup to take in the rich aroma.

"Not for me, thanks," said Martha. "I promised Officer Tomlinson I'd go to the police station later this morning and I need to shower and get over there."

A sympathetic murmur rose.

"*Mon dieu*," Joanne said. "An appointment with the police definitely calls for extra coffee. Hang on." She rushed into the kitchen and re-emerged seconds later, handing over a steaming mug. "You go shower. We'll clear out, and then meet up with you..." Her voice trailed off. The next time Martha would see any of these women would be at the funeral that afternoon.

Helen looked up hesitantly and spoke almost as if to fill the silence. "Martha, I don't quite know how to say this, but I had a visit early this morning from Officer Tomlinson. She was very nice, of course, but she did ask me an awful lot about Lorna and her comings and goings the past few weeks. I told her that we were friends and business associates, but not the kind of friends that keep tabs on each other. She seemed awfully persistent."

"Her *comings and goings*?" blurted Martha, louder than she intended. "Whyever for?"

Ethel Jean was never one to shy away from saying something awkward. "I'm no genius, but I'm guessing it might be to do with the dead body you found in Lorna's backyard."

Margaret's eyes widened and she looked down, as if searching for a hole to fall into.

"Well, we'll soon see about *that*!" snapped Martha, stomping up the stairs to the shower, cup in hand.

"I want to speak with her *right now*. And I don't want to hear any more of your excuses."

Martha spoke with the confidence and bombast of a true Bostonian, though she'd spent much of her childhood right here in Riley Creek. Even to her own ears, she sounded obnoxious and rude. She had never set foot in a police department, and even this modest-sized building made her feel edgy and out of her element. Her brusqueness came more from her own unease than any true irritation at the fresh-faced young officer behind the counter. He literally was wet behind the ears with his short-cropped hair combed into place and still damp from his morning shower.

"Please find Officer Tomlinson *now* and tell her Martha Sloane is here to see her."

The young man disappeared through a door after trying one last time to explain to Martha that Officer Tomlinson was not in the department at the moment, but another officer could be found to take her statement. She strained to hear the murmured voices beyond the door and was just contemplating sneaking behind the counter to get a better angle when a tall man in dress pants, pressed denim shirt with the cuffs rolled up, and a watch the size of Texas came through the door and up to the counter.

"I understand you're quite insistent about seeing Officer Tomlinson," he said.

"Damn right I am," said Martha, "and I've been out in your lobby waiting for about half a year while she pretends not to be here."

"And did you and she have an appointment?" the man replied, eyebrows raised. Martha guessed he was around six feet two, with black hair parted down the side and just brushing his collar. His bronze skin was one part Jimmy Smits and one part Antonio Banderas. The overall effect was one handsome drink of water, but Martha was darned if she was going to let *him* know she'd even noticed. Men equaled complication, complication took her eye off the ball, and taking her eye off the ball would keep her in Riley Creek much longer than she wanted. She had no time for that nonsense.

"Well...not exactly. She told me I could come over late morning and give my statement to an officer on duty. Look, I just need to talk to her to find out why she's asking around about my aunt, like she had anything to do with the body I found."

"Oh, I see," he said, nodding sagely. "And you are...?"

"Martha Sloane, the one who found the body and whose dead aunt you are all but accusing of murder!" Martha heard her own voice rise an uncomfortable octave.

"Ms. Sloane, I'm Detective Perry. Teddy Perry. Why don't you come back to my office and we can talk more privately?" Detective Perry came out from behind the counter and met her at the door from the lobby into the police station. He held the door open for her and led her to his office, such as it was. As she brushed by him, she caught the light scent of pine and wood smoke, suggesting a ruggedness that belied his sharply pressed dress pants. Martha had a fleeting vision of burying her head into his broad, strong chest and feeling his muscular arms around her.

Jeez, I must be seriously losing it, she thought.

They passed the young officer she'd assailed earlier. As she went by, he pressed his back into the wall. Martha cringed inwardly at her own behavior, but maintained her resolve as she entered the detective's office.

Detective Perry's tiny shoebox of an office bore little resemblance to the large corner room with conference table and wall-mounted TV monitor for teleconferencing that was Martha's own office back in Boston. He took a seat behind his desk and she sat in the rickety wooden chair across from him. Normally, she would have viewed this move as a power play on his part, but since there was literally no other place to sit in his office (*other than in his lap*, she thought randomly), she would at least play along.

Martha took in the room's sparseness: battered wooden desk; single file cabinet (equally battered); an outdated desktop computer with a monitor the size of a small suitcase; chairs that looked like they'd been rejected by Goodwill; and a single picture frame facing him. The most prominent feature in Detective Perry's office was books. They were stacked everywhere—on the floor; on top of the file cabinet; even on his ancient monitor. Various files and sheets of paper lay strewn about, but they clearly took a back seat to the books.

"Now, Ms. Sloane, how can I help you?" asked the detective politely, folding his hands over his flat stomach.

"I really want to speak with Officer Tomlinson and I'm not sure why I'm getting this runaround," said Martha, her steely attitude losing gas with Perry treating her so respectfully.

"Actually, Officer Tomlinson is already hard at work on this case. In fact, right now, she's attending the postmortem on the victim found in your aunt's leaf pile."

"Oh," said Martha, irritated at realizing she might have to eat some crow. She recovered quickly. "But I don't understand why she's asking my aunt's friends about her comings and goings the last few weeks, as if Aunt Lorna had anything to do with this dead person who just happened to be found at her cottage."

"Happened to be found under a neatly raked pile of leaves in her backyard," he corrected.

"Well, yes..."

"To begin with, the coroner's early examination showed that the body was only in a slight state of decomposition. Your aunt passed away five days ago. The man in the backyard probably died two to three days ago, so clearly she could not have caused his death. But still, you can imagine our curiosity. It is quite a coincidence to find two bodies in the same yard within the space of a week."

Martha was silent as she took in this bit of information. None of this made sense. Surely Aunt Lorna wouldn't have had anything to do with the dead man, right? Accustomed to being in the driver's seat, Martha didn't intend to be pushed around, even by police investigating a murder in which the body *just happened* to be found on her aunt's property.

As she opened her mouth to regain the upper hand in the conversation, Detective Perry spoke.

"Ms. Sloane, had you talked to your aunt recently? Can you tell me anything that might help us in our investigation?"

"Of course I want to help. But there's nothing..." Her voice trailed off as she recalled what some of the gals had said about her aunt's behavior in the weeks leading up to her death. "To be honest, I've been so busy at work that I hadn't talked to Aunt Lorna much recently," said Martha, suddenly deflated. "I'll regret that for the rest of my life. But I can tell you right now she had absolutely nothing to do with this guy or his death. Which happened after she was already dead, as you just said."

"We're doing our best to find out what happened. But you have to understand that the body was found at your aunt's house. That naturally makes us suspicious. And there is the manner of death... and the fact that he worked for your aunt..."

"What do you mean? What is this '*manner of death*'"—she added air quotes—"and what's it got to do with Aunt Lorna? And can we please stop saying 'the body'? Who was this dead person? What do you mean, he worked for her?"

"Well, I suppose there's no harm in telling you. Word will get out soon enough and we notified his next of kin this morning. The deceased's name was Curtis Sentrich."

"Curtis Sentrich? Who was he?"

"Well, he grew up in Riley Creek and attended Lewis High, but he never graduated. As far as I can gather right now, being a high-school dropout may have been the high point of a life otherwise filled with low points. We've gathered from talking to some of her friends that your aunt had a soft spot for him and allowed him to do small jobs around her house. Apparently, she thought it might help him get on his feet and dig himself out of trouble."

The irony of the phrase, juxtaposed with how Martha had found Sentrich, lingered in the air.

"But I still don't see why his body being found near my aunt's house means she had anything to do with his death," she said. "Maybe he was doing yard work or something for her after she'd passed, just to be kind, and had a heart attack in the leaves."

"A relatively young man, dying in the same yard of the same causes as your aunt days earlier? And somehow mysteriously being covered by the leaves he'd been raking?" Detective Perry gave Martha a few moments to realize the impossibility of what she was proposing.

"You said it yourself; she was dead before he was killed, so doesn't that take her out of the equation altogether?" Martha objected.

"I agree that it makes it impossible that she was the murderer. But him being found in your aunt's yard still must be handled as a suspicious death." He paused, and then changed the direction of the conversation. "Did your aunt own a rather large spotting scope?"

"A scope? Well sure, as do half of the birders that come through here," said Martha.

"And have you seen it since you've been back in Riley Creek?" he asked, eyebrows raised slightly.

Martha started an automatic yes, but then stopped a moment to consider.

"Well, now that you're asking me, I guess not," she said, crossing her arms over her chest. "But I also haven't thought to look for it."

Even as she said the words, she heard the same half-truth in her voice that the detective probably picked up. She had a distinct memory of seeing the scope's tripod and the strangeness of the scope not being affixed to its top. Aunt Lorna *never* took that scope out of the house, partly because she was not completely comfortable with having spent over four thousand dollars on it and partly because she enjoyed it so much, she would never have endangered it by taking it along the trail.

"To be honest, Detective Perry...." Martha hesitated a bit, not wanting to cooperate more than she had to. "There's a *chance* it's not where I expected it to be."

"Is that right?" the detective answered, the hint of a smile in his eyes. "That could be because it's sitting in my evidence room." He glanced sideways, as if nonchalantly reading some of the book titles on a nearby shelf.

"*Excuse* me?" Martha said, employing a tone of offended self-righteousness that came so easily to many Bostonians, but still sounded forced from her own mouth.

The detective sat up straight and leaned in. "Mr. Sentrich's skull was caved in and a birding scope matching the description of your aunt's was found in the shrubs at the side of her house, covered in blood and your aunt's fingerprints. And a Birds 'n' Beans business card with your aunt's phone number was in the victim's wallet."

Martha's head felt woozy as she took in his words. As much as she wanted to come up with a snappy retort, the truth was laid bare—in fact, it was practically sprawling naked in the air between them.

Chapter Five

By four that afternoon, Martha was standing just inside the door of Birds 'n' Beans, over to the right and greeting people as they entered while waving to others as they left. The burlap sacks of coffee and the antique Royal coffee roaster (it had done time in its earlier life as a peanut roaster) that usually took up a large part of the front of the shop had been moved to the storage room to make way for the guests.

The celebration of life for Aunt Lorna had been held at the First Methodist Church. Aunt Lorna had never been particularly religious—"*Those big churches just cash in on guilt,*" she'd said on several occasions—but she had been known to contribute fancy birdhouses when First Methodist put on a fundraiser. And she'd taken Martha there for a few Christmas Eve services over the years. Martha thought it made as good a venue as any to host the special event.

While she'd expected a somber teary-eyed affair, to her surprise, it had been anything but. The gals had arranged everything, from flowers to the bluegrass music Lorna had loved, to the revolving slideshow of Lorna's life that ran on a large screen throughout the celebration. Martha was surprised to see pictures of herself figuring prominently in the flickering images. She'd sat in the front pew, surrounded by PJ, Joanne, Margaret, Mary Jane and Helen. The Ritzenwallers sat right behind her. Ethel Jean was there, but kept her distance by sitting in one of the back rows, off to the side and away from most of the crowd, pretending like she was doing so to keep an eye on things.

She really is an odd bird, thought Martha. *As different from her sister as night and day.*

Most of the town merchants were there, and she'd spotted Officer Tomlinson in one of the middle rows, speaking with those around her.

What in the heck was she doing there? Martha thought now. *Getting mourners' thoughts about Aunt Lorna as a possible murderess once they signed the guest book?*

One by one, several of the mostly older crowd had come to the lectern that stood on the altar. They shared a story or a memory of Lorna, many of which were so funny, they drew laughs and applause. Martha realized through the stories that she'd only known one small part of her Aunt Lorna, who'd had a rich life here in Riley Creek, with a bowling team, birding trips, card and dinner parties, and many dear friends whose lives she'd touched. As people spoke of her aunt, Martha saw that Lorna had been a caretaker to the town; someone who could be counted on and always helped those in need. Martha knew Lorna had been that kind of person, but hadn't previously understood the depth and breadth of her giving spirit.

Martha snapped herself back to the reception in the shop and looked down to find a tiny woman in a sleeveless black silk tunic, flowing black pants, and black Birkenstock sandals holding her hands, tears rimming her eyes. Though the woman appeared to be in her late sixties or early seventies, Martha felt a surprisingly strong grip and noted the sinewy muscles in her bare arms.

"Mavis Settler," the woman introduced herself. "Your aunt and I attended Lewis High together; we were close."

Martha recalled Mavis telling a funny story at the celebration of life about her and Lorna setting something on fire in a chemistry class. Martha couldn't remember her aunt ever having mentioned Mavis, but here the woman was, shaking her head and starting to cry again as she reminisced about Aunt Lorna.

"Your aunt," Mavis said, "accepted me back here in Riley Creek as a true friend, even though I had not seen her in ages. I only regret that we had so little time together again before she was taken from us." A few tears overflowed and rolled down her cheeks. She raised a hand that sported numerous silver bangles, which clattered and jangled down over her wrist toward her elbow, and sniffed. "Do come and see me at Ohm Mama, my yoga studio sometime. We can do some energy work together. It'll be good for both of us." With that, Mavis made her way out the door. Martha looked up to see Ethel Jean nursing a coffee at the counter and nodding toward the departing Mavis with an eye roll.

Before Martha could puzzle through Ethel Jean's message, a deep, booming, "Oh my dear, my dear," brought her back to reality. "I am Albert Jeremiah, one of your aunt's oldest friends and, as luck would have it, her attorney. I'm as sorry as I can be about Lorna's passing, but so pleased to finally meet you. Your aunt had only the nicest things to say about you and your many adventures up in Boston." Still pumping her hand up and down, the short, slightly built man drew in close to her and said quietly, "Do come and visit me as soon as you are able. Tomorrow perhaps? I have some news to share with you and it would be best for you to have it sooner rather than later."

As Martha opened her mouth to respond, he gave an old-fashioned bow and withdrew. She had heard of Albert Jeremiah many times in passing, but had she known he had been one of Aunt Lorna's oldest friends?

The long line of visitors, some familiar members of Lorna's birding club the Hot Spotters and some unknown to Martha, finally let up as the shadows across the square grew long. With the pause, she realized how exhausted she felt. As she looked around the shop to locate any visitors she had not yet greeted, Ethel Jean sidled up to her. Not surprisingly, she hadn't changed out of her usual garb too much, but had given a nod to the occasion by swapping her field watch for a sturdy silver bracelet inlaid with turquoise.

"Randy old coot," said Ethel, nodding her head at Mr. Jeremiah who was receiving some friendly handshakes as he exited the shop. "He wanted nothing more than to get with your Aunt Lorna, but she wasn't having it."

Martha cringed inwardly at the thought of her beloved aunt being someone's romantic interest.

"*What?*" she said. "I thought he was just her attorney."

"If that's what you call someone that helps an old lady just to get in her pants," said Ethel Jean, lifting her shoulders in a shrug.

"ETHEL JEAN!" Both Martha and the owner of the shouted name turned to see PJ striding across the shop toward them, decked out in a long black skirt, black blouse and enough rings and bangles to start a jewelry shop. He'd taken his hair out of its customary ponytail and rolled and curled it into beautiful thick waves. "That's enough. Mr. Jeremiah did nothing more than help our Lorna with her legal needs. You and I both know he'd been pining after her for years, but that doesn't mean he did anything wrong. He just loved her from afar."

Ethel Jean raised her eyebrows cynically, as if indicating she knew better, then turned to go help with the cleanup. PJ patted Martha's arm.

"Don't listen to that cranky old thing. Albert Jeremiah and your aunt had been dear friends for years. I believe she told me once that they had been neighbors as children." PJ looked off, as if trying to dredge up the right memory. Not able to bring it to mind, he shook the effort off and continued. "He always understood that for Lorna, there was only ever one man and that was your uncle. I never met your uncle, but I hear he was a wonderful man and the apple of Lorna's eye. Albert always understood, and somehow he and Lorna managed a very special friendship within certain boundaries. He'd been helping her a great deal these last several months. On what, I don't know, but I know she'd been to see him more often than was usual."

Martha sighed and looked all around the shop with its brightly colored birdhouses suspended from the ceiling, the flat screen mounted over the coffee bar displaying what the birdfeeder webcam captured out back, and the whirligigs wedged here and there, twirling slowly thanks to the shop's steadily rotating ceiling fans.

"This is all so strange, PJ," she said tiredly. "It's such a terrible thing to say, but for the past hour, all I've been doing in my head is trying to figure out how to solve Sentrich's murder so I can clear Aunt Lorna's name and get back to Boston. Who would want him dead? How do I even begin to figure that out? And what was he doing hanging around Aunt Lorna anyway?"

"Honey, I sure don't know how to help you answer all of those big questions. But I *do* know that right now is not the time to figure all that out." Hesitating for a moment, PJ then said, "I can tell you why he was hanging around the shop and Lorna's house, if it helps. You see, your aunt had taken that young man on. Almost as a project. She really felt she could turn him around, help him make something of his life. All I know is he'd been after Mavis for something—I don't even know what—and next thing, he's your aunt's handyman."

It was all very confusing to Martha. Her aunt hadn't even mentioned Sentrich on the phone. Or had she?

PJ asked tentatively, "Martha, I know it's soon to ask, but have you given any more thought to your plans?"

Martha gave a small smile. "Oh, PJ, I don't know. I'm only supposed to be here for a few more days, and then my boss expects me back to deal with some major issues at our university. We're facing a possible merger. Now all of this with Sentrich has come up and I'm just not sure what I'm dealing with here."

PJ put his large arm around her shoulders. "Well, it's nothing you have to decide today. One look at you and I can see you're exhausted. Why don't you head on home to the cottage and let us deal with this place? We insist."

Martha looked around. There were only a few stragglers and she'd already greeted them. Otherwise, it was the rest of the gals: Margaret, Ethel Jean, Mary Jane, Helen, Delores and Joanne. Helen's husband Don, along with Jimmy Ritzenwaller, was among those carrying cups and plates back to the dish station, but mainly Martha saw the friends who'd made up the circle of Aunt Lorna's life.

How right it is, she thought, *that they should be here with me in my aunt's shop, just keepin' on keepin' on.*

Chapter Six

The gals (and their guys) finally succeeded in shooing Martha from the shop with a promise from her that she'd get some rest. She went back to the cottage, changed clothes, and took an excited Penny out for a short walk along the river. At the end of their walk, although the thought of covering herself up with blankets and reading her mystery was appealing, Martha still felt too much adrenalin from the day's events to go to bed just yet. Instead, she decided to sit out on the front porch swing for a bit.

She took a Pendleton blanket from the back of one of Aunt Lorna's leather club chairs and sat, swinging as Penny pressed up next to her. It was what Aunt Lorna had always called the "middle time," just as the sun was going down, but before the moon came up. The birds were nestled in their nighttime places, their daily cacophony giving way to the sound of the wind in the tall trees.

As Martha swung, she sifted through the many things that had been said about her aunt that day and considered possible suspects in Sentrich's murder. Mr. Jeremiah? Maybe he'd thought Lorna was having an affair with Sentrich and killed him in a crime of passion?

Sure, as long as Sentrich had helped Mr. Jeremiah lift the scope first, and then bent down low enough so that Mr. Jeremiah could bash him on the head with it.

An oddly familiar male voice calling out from the near-darkness broke into her thoughts. "Martha? Martha Sloane?"

"Hello?" she replied, Penny's head jerking up and a low growl bubbling deep in her belly.

From the road, a tall figure moved closer. "Hey there. Well, aren't you a sight for sore eyes?" As the man moved up the walk, Martha watched his John Wayne-like amble as if he had all the time in the world, so different in every way from the hurry-scurry she had come to know in Boston. He stopped with one hiking-boot-clad foot resting on the bottom step of the porch, an arm extended lazily on top of the handrail.

"Jason?" she said in a combination of question and exclamation. "What are you doing here?" Jason Turngate was a man she hadn't seen since they were both about seventeen years old. Her reaction to seeing him now was... complicated. On one hand, she couldn't deny how attractive he'd turned out to be: tall, lanky, a ginger beard trimmed perfectly. He was dressed in canvas pants, a crisp flannel shirt and a corduroy baseball cap. A hint of clean, spicy aftershave floated over to her across the porch. On the other hand, seeing him brought to the surface irrational feelings of irritation. She suddenly felt disarmed, unprepared, and at a disadvantage.

"And hello to you too. It's been a while. I actually came back to the R-C last year. Guess your aunt never told you..." It could have been a trick of the shadows, but he appeared to flush just a bit.

"Not a word," she said, shocked that Aunt Lorna wouldn't have passed along this tidbit of information, even though Jason was a chapter of Martha's life that had ended long ago. "What brought you back? Last I heard you'd headed out West for money and adventure."

"Well, I left this one-horse town ready to find fame and fortune, and spent a good long time out there. Sure had some adventures, but money, not so much. Once I did manage to scrape some together, I guess it was time to come home. How about you?"

"I've been living in Boston since college. I stayed for grad school, joined the rat race and never left." She heard herself gloss over this recitation of the last twenty-plus years, failing to acknowledge that parts of it had nearly broken her. She also heard how pathetic and dull her life sounded.

"Your aunt told me some of that, mainly that you were doing really well in your job and that she didn't see you as much as she wished. But she was proud as heck of you." He paused a moment, a smile forming on his face. "You always did fancy yourself a big city gal."

"And what's that supposed to mean?" Martha snapped back, hearing herself for the second time that day sound like a person she barely knew and didn't much like.

"What do you mean, '*What's that supposed to mean?*'" Jason replied, not in the apologetic tone Martha had hoped for. "Riley Creek was always too small for you. Even when you came here to spend the summers with your Aunt Lorna, you were always dreaming of going away, being something more, doing something more. Well, sounds like you managed to do just that." In his even tone and rich, deep voice, Martha recognized the old confidence that she remembered so well.

"You say that like it's a crime. And besides, I wasn't the only one that wanted to get away to somewhere else." She hated the childish tone in her own voice, but was unable to hold it back.

"True enough. There was plenty to get away from here." He looked off into the night, and Martha suddenly wished she could take her words back. Jason's reasons for wanting to leave were far more painful than her teenage wish to become a famous writer, to break away from her boring old life in Ohio and go off on grand new adventures. What had driven Jason to leave Riley Creek was a verbally abusive alcoholic father who owned the only car dealership for miles around. Once the town mayor, he was perpetually disappointed in his son.

"Is your dad still in town?" Martha asked.

"Oh, he's around," replied Jason, clearly not interested in expounding on the subject. "Anyway, enough of that. Listen, I wanted to stop by today to pay my respects, but I had to watch the shop so I couldn't make it. I'm really sorry about your aunt. She was an amazing woman and one of the nicest people this town ever produced."

Martha felt like an utter heel. "Thanks, Jason," she said. "But what shop? Or did you go into business with your dad? How is he?"

Jason's eyes looked interminably sad. "No, no. Dad gave up the car business years ago, after my mom died. I bought a small shop on the square and turned it into an outdoors store. Fins to Fur. That's me."

"I'd heard about your mom from Aunt Lorna. I'm sorry I didn't send a card or anything. Your mom was so kind to me when I lived here for a while after losing my folks." Martha reflected on why she hadn't followed through on this most basic of kindnesses. Had she really been too busy at work to send a card offering condolences?

"It's OK. What were we, seventeen or something last time we saw each other? And besides, it's not like you'd have known where to find me. And Dad? Well, he probably never noticed who sent cards and who didn't. When Mom passed, he went even more downhill, if that was possible. Couldn't even hold it together through the drinking anymore. He's in a nursing facility over in Park Ridge now."

"Jason, I'm so sorry. I had no idea." To herself, Martha wondered why Aunt Lorna hadn't told her any of this. Jason had been both her best friend during those childhood summers she'd spent in Riley Creek and, somehow, her nemesis. He'd always known how to get under her skin. But, still, they'd been important to each other all those years ago.

Her thoughts were interrupted by Jason speaking. "We sell outdoor gear and do some guiding in hunting season. Deer, turkey, lots of fishing trips—you know." At this, he peered up at her inquiringly. "That's maybe the one topic your aunt and I didn't see eye to eye on. She could never quite settle her mind on the idea that I helped people shoot the beautiful turkeys that roam these mountains. But we agreed to disagree and always stayed friendly."

Martha could easily imagine her aunt, who loved every feathered thing in the mountains, having a hard time condoning someone killing a wild turkey. After all, as her aunt always reminded her, the turkey came *this close* to being named the national bird, only losing to the bald eagle by one vote. Martha recalled her first time seeing one during a wildflower walk one spring. She had stopped to tie her bootlace and stood up to see an elegant, gigantic turkey slowly moving through the woods just feet from her. She still remembered the flashing greens, blues, and silvers of its feathers as it stood on a downed tree before jumping off and disappearing into the forest.

"So, will you be staying in town long?" Jason asked, squinting at her through the now dark night.

"To be honest, my plan was to come in for the funeral, sort out Aunt Lorna's affairs, and get back to Boston," she said. "But since I found Curtis Sentrich dead in the backyard and there's some suspicion that my aunt had something to do with it, things aren't quite so clear cut."

"Sentrich? Yeah, I heard about that in town today. I know you shouldn't speak ill of the dead and all, but..."

"I hear he was sort of a bad boy around town, but I really don't know much else about him," said Martha. "How in the world did he get connected to my aunt?"

"I don't know too much about him either," said Jason. "Hadn't spoken to him since returning so I don't know why your aunt would have had anything to do with him. Let's say he and I had our differences and I don't exactly think back on him with fond memories. But I'm sorry you had to find him like that. I'm sure the police'll sort that out soon enough and find that your aunt had nothing to do with it whatsoever." He paused, and then said, "Well, Martha, if you end up in town for a bit, maybe we could have dinner together sometime. Talk about old times."

She stood with Penny in her arms and yawned. She wasn't sure she wanted to talk about old times, since old times included her parents and Aunt Lorna.

"That might be nice, Jason, if I'm here that long. But thanks for stopping by. It really was nice of you."

Jason tipped his ball cap at her, told her goodbye, and ambled down the road and into the night.

This day just gets weirder by the hour, she thought, heading for the screen door. *Think I'll call it a night before one more strange thing can happen.*

The next morning, after walking Penny and having some breakfast, Martha decided to pay a visit to Mr. Jeremiah. While she was in no mood to discuss her aunt's will or business affairs, she knew she only had so much time left in Riley Creek. The College President had been understanding of her need to be away for her aunt's funeral, but that understanding was dependent on an unspoken agreement that she would hightail it right back to Boston as soon as she could.

Martha drove the few miles to Mr. Jeremiah's "office," which was a fancy term for a large room off the back of his modest cabin set in the woods off the old State Route 2. The long room featured all the necessities at one end: a large desk heaped with files, papers, and a high-end laptop computer. At the other end, far from looking like a typical legal office, it had a comfortable arrangement of chairs and sofas grouped next to a picture window that let out onto a stone patio ringed with large, tasteful pots of trailing herbs. Beyond that lay the forest. It was a breathtaking setting.

After settling in one of the couches with a cup of the fresh coffee he'd had ready—she'd caught a glimpse of a brown coffee bag with the Birds 'n' Beans logo on it on the kitchen counter, but wasn't sure what kind it was—Martha watched Mr. Jeremiah bend into one of the overstuffed chairs and fold his hands together. She breathed in the aroma of the steaming mug, in part to brace herself for this conversation.

"Viennese Melody," said Mr. Jeremiah. *What is it with people around here announcing the flavor of coffee they serve?* "Your aunt advised me to always serve Viennese Melody to my clients, swearing that it was just the right flavor for intimate conversation."

He shook his head, smiling at the memory. Then he was down to business, the keen legal mind inside the small body on full display.

"Martha," he began, "I'm sure you know that your Aunt Lorna was a savvy businesswoman. She started Birds 'n' Beans ten years ago before coffee shops were popular and when birding was a hobby for the few. I told her at the time that I didn't think it was a smart investment, but she had other ideas. She had money saved up in her retirement account from her time working as a science teacher for Riley Creek Schools and wanted to set out on something new. I helped her secure a small business loan, buy the property, find a coffee distributor, and get things started. The rest is history.

"For ten years, she surpassed even her own expectations for success. Once the coffee shop craze took off, she did exceedingly well. The birding tourists that came through were icing on an already-thriving cake. Over time, she built up her profits, paying off a great deal of what she owed on the property and making payroll to boot."

He paused, took a sip of his own coffee, and sat back, his hands wrapped loosely around the mug.

"But that's great, right? There must be someone who wants to buy a business that's doing so well? To take it over and keep it going?" Martha felt a sense of relief washing over her for the first time since her arrival. "I can make the sale contingent on Helen and PJ continuing to work there."

"Well, not exactly. You see, over the last year, your aunt had been to see me numerous times. She wanted my help taking money out of both her house and the business." Mr. Jeremiah frowned into his cup. "She had nearly paid off her cottage after years of careful money management, and was well on her way to paying off the shop, too. But she began borrowing deeply against the equity she had built up in both properties."

Martha looked at him, confused. "I don't understand, Mr. Jeremiah. Why would she do that? What was going on that she needed money so badly? Was the business suffering?"

"My dear, if only I knew," he replied. "I have asked myself that very same question more times than I care to count. And by the way, I insist that you call me Albert. I tried talking to Lorna on multiple occasions, asking her to reconsider what she was doing and the impact on her financial situation long term if she didn't reverse course. But she was quite determined, and you know how she could be when she had built up a full head of steam."

You can say that again, thought Martha. "So where does this leave the business? And her cottage?" she asked.

"It leaves it all to you," Albert replied, gazing at her.

"To *me*?" said Martha, mouth agape.

"Indeed. As you know, you are Lorna's sole living relative, and she had always intended you to be her beneficiary. I'm only sorry that I can't tell you exactly *what* you've inherited. I'm not certain where her heavy borrowing left her at the time of her..." Albert's eyes became misty and he coughed and looked away, regaining his composure before turning back to her and taking a sip of coffee.

"But what do I do now?" asked Martha, still stunned from this new information. "I'm supposed to be back in Boston in just a couple of days, but the police are investigating Sentrich's body being found in Aunt Lorna's yard, and now this. I don't even know where to begin." Martha had always assumed that Lorna would leave everything to... well, she had never really stopped to think about it. Aunt Lorna was such a constant presence in Martha's life that she'd never thought of her not being there, and had certainly not contemplated the future of her worldly goods.

"You and I both know your aunt would never even have hurt a fly, so the police are most certainly barking up the wrong tree if they think she had any connection with his death. As far as I know, Mr. Sentrich did odd jobs around the cottage for your aunt; she hoped that she could help him gain his equilibrium in life by providing him with meaningful work to complete. I'm not certain anyone could really help someone with his history, but your aunt could only ever see the best in everyone."

Again, he gazed down, as if lost in a memory. Then he looked up.

"But on the topic of the cottage and business, let me say this; I always told your aunt that the best place to start is to do your homework. And now I suggest the same to you. The last time she visited me, your aunt had copies of all of the loan documents, as well as the bank statements and business accounts, in an old leather briefcase. Perhaps work forward from there. I am at your service, of course. Your aunt was a dear friend of mine for many a year, and if I can help you in any way, I hope you will avail your-self of my assistance."

Albert dipped his head in the old-fashioned bow he had given her yesterday after the funeral. They chatted for a few more minutes, but Martha was too rattled by all she'd heard to be much of a conversationalist. Albert saw her to the door, where she turned to him and shook his hand.

"Thank you, Albert. And thank you for being such a good friend to my aunt all these years. I need to get my head wrapped around all of this and figure out what she was up to. A dead body in the backyard? And Aunt Lorna mysteriously taking money out of her accounts? Something definitely does not add up here. And I'm going to find out what."

"My dear, I recognize that fire in your eye and have no doubt you will do just that."

Chapter Seven

Next morning, Martha decided to start the day with a long hike. First, she had breakfast and let Penny out for a stroll, the little dog coming back up onto the porch fifteen minutes later and passing out exhausted on her pillow in front of the empty fireplace.

It may get cold enough tonight for a fire, Martha reflected. She made coffee—some Brazilian Tailfeather PJ had sent over with a promise that it was perfect for cold mornings—and took a mug into the bathroom with her while she showered and got ready, all the time feeling the nagging stress of her situation on the outskirts of her brain.

She was so glad she'd decided to throw in some hiking clothes among her luggage: breathable pants with zip-off legs in case she got too hot; a quarter-zip top to keep her warm, but wick moisture; a bandana to keep her hair back or the sun from her neck; and her sturdy boots with wool hiking socks. Her fleece vest was the finishing touch. She grabbed her old hiking pack from the storage closet where Aunt Lorna kept all of their gear—sticks, backpacks, sleeping bags and such—and filled the water reservoir from the sink. Scrounging a granola bar from the pantry, she recalled that Aunt Lorna kept each pack fully stocked with essentials: she had already spotted a small first aid kit, a pocketknife and compass in a side pocket.

Always the caretaker, Martha reflected. If it had been up to her, a candy bar and soda might have comprised her pack's only contents.

The one thing she was missing was the pair of compact Leica binoculars she liked to take on her hikes with Aunt Lorna. Usually they were hanging on a peg in the storage closet, but she hadn't seen them.

"Now where would those be?" she asked herself. She gazed around the living room and kitchen, the most likely locations for them, then went to the closed secretary and turned the key to open the large front panel. She spotted her small binoculars immediately, pushed back and into one of the many nooks in the desk.

Right in the center of the desk lay a bulging leather portfolio with the initials LJS on it. A quick peek told her it contained the papers Albert Jeremiah had mentioned seeing when Aunt Lorna had visited him. Under the portfolio were two watercolor pictures, each about the size of a piece of legal paper, encased separately in a clear plastic sleeve. They were of birds, one that looked like a stylized cedar waxwing on a branch with berries and the other a blue jay on a pine bough. They both reminded her of something one would see in a John James Audubon book.

Perhaps they are something Aunt Lorna bought to hang in her house and had never gotten around to it? thought Martha.

Getting a little warm in her vest, Martha harnessed the binoculars to her chest, moved the portfolio and pictures to the dining table, closed the secretary, and turned her attention back to her hike.

"See ya, girl," she said to the schnauzer, who looked up sleepily but remained in her bed. The little dog seemed to sense that whatever outing Martha was going on would be too strenuous for her already-tired legs. Martha closed the French doors and headed down to the riverside path that connected to the Talisman Trail about a mile downriver.

Crossing a small footbridge that spanned the river, Martha spotted the blue blazes and small sign that marked the Talisman trailhead. She could see farther up the inclining trail than usual, a sure sign that the leaves were mostly down and deep winter not too far away. Adjusting her pack and retying her boots, Martha began her hike. She only planned on a short loop today, a couple of miles since she hadn't hiked for some time and knew she was in no shape for the eight-miler she'd completed so many times with Aunt Lorna.

All the same, she hoped to catch at least a glimpse of a bird that had always been a favorite of hers; the Cooper's Hawk. With its dark cap, which the young Martha loved to imagine it raising in a greeting like an old-fashioned gentleman straight from the pages of a Jane Austen novel, and the wonderful reddish-brown barred plumage on its breast, this was a bird that it was impossible to forget. And that's before Martha contemplated the Cooper's Hawk's most distinctive feature; beautiful red eyes that spoke of wisdom and mystery. Wrapping her fingers around her binoculars in anticipation of a reunion with an old friend, Martha stepped out with renewed vigor and a smile of satisfaction upon her face, her troubles momentarily forgotten.

Talisman Trail was just one in a series in the Paris Mountains, and Aunt Lorna had hiked them all hundreds of times. In fact, she was the fittest seventy-year-old Martha knew. As the trail climbed up and the early sun faded to sharp rays reaching through the tall canopy, Martha felt the temperature drop and her heartbeat pick up. She followed the broad trail up the mountain, a drop off on the left edge plummeting down about twenty feet into what was now a clear mountain stream, but would become a rushing river once the winter snowpack thawed in early spring. On the far bank of the stream, which the sun had not yet risen high enough to touch, Martha thought she could make out the flash of ice crystals forming at the edge.

She had wondered if she'd dressed warmly enough, but was now perspiring as she hit her stride. The trail was soft from the bed of rotting leaves underneath her feet, and she took in the familiar sights and sounds of the deciduous forest. All around her were tiny scurryings of birds, chipmunks and squirrels, many clearly visible, but just as many out of sight under the leaves and back in the thickets of rhododendron and mountain laurel. She recalled Aunt Lorna teaching her how to distinguish these two shrubs from one another; they often grew together into massive clumps some in this area called "laurel slicks."

"It's easy to remember," Aunt Lorna had told her many times. "Short leaf, short name. Long leaf, long name." Martha felt somehow comforted by this fond memory, and by how much of her aunt's teachings about this place had stayed with her. How many more hikes up here would she have once she sold Aunt Lorna's cottage and business? How many more reunions with the Cooper's Hawk and all the other wildlife that had held such an important place in her childhood? Just the thought brought back the stress she had managed to keep in abeyance for the last hour or so. How could she not come back here, the place where she'd spent so much of her childhood? Or was this what growing up was all about; having to cut ties with all that connected you to your childhood?

This didn't feel quite right to Martha, but she couldn't think of a solution, either. She could still come and hike these mountains, staying at a hotel and dropping in to town to say hello to old friends every once in a while, couldn't she? The thought felt instantly wrong in her mind. She couldn't visit here as some kind of outsider, some kind of tourist. It had been her home, and she'd rather never return than do so as a virtual stranger.

Suddenly, against a backdrop of numerous birds singing off in the distance came a sharp call. It was loud and distinct enough for Martha to stop in her tracks and lift her head to locate its source. She listened carefully for a few more seconds and it came again.

Teakettle! Teakettle!

She spotted the small bird perched about eight feet off of the ground in a pine tree. Lifting her binoculars, she focused on it and made out its rusty coloring, long up-cocked tail, and distinctive white eye stripe. A Carolina wren. Even though some birders would categorize this beauty as "common," to Martha, it was always a treat to spot the familiar little creature.

In another fifteen minutes, she felt the pressure of the morning's two cups of rich, dark coffee weighing on her bladder and knew she'd never make it all the way back to the cottage without a pit stop. Pulling some biodegradable toilet paper from her back pocket, she removed her pack and went about twenty feet off of the trail until she found a secluded spot. Swinging her leg over a downed tree, she simultaneously heard and felt a squeaking *THWAP!* as something metallic flashed up and out of the deep layer of dead leaves on the other side. Confused, she took a moment before her brain realized that a small steel trap had closed on the edge of the heel of her leather boot. Seeing a linked chain running from the trap into the leaves, she pulled on it and saw that it was attached to a metal stake the size of a railroad peg. Tugging as hard as she could, she pulled the peg from the ground and used it as a wedge to pull the edge of the trap off of her boot. It closed immediately, the force of the snap causing the trap to jump up the air.

Disgusted as much as she was shocked, Martha sat for a minute. She had never encountered a trap up here in all of her years of hiking with Aunt Lorna and couldn't bear to imagine what the powerful device would do to a small paw.

What if Penny had come along with me and gotten her tiny, delicate leg snapped up into this horrible contraption?

Feeling almost sick at the thought, Martha wrapped the trap in her bandana, stowed it in her pack, and decided to head back down the trail toward Riley Creek. She was sweaty and shaky and just wanted to get home, her urge to hike and catch up with her feathered friends gone.

Showered and changed, Martha placed the bird pictures in her aunt's portfolio, put it, along with the wrapped trap, into her backpack, and headed out toward the square. Overwhelmed by Albert's news that her aunt had left her the cottage and the shop, and that she now had to sort out some kind of financial mess, Martha was not sure what to tackle first. But she still had the simmering anger inside of her from literally stumbling over a trap on her beloved mountain, and she knew what to do about *that*.

As she emerged from the side road onto the green, much looked the same as it had yesterday, except for down at the west end where Mr. Bennett was outside of his bookshop, struggling to handle a large sign. He spotted Martha and she waved awkwardly to him.

Just because you think someone is strange, Aunt Lorna would always say, *it doesn't cost you a thing to be kind to them.*

"Hello, Mr. Bennett," she said, watching him as he continued to try to pry open the wooden legs of an ancient-looking sandwich board. "Can I help you with that?"

"Martha! How lovely to see you," he said in a lilting British accent, which for a fleeting moment had her imagining him and the Cooper's Hawk tipping their caps to each other in polite greeting. "Why yes, yes, that would be grand." He stood and rubbed his back. "I haven't had this thing out of the attic in years, but decided I might see what good it can do me. One must keep up with the times," he added, looking pleased with himself. Martha, unsure that this antique chalkboard sign had any relationship to modernity, put down her pack and wrestled with its cranky springs. Eventually, she was able to pry them apart widely enough that it stood open and upright.

She looked down at herself and brushed off the dust stains of what was probably fifty-year-old chalk.

"I can bring over some spray for those hinges," she said. "It'll make it easier to open and close them."

"Why, thank you," he said, patting his hands together. "I must begin preparing for love's bitter song!" He seemed so excited, Martha thought he might kick up his heels and break a hip, and she wondered from his statement whether he was going a little senile. She'd have to check with PJ.

"Yes, well, all right. So nice to see you," she said as she shouldered her backpack and walked away. She left him there, dusting off the sandwich board and humming some old-fashioned tune.

Stopping by Fins to Fur, she pushed open the door and heard a far-off electronic chime announce her entry. Jason was standing behind the checkout counter, pinning tiny fishing flies to a felt panel in a revolving display case whose glass door stood open. She crossed the floor of the shop in a flash and unceremoniously dropped her pack onto the shiny glass countertop.

"Well, hi there..." He stopped as he read her face and frowned. "What's the—"

"I'll tell you what's the matter," she said. "As usual, you're taking shortcuts to get what you want, and I for one do *not* think it's OK." She unzipped her pack, pulled out the trap, and unwrapped her bandana. Fortunately, she had the presence of mind not to slap the steel contraption down onto the glass counter and shatter it. "How could you even *think* of placing these on Talisman Trail? Do you know how many children and families hike that trail? How many of these are up there?" She noted with satisfaction the grimace of discomfort on his face.

"I have no idea—"

"Oh, that's great. Just great. You don't even know how many you put up there? Typical. Why should I even be surprised? Well, know this; I'm not going to stand by and let you trap small, defenseless animals just to help your business. I'm not going to stand for this, and neither is anyone else around here!" Without another word, she turned on her heel and headed for the door, seeing in her peripheral vision Jason fingering the links of the trap attached to the peg.

And to think I even contemplated having dinner with him.

Chapter Eight

A few minutes later, she was at the door of Birds 'n' Beans, her mood lightening as she took in the colorful yard flags and birdfeeders hanging from the shop awning. The place was bustling. PJ was behind the coffee counter, confidently working the knobs of the espresso machine and prepping drinks for a couple of hikers already seated with delicious-looking muffins on plates in front of them. Martha took in the familiar scent of roasted beans and felt at ease for the first time since she'd discovered the trap.

"Morning, sweetie!" PJ shouted as he looked up and saw Martha walk in. She waved a greeting in response, not sure if she should find an apron and help, since technically the shop now belonged to her. Given her relative ignorance of all things bird and bean, she settled on taking a seat at a wooden table by the rear windows. She laid her backpack on one of the other chairs, took Lorna's portfolio out, and rested her arm on it as she took in the bird scene beyond the window.

A green suet basket held a protein-rich square of feed. A tubular feeder containing nyger seed was meant to attract small birds like goldfinches, and several house-shaped feeders contained what looked like standard birdseed. While she watched, red-bellied woodpeckers and blue jays flew in to partake of the morning's offerings, and the platform birds continued to gorge.

With the rushing river sounding in the background, the whole scene was something right out of *National Geographic*.

She was jarred out of her reverie by Joanne, who walked up to her with a cheery *"Bonjour*, Martha!" and sat down next to her. Apparently, yellow was the color of the day, as Joanne was decked out in it from head to toe, right down to a pair of bright yellow Chuck Taylors with yellow and white striped socks peeking over the tops.

"These birds really are something," said Martha, shaking her head. "Once you start watching them, it's kind of hard to stop."

"Yes, your aunt Lorna felt just the same. Her favorite part of the day was heading out there to clean and fill the feeders each morning. Some of the birds became so used to her that they'd even land on the feeders while she was filling them! I think she got us all a little hooked on them."

Helen came rushing by, a cardboard box in one hand and a box cutter in the other. "Morning!" she said, not stopping to chat.

"Delivery day," said Joanne conspiratorially. "Usually, Lorna would have been here to deal with the feeders and stock anything that had arrived the day before. I think Helen is a bit frazzled."

"Oh my gosh, I should be helping," said Martha, getting up. Joanne quickly pulled her by the arm back down into her seat.

"My dear, no one expects you to jump up and help right now. That'll all sort itself out. Don't let Helen kid you; she loves this place and she's happy to do anything that needs doing while you sort out Lorna's affairs. Speaking of which... *quoi de neuf*?"

Martha looked at her quizzically, knowing only that Joanne was dropping something in French, but not knowing much more.

"Stop with your nosiness!" Mary Jane came striding over from the counter, dressed in leopard-print spandex leggings that went down to her mid-calf, a black zip-up warmup jacket, and a pair of serious-looking running shoes. Her short hair was pulled out of her face by a black headband, and it was clear from her pink cheeks that she had recently been exercising. She had a chocolate croissant on a plate and a glass of chocolate milk. Nodding at the croissant, she said with feeling, "Don't say one word until I have a bite of this."

Settling in at the table, she draped a paper napkin over her lap, took a bite from her croissant and closed her eyes, uttering an "Ohhhmmmm..." Martha was pretty sure this was not a meditation chant.

Mary Jane's eyes opened and refocused on Joanne. "I've been over at Ohm Mama at a hot yoga class. Mavis says we should be mindful of everything we consume, taking in the flavor, the texture, the *meaning* of each bite. So I stopped in here for a glass of protein." She nodded in the direction of her chocolate milk. "I believe I caught you in the act of being nosey?" she asked her yellow companion cheerily.

"I'm not sure there was anything particularly *mindful* about the way you scarfed that croissant down," Joanne replied. "Anyway, I was just 'checking in,' as the young people say, to see how Martha was doing and ask if she'd made any decisions about things."

"*Things* are none of your business, nor mine," said Mary Jane. "Martha will figure out her plans all in good time and will tell us when she is ready to tell us." But she did also look at Martha with a question in her eyes on the off chance that Martha was ready to share those plans *now*.

"Right now, I'm so confused, I don't know which end is up!" said Martha, her elbows resting on the portfolio and hands in her hair. "My boss is expecting me back in Boston soon, but after what Albert Jeremiah told me yesterday... well, I just don't know what to think." She paused as PJ joined them at the table and slid a coffee in front of her. "Thanks, PJ," she said, picking up the cup. "Apparently, Aunt Lorna left everything to me in her will... but it's a little complicated. According to Albert, she'd been taking money out of the cottage and the shop's equity, so now she... well, I guess now I may have a difficult financial situation on my hands." She glanced from one friend to the other. "Do you have any idea why Aunt Lorna had been taking so much money out? Did she buy something? Or give it to someone?"

"I have no idea," said Joanne, looking shocked. Mary Jane's shaking head echoed her answer to Martha. As the hikers headed out the door with a wave, PJ waved back to them.

Turning to PJ, Martha said, "And I don't mean to worry you, PJ, since you work here. I just learned about all of this and so I'm freaking out a little at the moment. I don't know how to figure it out."

PJ patted her arm. "Don't you worry one second about me, little one. I am a master—or, you might say, mistress—of transformation and survival. If you have to sell the shop, I'll either work for the new owner or find a new place to be."

Martha felt her heart break a little at the thought of PJ not being in this shop with these people and this smell of coffee and these beautiful birds outside the window.

"It does begin to make sense of why Lorna had seemed so out of sorts, though, doesn't it, girls?" PJ asked as he glanced at the faces around the table. "I mean, if her financial situation was becoming so difficult. But why didn't she tell any of us if she was in trouble?"

Joanne, Mary Jane, Martha and PJ all looked at each other, sharing a glance of mutual grief and confusion about their beloved Lorna shouldering such worry and none of them being any the wiser.

"Who says you can't figure it out?" Joanne blurted out.

"Joanne, hush," Mary Jane countered. "Now is not the—"

"Wait, Mary Jane, let's hear her out," said PJ evenly. "Joanne, honey, what do you mean?"

"Well, you girls know that since retiring from teaching French at the middle school, I've taught the odd online class for River Bluff Community College. It helps to have the extra money and to keep up my fluency. I also have such a nice time meeting the stu—" PJ's soft eyes turned a bit flinty, reminding Joanne she was getting off track. "Anyway, I was just thinking—and it's probably not a good idea—that maybe you, Martha, could work from here for a bit while you figure out your aunt's estate and decide what you want to do with everything."

"But how could I work from here? Everything is on my computer back in Boston. My boss is there." Martha shook her head, exasperated.

"Well, I've become a fair hand at information technology, and I think I could help you set up a home office at Lorna's... I mean, *your* cottage. And if you have a computer, I can help you set up a virtual private network. That allows you to access your computer at work to retrieve files and documents. Plus there are lots of programs to help you have virtual meetings with your boss and your team through your computer so you can talk in real time."

Joanne sat back. Martha thought for a moment, opening her mouth to declare such a scenario impossible, then closing it again.

"You know, Joanne, that's not such a bad idea. I don't know if my boss would go for it, but it could actually work. At least, just until I sort everything out here in Riley Creek." She touched the cover of the portfolio, her momentary flash of hope brought back to reality. "But there are so many papers and statements showing negative dollar signs. I'm not an expert in finance, so I'm not even sure I *can* do my regular job from here while sorting out this mess."

She saw the gals exchange knowing looks.

"What?" she asked.

PJ leaned in. "Well, Riley Creek has a secret weapon you may not know about; Margaret. She does the books for the Methodist church and the Minister always says that if she wanted to go into business as a Certified Public Accountant, she'd make money hand over fist. I'm sure she'd be willing to help you sort things out."

"*Margaret* is a financial whiz?" Now Martha understood what Margaret must be working on all the time with that laptop of hers. She sat back and gazed out the window at the birds for a moment. Then she looked at the gals circled around her, watching her and asking her with their eyes what she was going to do.

A group of honest, kind people trying to help me, she thought. *I sure could get used to this.*

"You know, I think you are onto something. I'm calling my boss this afternoon. Do you really think Margaret would be willing to help me?"

The gals around the table all smiled. "Oh yes," said PJ, clasping his perfectly manicured hands together over his frilly apron and speaking in a deep voice. "I most certainly think she will."

Chapter Nine

Martha glanced down at her watch, pushing herself the last half mile when she saw the time. She had gotten Margaret's phone number from PJ before leaving the shop yesterday, and Margaret had agreed to help her take a look at Aunt Lorna's financial papers the next morning. They were meeting at the shop in just forty-five minutes, but Martha had felt the need to get outside, if just for a three-mile run to get her blood flowing. Penny's blood had been flowing nice and slow, thank you very much, as evidenced by her refusal to leave her doggie bed after a brief trip around the back yard.

Martha ran back to the cottage, quickly showered and changed, grabbed her backpack and went off to the shop. While she was sure the reserved Margaret would have arrived early and been waiting for her, as she entered the square, Martha saw her standing in front of Toad in a Hole, talking quietly with Mr. Bennett. When Martha made eye contact with her from across the expanse of the square and raised an arm in a wave, she could have sworn that Margaret looked embarrassed to have been caught talking with the bookshop owner. Perhaps she was simply surprised. While Margaret was bedecked in her customary black—today, skirt, tights, cardigan and turtleneck, a black leather briefcase over her arm—Mr. Bennett was dressed in an unusually colorful argyle sweater of green and pink diamonds over his trademark white shirt and tan khakis.

As Margaret quickly ended her conversation with Mr. Bennett and headed to Birds 'n' Beans, Martha spotted a small delivery truck parked in front of the shop. It was a short white-panel truck with a logo on the side that featured a steaming black cup of what was presumably coffee emerging from a nuclear-blast-shaped bundle of fruits and vegetables. "Nature's Way," the logo read. Coming around the back of the truck as she approached the store, she saw a broad-shouldered young man in a uniform, muscling bags of coffee onto a dolly inside the cargo area. Just as she got to the shop, he rolled one down the truck's ramp and she held the door for him.

"Thanks," he said, whisking by her in a manner that belied the weight of the load.

Martha emerged into a bustle of activity. PJ was in the front right corner of the shop, overseeing the unloading of the coffee bags, checking the tag on each against whatever was listed on the clipboard in his hands. Helen was behind the coffee counter, looking a little harried and glancing over at the small line of people waiting at the cash register to buy bird-related items.

Martha looked at Helen with a "What can I do?" expression on her face. Helen met her at the counter and almost pulled her backpack from her shoulder.

"Look," Helen said, "the coffee delivery is late today and we've got a birdhouse class just breaking up"—here she nodded over her shoulder toward the connecting doorway between the shop and Silent Sisters Antiques—"and we haven't even had a chance to go get the morning baked goods order. Would you be a dear and run to Carl's before we're overrun with hangry bluebird fanatics?" Before Martha could answer, Helen turned around and headed back to the coffee counter, slinging Martha's pack behind it.

Well, thought Martha, *if I own this place, I guess I need to make myself useful.* She met Margaret who was coming in the door, her eyes widening as Martha whisked past her.

"Sorry, Margaret. Gotta go to the bakery. Be right back."

Martha rushed diagonally across the square as the wind picked up, creating mini-tornadoes of leaves here and there. Though she hadn't been in for some time, since her visits to Riley Creek had been so short and sporadic, she knew exactly where An Early Riser bakery was located. And even if she hadn't remembered, the yeasty smell blowing on the wind would have led her there. Taking a turn into a side street, she spotted the small storefront with two bistro tables covered in blue tablecloths. One was occupied by none other than Jason Turngate, *Wall Street Journal* in hand, sipping from a to-go cup emblazoned on the side with "Birds 'n' Beans" while a cinnamon roll the size of a salad plate sat waiting. He opened his mouth to greet her, but she walked right by and into the bakery.

Focus, she told herself.

The aroma that hit her made her weak at the knees. It was a combination of yeast, cinnamon, brown sugar and exotic spices that brought her up short. A tall young man stood behind the cash register next to the glass displays of baked goods, handing a twine-wrapped box to a departing customer.

"*Lewis?*" Martha said, surprised.

"Yes, ma'am?" the young man answered, politely yet warily. Little Lewis Shipman was not very small anymore. The last time Martha recalled seeing him, he was perhaps in the fifth grade, still shy and hardly talking to anyone except his mother, Catrin

Shipman. Martha knew that Aunt Lorna had been buying the pastries and other baked items for Birds 'n' Beans from An Early Riser for years. And somewhere during those years, the small, shy boy she remembered had blossomed into this earnest young man.

"I'm Martha Sloane and I'm here for PJ and Helen to pick up the order for Birds 'n' Beans," she said, feeling a little awkward.

"I was just going to send Lewis over," came a booming voice. Cat, Lewis's short but sturdy mother, came out from the back of the shop, cheeks blazing, fiery red hair held up in a cloth cap, long white apron fixed firmly around her middle. "It's been too long, Martha," she said. "And I'm that sorry to hear about your aunt and all the troubles over at the cottage." Cat's Irish accent had all but disappeared, but it came out now as she handed the four twined boxes over to Lewis and came around the counter to give Martha a firm hug. "You must think us awful for not coming to the funeral, but we had a catering event. At this time of year, we just couldn't afford to turn it down."

Martha knew from Aunt Lorna that the tourist trade was thin as the fall months turned to winter. "Oh, Cat," she said, "don't even mention that. I know you were great friends to my aunt, and that's what counts. Look, I'd love to chat, but if I don't run this food back to the shop, PJ and Helen will have my head. Let's catch up soon, though." She nodded at the tall Lewis standing next to his mother. "Clearly lots has changed since I spent much time around here."

Cat looked proudly at her son. "Yes, well, they do grow if you keep feeding them. Carl will want to see you too and pay his respects, so don't be a stranger."

Lewis offered to carry the load of sweet-smelling boxes for Martha, but she declined so he held the door open for her to exit the shop. She purposely angled the armful to her left so that she would not see Jason's face as she whisked by.

Why do I regress to middle school just by virtue of being around him? she wondered.

When she got back to the shop, the coffee delivery man was standing at the rear of his truck, typing something into a hand-held computer device. "Here, let me get the door," he said when he saw her coming with her heavy load. "By the way, they told me you're the new owner. I just wanted to say sorry for being late this morning. Won't happen again."

He let the door close behind her before she could respond. She noticed her tinge of excitement and pride at being called "the owner," but quickly dismissed it as she made her way to the coffee counter.

I'm only the owner until I can sell this place.

PJ was back there now, clipboard exchanged for his usual apron, working the knobs of the espresso machine as quickly and deftly as a pianist's hands move across the keys.

"Oh thanks, Martha. Do me a favor? Grab some plastic gloves and stock the cases?" He gestured to the many free-standing glass cases along the counter that currently held only sad-looking remnants of the previous day's fare. Martha worked methodically to refill them with goodies, and as quickly as she stocked them, PJ unloaded them to the birders who looked like mangy cats waiting to pounce upon any available carbs. Helen, further down the length of the counter, cashed them out.

Martha noticed that most customers carried a to-go coffee from the self-service station that held hot carafes of various types of brews, as well as a bagged goodie. Most also dangled a long and slender birdhouse by a sturdy chain.

Ah, recalled Martha. *Those are from the* Make Your Own Bluebird House *class.*

Don Chelton, clad in jeans and a denim shirt sporting a state park emblem on the chest, emerged from the doorway that led to Silent Sisters and greeted Martha warmly.

"How are you doing?" he asked sympathetically. Martha recalled that she hadn't really had much time to talk to him at the celebration of life for Lorna.

"Doing OK," she said. "You, on the other hand, have had your hands full this morning." She gestured at the mingling bird aficionados holding their bluebird houses.

"Well, Lorna's had me teaching this class for years. I hope you don't mind that we held it so soon after..."

"No, no, not at all," said Martha. "It would make Aunt Lorna happy to see so many people in the shop learning about one of her favorite birds."

"I know it seems like an odd time of year to help people build bluebird boxes, but Lorna knew it was as important to provide boxes for winter roosting as for spring nesting. Plus it keeps people thinking about birds and reminds them to come in for seed throughout the winter." He winked at her, both of them acknowledging that her aunt's kindness to feathered friends did not preclude interest in sales remaining steady. "Having the classroom over at Silent Sisters has really helped too, so we don't take up all of the tables at Birds 'n' Beans."

Martha recalled Lorna mentioning something about a classroom at the antique shop, but now realized she hadn't really listened to the details these past years. *Why was I always too busy?* she thought regretfully.

"Oh really?" she said. "Will you show me?" Even if she hadn't paid attention when Aunt Lorna had told her, perhaps she could make up for that now the shop was her responsibility.

Don led her back through the connecting doorway and into Silent Sisters Antiques. It was like walking into another world, one only glimpsed through a looking glass. All around were signs of another age: ancient birdcages hanging from the ceiling; antique tricycles on shelves high up; racks and racks of vintage clothing; glass cases of elaborate antique jewelry and silver.

Don raised his voice at no one in particular. "Just showing Martha the classroom."

From behind an assortment of matching china came Ethel Jean's cynical, "Be my guest, why don't you?"

Don led Martha through a heavy green curtain and into a compact classroom. There were six two-person tables lined up chevron-style, and a head table that could seat four at the front of the room. It was tidy and comfortable, and each table had the requisite number of stools standing ready. The head table held some wood scraps and a toolbox, and surprisingly, Margaret sat at one of the small tables, teacup in hand and reading a novel.

"Oh, Margaret!" said Martha. "Here, I've kept you waiting all this time. I'm so sorry!" Turning to Don, she thanked him for showing her the classroom and for helping with cleanup after the funeral. He nodded to her.

"Say, Martha, not sure the time is right or that you'd be interested, but we're leading an owl walk soon," he said. "I know Helen would love to have you along." Martha thanked him, making a mental note to ask Helen more about it. Although her list of things to do was growing instead of shrinking, an evening outside sounded like a welcome distraction.

As Don cleared up the remains of the class, Martha darted back to the shop, grabbed her pack, and returned to seat herself next to Margaret. When Don had packed up, he nodded a goodbye to both women, and made his exit.

Martha glanced at the book Margaret had been reading. "Wow, *Moby Dick*? That's no easy read!" she said.

"Well, as Melville said, 'I try all things; I achieve what I can,'" said Margaret, tucking the book into her briefcase and pulling out a legal pad and pen. "Now, how can I help you, Martha?" Martha noted an uncharacteristically confident tone in Margaret's voice, as if she had told herself that morning to sound businesslike.

Martha withdrew the portfolio from her bag. Putting the bird paintings aside, she revealed the thick sheaf of statements, receipts, and past due notices, and explained what Albert Jeremiah had told her about Lorna's withdrawals over the last year.

"I really need your help with all of this. So far, I've only been able to put things in order by date, but beyond that I'm clueless."

"Hmmm," muttered Margaret as she pulled the portfolio close and leafed through the papers. "Yes, I see why you're confused. This *is* rather a mess," she said, still turning the pages. "I need to input all of these details into my accounting software at home to make heads or tails out of it all. Would that be all right?" Margaret peered at Martha through her kitty-cat glasses and picked up her teacup to drain the last of its contents.

"Of course," said Martha, "but I also need to know your rates and when I should pay you."

Margaret's eyes grew wide and her neck turned red, the color moving steadily up to reach the roots of her salt-and-pepper hair.

"Oh, but I don't want you to pay me. I would *never* let you do that," she said. "Lorna was one of my dearest friends, and I want to help you figure this out. In a way, I'm helping Lorna too." This outpouring of emotion was so unusual for Margaret that she looked away and the two women sat in an uneasy silence for a couple of moments.

"Thank you," Martha said, as unaccustomed to freely given kindness as Margaret was to speaking of her feelings aloud.

I've lived too long in Boston, Martha thought. *I've forgotten that some people are kind because they are kind, not because they have an agenda.*

Ethel Jean walked in. "I see you've found your aunt's secret weapon," she said acidly, gesturing around the room. "She talked Mary Jane into clearing out this back room and converting it to a classroom. Now my duplex and hers are piled high with extra inventory we haven't yet gone through *and* we have crazy birders traipsing back here three times a month."

Martha thought of the sisters' duplex building, which was just a block from the village square, and imaged the grumpy Ethel Jean carrying antiques back and forth to the store. Not a pleasant thought.

"Methinks she doth protest too much," Margaret said, almost under her breath.

"What was that, Johnny Cash?" Ethel Jean shot back. Martha recalled her aunt telling her that Margaret had worn black since the death of her husband on their wedding night almost fifty years ago, and everyone had become so accustomed to it that no one even noticed anymore. Except Ethel Jean, apparently.

"Nothing," Margaret mumbled.

"Sister, what are you up to back there?" came Mary Jane's singsong voice.

"Oh sheesh," said Ethel Jean, looking up at the ceiling as if beseeching a higher power to turn down her sister's happy dial. Mary Jane came flouncing in, wearing a man's oilskin hat with the wide brim set at a jaunty angle over her outfit of a tweed jacket, breeches and tall leather boots. Ethel Jean looked back at Margaret and Martha and rolled her eyes once more skyward. "Well, if it isn't Mr. Darcy," she said wryly.

"Oh, Ethel Jean," said Mary Jane, dismissing her sister with an aristocratic wave of her hand. "You know how I enjoy dressing up when we have classes back here. And besides, we made three hundred dollars in sales this morning, which you know would *not* have happened if those wonderful birders hadn't come through. Lorna had such a head for business; if it hadn't been for her, this would still be a storage area and we wouldn't have had a soul in the shop so early in the day." Mary Jane removed her riding gloves, carefully pulling the end of one finger at a time as if she really *had* been out riding with the hounds all morning.

"I can't take it," said Ethel Jean disgustedly, turning back to the store. "You're ridic—" She stopped mid-sentence. "Where did you get those?" she asked, her deep, accusing voice taking all levity out of the room. She was staring fixedly at the bird paintings Martha had removed from her aunt's portfolio. Tentatively, Ethel Jean reached out to touch the corner of one of the plastic sleeves and straighten the angle.

"Oh my," Mary Jane said, nervously fingering the riding crop in her hand.

"They were in Aunt Lorna's old secretary," replied Martha. "I threw them in the portfolio yesterday after I'd met Albert and they were still in there when I came in to meet Margaret this morning."

Margaret gave out what sounded almost like a squeak, picked up her teacup, the portfolio of statements, and her own briefcase, and swept out of the room. Martha looked from Ethel Jean to Mary Jane, trying to understand what was going on.

"Well, I'll be damned," said Ethel Jean acidly.

"Now, Ethel Jean, don't start again," said Mary Jane, her tone of voice more pleading than any Martha had heard her use with her sister before. "Lorna was a friend and it was the right thing to do."

Ethel Jean looked at her sister and, too exasperated for words, brushed out of the room.

"Is everything all right?" asked Martha, unsure what had just happened. "Why is Ethel Jean so upset? Was it something I said?"

"No, my dear, it has nothing to do with you," said Mary Jane. "But it does have everything to do with me and your aunt. You see, these came into the shop from an estate sale I visited. They were so beautiful. I was in the midst of pricing them a few months back when your aunt came over to the shop for a visit. She saw them and was admiring them so much, I gave them to her. My sister feels they are quite valuable—"

"NOT VALUABLE, PRICELESS!" came a shout from the front of the antiques shop. Mary Jane pressed her eyes tightly shut and cringed slightly.

"It's left my sister quite upset with me, you see. The set—particularly the mockingbird, being our state bird—could have significant value."

Martha looked at her, confused. "But there were only these two in the secretary," she said. "The cedar waxwing and the blue jay."

"Ethel Jean is quite the birder, as you know, and I can assure you that there was also a mockingbird lithograph. I heard about it all the rest of that day and, as you can see, it is still a source of contention between us. I'm only glad we don't live together or else I would likely never hear the end of it."

"I can't imagine where the other one is," said Martha. "And what is a lithograph, anyway? I've heard the term, but thought it had something to do with museums."

Mary Jane went into full antique-dealer mode. "Lithographs were created in the 1800s as a way to make copies of works of art. Pictures were etched on wood or other surfaces, covered in paint or ink, and reprinted onto fine paper. Think John James Audubon's famous renderings. Though the medium is rarely used now, except for modern letterpresses that produce unique greeting cards and such, it was very cutting edge in the early 1800s."

"Are you saying these are Audubon lithographs?" asked Martha, looking down nervously at the two pictures on the table in front of her.

"I seriously doubt it," said Mary Jane. "From what I could find out, only about a hundred and twenty full sets of his prints survive, and most are in public museums and libraries. But I have to agree, the three I found at the estate sale sure looked old and possibly valuable."

"Mary Jane, you should have these back," said Martha, pushing the lithographs partway across the table toward her. "They belong to you."

"Nonsense," said Mary Jane. "I gave them to my friend Lorna and now they pass on to you."

A strangled moan was audible from the antique shop beyond the green curtain.

When Martha and Mary Jane finally emerged from the classroom, the older woman stayed in the antique store to assist a few lingering birders and Martha headed back through the hallway to Birds 'n' Beans. Things had calmed down somewhat, the last of the workshop participants having made off with their purchases and a coffee to go. PJ was moving around the fifty-pound bags of green coffee that had been dropped off that morning, mumbling to himself under his breath.

"PJ, can I help?" Martha asked tentatively.

"Yes. You can sub in for Mavis on our bowling team tomorrow," PJ said with uncharacteristic bluntness. "This is the fifth time she has cancelled on us; she claims she has plantar fasciitis. Last time it was her bunions. It's amazing she can actually walk, let alone do yoga." He grunted as he moved another bag to lean up against the massive antique roaster. "Any chance you would stand in for her?"

Martha recalled Mavis, the small woman she'd met at the celebration of life; the one who'd mentioned she'd gone to high school with Aunt Lorna.

Helen walked up to them, hands on hips. "Please tell me you've talked Martha into bowling with us tomorrow," she said to PJ, exhaling either in relief at the shop calming down or anticipation at the prospect of Martha agreeing to bowl with the team, or a combination of both. PJ straightened up and looked at Martha, his shapely eyebrows raised in a question.

"It's entirely her decision. I'm sure she's very busy at the moment."

Martha looked back and forth between the two, remembering all that they'd done that morning to keep her aunt's shop running like a well-oiled machine.

"What time is the game and where shall I meet you?" she said, blowing on the tips of her fingers through a conspiratorial grin.

Chapter Ten

Martha focused as she grasped the ruby red bowling ball upright just below her chin. She began her familiar approach, drawing her right arm back, swinging forward, and then SNAP! She let the ball go as the toe of her bowling shoe touched the tip of the black line at the top of the shiny oiled lane. The ball shot down the wooden alley, skirting the edge of the right gutter before arcing slightly left and smashing into the ten pins triangled at the end.

"Stee-RIKE!" yelled Joanne, apparently unable to think of an appropriate equivalent in French so going with the good old English standby. Martha felt elated; everyone on the team was jumping up from the crescent-shaped table situated about fifteen feet back from the alley and high-fiving her.

Joanne had forgone selecting a color and opted instead for a design *du jour*; peacock. Everything on her, from her earrings to her stretchy pants to her hair accessories, managed to incorporate the turquoise and royal-blue pattern with a dark eye-like center. The overall effect was striking.

Perhaps, thought Martha, *she meant to distract the bowlers from the opposing team playing in the next lane?*

Martha sat, taking in the familiar sights and sounds of the bowling alley. This one, Splitsville Bowlorama, was like so many others she'd frequented since first discovering the sport as part of a team-building exercise at work. Ubiquitous large-screen televisions were situated strategically all over, so that no matter where you sat, one was in view. The televisions showed a combination of college and pro football and basketball, and one near the small restaurant area showing revolving live feeds of the lanes and bowlers themselves. This alley was a bit smaller than those she'd frequented in Boston—they had around thirty-two lanes to this one's eight—but it had the same carefree vibe.

The members of the team—coach PJ, Officer Tomlinson, Joanne, Carl and, for today, Martha—all sported long-sleeved black t-shirts that read "Bowling is for the Birds" on the back in Comic Sans font, with "Birds" down one sleeve and "Beans" down the other. On the chest pocket of each was the shop's logo. There was no doubt which local business backed this team.

Officer Tomlinson was just coming back to the table with a family size basket of wings, sides of bleu cheese dressing, carrots and celery, and a giant stack of napkins. She sat down next to Martha and held out the napkins.

"Care for some wings?" she said, her tone friendly. Martha felt herself go frosty at the offer.

"No thanks," she said, pretending to be engrossed in the six-foot-five Carl pulling back his beefy arm to let fly a giant purple bowling ball.

"Your aunt really loved this team," said the officer, dipping a wing into some bleu cheese and taking a bite. "I had never even picked up a bowling ball until she encouraged me to join a practice when I had just moved to Riley Creek. I didn't really know anyone and had stopped into the shop for a coffee. Next thing I knew, I'd committed part of my Sunday afternoons to this motley crew."

Martha nodded aloofly, still uneasy about Officer Tomlinson questioning Aunt Lorna's friends as part of the murder inquiry. Turning to her right, she leaned over to Joanne.

"Thanks again for your suggestion that I work remotely from Riley Creek while I sort things out," she said to the colorful French teacher. "I called my president that afternoon and talked him through it. It seems to be working well, at least for now. I can accomplish twice as much as I did when I was in the office. Anyway, thanks."

Joanne, moving her head slightly in Martha's direction, but not taking her eyes away from PJ's bowling ball as it spun down the lane, replied, "Good, yes, good... I'm glad it is working out."

Martha smiled. *This may be a friendly neighborhood bowling league, but there's no shortage of competition going on.*

Once they'd finished their third game and said goodbye to the other players from their league, the Birds 'n' Beans team sat down to change back into their street shoes. Martha was beside Carl as she removed her rented red, white and blue-striped bowling shoes while he bent his huge frame down to take off his size fourteens.

Carl had only two interests in life, as far as Martha could tell: baking and his family. He had always been a man of few words, something Martha appreciated since so many people in her professional life seemed to take joy in the mere sound of their own voice. He had certainly not said much the whole afternoon, only erupting in deep-throated cheers when someone bowled a strike, so when he leaned over to speak to her in his slightly accented English, Martha was taken by surprise.

"It is not my business, but PJ told me you are angry with Allison, so I am saying this anyway. Allison means no harm to you. She lost a friend too and is only doing her job."

Those three sentences had clearly cost the quiet German giant; he was flushed and perhaps a little embarrassed at his outpouring. He finished packing up his leather bowling bag and headed out the glass doors with most of the others, while Martha remained seated on the bench for a few moments, considering what Carl had just said.

PJ and Officer Tomlinson were the last of the team to pack up, and Martha walked over to them.

"Thanks again for inviting me to join you," she said.

"Are you kidding?" said PJ. "Thanks to you we might just qualify for the Thanksgiving Tournament! We haven't turned in that many strikes since Clint the barber was on the team. Once he hurt his back, we started hurting too."

Martha turned to Allison Tomlinson. "Hey, can we start again? I'm afraid I haven't been very kind to you since I learned the police are looking into my aunt's connection to Sentrich. I understand you and she were actually friends, so I wonder if I could buy you a beer." Martha glanced at PJ to see him give her a knowing smile and a nod. "PJ, join us?"

He shook his head as he tightened up his ponytail. "You girls go ahead. I've got to get cleaned up and head over to Toad in a Hole. Mr. Bennett wants to talk to me about catering a possible event, though what 'event' he could be holding is a mystery to me." He shrugged his shoulders, then hugged them both, picked up his custom black and red leather bowling ball bag with one beefy arm, and departed.

Martha asked Allison what her poison was.

"Actually, they sell some of our best local microbrews here. I think I saw Tempestuous Ale on tap. That would be great."

Martha went to the bar to purchase their drinks while Allison grabbed a table. When Martha came back, she handed Allison's beer to her, then took a sip of her own, enjoying the crisp hops of the brew and detecting a hint of orange at the back of her throat.

"So," she said, "since you're not interviewing me, should I still call you Officer Tomlinson?"

"Oh, jeez, please call me Allison," the other woman said, shaking her head and grinning in embarrassment.

"OK. And look, I'm sorry I've been such a jerk. It's just that one of the gals told me that you'd been asking about my aunt and there's no way she could be connected to what happened to Sentrich. I don't care if her fingerprints *are* on the murder weapon. The whole situation has me on edge, but I could have behaved a lot better toward you."

"No problem. I totally understand. And don't bite my head off, but your aunt did know Sentrich, fairly well from what I can tell. But having known your aunt personally, I agree with you that Lorna could not have had anything to do with his death, literally or figuratively. It just makes no sense. From what I gather, she was one of the most upstanding, solid citizens this town's ever had. What would her motive have been?"

"Wait a minute—just how well did they know each other? What did you find out? I only know from the gals at the shop that he did odd jobs for her."

"Apparently, Sentrich had been doing lots of jobs around her cottage on a fairly regular basis—helping her sort some things in the attic; stacking wood. It sounds like she wasn't on top of her game physically and he was helping her with her projects. According to Delores Ritzenwaller, Lorna hoped to get him back on his feet until he could find a regular job and she was really invested in him. She even had coffee with him on the porch, as if they'd become friends of a sort..." Here Allison trailed off and gave an almost imperceptible shudder. "We figure the Birds 'n' Beans business card that was found on him came from your aunt."

"None of what you just told me sounds out of character, except for the part about her not doing well physically. I had no idea."

Allison nodded. "I'm sure she didn't want to worry you."

"But now what?" asked Martha. "Do you have any suspects? I'm really concerned about Sentrich's death being connected to Aunt Lorna, even though we know she was dead before he was." *That might be the weirdest sentence I've ever uttered.*

"I'm sorry, Martha, but I can't discuss too many details of an open investigation. I can tell you we are trying to talk to Sentrich's grandmother to get some background on him. She lives out on Rhubarb Pike, but she gets so upset when any officer speaks to her, we haven't been able to gain any information so far. Other than that, all we've gathered is that Sentrich was a ne'er-do-well who rarely held a steady job. His grandmother is the only one expressing any remorse at his passing." Allison shook her head and took a deep swallow of her beer.

They sat quietly for a few minutes, sipping their beers and half-watching the bowlers around them. Allison waved at a group of men who'd walked in and were heading toward the shoe rental counter. One of them peeled away from the group and came to their table. Martha's smile froze when she saw who it was.

"Officer," he said, nodding to Allison.

"Hi, Jason. How are you? This is my friend Martha Sloane."

"Martha and I know each other from years back," replied Jason Turngate. "How are you, Martha?"

"Just fine," replied Martha frostily.

"Well, good to bump into you, Allison," said Jason, tipping his ball cap at them before turning to rejoin his friends.

"You guys friends?" inquired Allison.

"Once upon a time, you could have said that. I spent summers here as a kid with my aunt, and Jason and I passed a fair amount of time together. But lots has changed since then. You could say we're more... acquaintances now." Martha crossed her arms in front of her as she recalled her recent run-in with Jason at his store.

"Sounds like you and your aunt were really close," said Allison softly.

"We were. In fact, I stayed with my aunt right after I was born because my mother was so sick from complications. Then, growing up, I was here all summer, every summer, since my parents were busy building a real estate business and renting out apartments to college students. Every summer, they were turning over apartments to get them ready for fall rentals, and I always preferred to be here in Riley Creek anyway. It worked well all around.

"I lost both of my parents to a car accident just before college, and it's been me and Aunt Lorna ever since. Or, at least, it *had* been us."

"I'm so sorry," replied Allison. "What a loss for you."

"It is," said Martha, tearing up. "And I feel so bad I hadn't been able to visit much this past year or so, what with work and all. Aunt Lorna said she understood, but now I see I should have done better by her. Maybe if I'd known she wasn't doing well, I could have done something to help."

"You need to lighten up on yourself. I didn't even know you before meeting you last week, but I can tell you that you were the apple of your aunt's eye. She was so proud of you and your success, and you meant everything to her. She talked about you often when I stopped in at the shop. And... I don't exactly know how to put this, but the coroner tells me that the massive heart attack that took her was a ticking time bomb. No matter what anyone had done to help her, her time to leave us would have been about the same."

Allison looked at Martha sympathetically and dabbed at her own eyes with the cuff of her t-shirt. Martha sniffed and laughed.

"Gosh, you are in the right line of work," she said. "Here I am, spilling my life story to you when I hardly know you."

"Oh, it's OK," said Allison. "Family is complicated, and sometimes it's easier to share with a complete stranger."

They sat in companionable silence until Martha spoke.

"Well, I should probably get back to Penny. She's my schnauzer and I bet she's saying some pretty creative doggie curse words at me right about now."

"Oh wow, you have a dog? I have two. I'm part of a local rescue group—goldens, mostly—who meet up to do various service activities around the area. Join us sometime?" Allison asked.

"That sounds like fun," said Martha as they headed for the exit. "I'm calling Lorna's cottage home for the next several weeks or so while I sort out her finances and figure out what's next with the cottage and the shop."

"Well, I think I can speak for the rest of the team when I say I'm glad you're calling this place home for a bit," said Allison, laughing and opening the door for Martha.

Team. Home. Martha felt those words wash over her and had to admit that they sure felt nice.

Later that afternoon, Martha decided that it was time to give Penny some much-needed attention. After a nice long ramble along the river, she popped Penny inside for a drink, and then went out to the storage shed to get the large rubber tub kept there. She placed the tub on the back deck and filled it halfway with a nearby hose, then went to the kitchen to fill a kettle. Once it had reached an almost-boil, she carried it out and added its contents to the tub. Testing the temperature, she decided it was just right. She ducked inside to get some old towels and threw them and Penny's lavender shampoo onto the deck next to the tub.

"Come on, gal, time for your bath," she yelled inside. Penny came trotting out onto the porch. She was all doggie smiles until Martha turned to pick her up and put her into the tub. When that particular moment of this day's adventure arrived, she cowered under the picnic table, her ears and tail drawn down until Martha snagged her collar and pulled her out.

It was while Martha was toweling Penny off some sudsy minutes later that an idea came to her. She set Penny down to shake off the last drops with dramatic schnauzer-like flair, then let her back in the house to snuggle in her doggie bed. After dumping the sudsy water, rinsing the tub with a hose and hanging out the wet towels, Martha grabbed her backpack and keys and ran out the door.

Nothing is more complicated than family, she thought. *But Sentrich's family may just hold the key to this mystery.*

Chapter Eleven

Martha had given Delores, a walking *Who's Who* of Riley Creek, a quick call to confirm Curtis Sentrich's grandmother's name and whereabouts, but it was pretty hard to miss once she got close. Hardly anyone lived out on Rhubarb Pike besides some grazing cows and the odd horse in a field. The only other buildings on the winding rural road were a Kubota farm machinery outpost and a Chevron gas station sporting dated pumps that required patrons to pay cash inside.

The first sign Martha was getting warm was a metal mailbox mounted on two thin posts sunk into a plastic bucket of concrete. Even with this solid base, the jaunty angle and multiple dents on the side of the mailbox bore evidence to it being a favorite target of mischievous passersby. On the side of the mailbox, faded gold letters on individual stickers spelled out the name "RIGGS," while below it "SENTRICH" had been added in thick Sharpie letters.

It was a stretch to call the two deep ruts that ran from the mailbox a driveway, but Martha turned her Subaru into the track and followed it about five hundred yards before it opened onto a clearing. *Clearing or cluttering?* Martha wondered as she took in the yard, which was surrounded by a chain-link fence. It was filled with every variety of junked-out Trans Am she could imagine. Some were newer, but had experienced severe bodily trauma and were crinkled into near-unrecognizability. Others had been so scavenged for parts that only the general shape of the skeleton could prove their provenance.

At a quick glance, she took in fifteen car bodies in various states of decay, a few with cats asleep atop the roof and the oldest with saplings growing up through its open hood. Piles of discarded Trans Am doors stood against the fence on the left of the yard and a long, lopsided heap of tires eclipsed much of that which ran along the right.

The trailer home set at what might once have been a jaunty angle in the center of the yard had seen better days, but those days were long gone. Once-white siding was now graying and splotches of lichen provided uneven splashes of green along the front. On the end of the trailer closest to Martha, the gypsum exterior wall had peeled off from the main body and lay in the grass where it had fallen. On the ground and to the right of the cement block porch sat a lime green baby pool, faded and full of stagnant water. A wild-haired calico cat that had been drinking from it disappeared under the trailer the moment Martha got out of her car. A couple of worn La-Z-Boy chairs sat upright in the yard, one with the footrest pushed out and tall tufts of grass growing up through the gap.

The faded "NO TRESPASSING" sign nailed to the empty air conditioner ledge outside one of the trailer's windows gave her a moment's pause and she briefly reconsidered the likelihood of her plan's success. She climbed the wobbly porch and knocked on the door, letting her eyes rest on a newish satellite dish on the trailer's roof while she waited. Nothing. She knocked again. Nothing. Knocked one last time, a bit harder.

"GO AWAY!" yelled a gravelly voice angrily.

"Miss Riggs, my name is Martha Sloane and I'd like to talk to you," Martha said loudly, using her friendliest version of herself.

"I already told you people I got nothing to say," came the response.

Martha figured straight-up honesty gave her the best chance at talking to this lady. "Miss Riggs, I'm not with the police; I'm a visitor from out of town. Curtis was found in my aunt's yard and I just want to talk to you."

Silence.

Martha tried one last time. "Please, Miss Riggs, I need your help. I'm trying to find out what happened to Curtis."

Then Martha heard the floor creaking and could actually *see* the flimsy walls of the trailer quiver as someone inside moved around. The inside door opened and a grizzled face peered out at her.

"What do you know about my Curtis?" the old lady asked, frowning. She was short and wiry, with a wide halo of dark roots at the center of a bed of long blond hair. Hot pink tights, black V-neck t-shirt *sans* bra, and fuzzy well-worn house slippers completed the picture. Based on Sentrich's age and the woman's heavily wrinkled appearance, Martha clocked her at about eighty.

"Honestly, Miss Riggs, I don't know much at all, which is why I'm here," said Martha. "Could I come in for a minute? I just want to talk."

Pausing for a moment to consider, the old woman then snaked a hand out and pushed the torn screen door open. As soon as Martha had the doorframe in her hand, the woman turned to plod back down the narrow hall of the trailer. Martha took that as an invitation to enter, so she did.

"I haven't been Miss Riggs for going on sixty years, honey," the woman said in a slightly less gruff voice. "Might as well call me Donna."

Martha's eyes stung as the ammonia scent of cat urine washed over her. Following Donna Riggs, she entered a living room that appeared to double as a bedroom. The couch was made up with graying sheets, some homemade afghans of garish greens and yellows, and a flattened gray pillow. The rest of the space in the room was nearly filled by two huge brand-new leather chairs, one of which Donna flopped down into. The other was occupied by two scrawny orange cats, both of which darted out of the room and back down the hall past Martha.

"Have a seat," said Donna, pushing a button on the arm to make her own chair recline. Opposite her, a new-looking flat-screen television took up nearly the entire wall. Donna seemed to have been watching a program about the rich and famous in some glamorous far-off city. She glanced at the TV periodically, keeping track of the action while talking with her surprise visitor.

"Now what's this you want to know about Curtis?" she said, not so much asking as commanding Martha to answer. She took a deep drag from her e-cigarette and blew the smoke in Martha's general direction.

"Well, he was helping my Aunt Lorna. That's Lorna Sloane who owned Birds 'n' Beans in Riley Creek. I want to understand more about him and why he was found dead in the backyard of her cottage." Martha tried to make herself comfortable amidst the smoke and the cat hair that had already been making her eyes water. Her gaze did not miss the deep golden splotches in various spots on the carpet.

Focus, she told herself. *Do not cringe.* She was a dog person, after all.

"Honey, I don't know a thing about your aunt," said Donna, "but I can tell you what I told my Curtis. You watch what you get up to over in town. There's not much good that ever comes from mixing with that bunch, and getting them to part with their money is like trying to part the Red Sea." As emphasis, she reached over and laid her hand on a large book with "Holy Bible" inlaid in silver on the cover. The rings on top of the book suggested it sometimes doubled as a coaster, but currently, it lay next to a brand-new gaming console with wires snaking across the cream-colored carpet to the back of the flat-screen TV.

"When you say 'part with their money,' do you mean the odd jobs he was doing for my aunt?" asked Martha.

"Yeah, I knew he was doing those, but Curtis said he was on-to something bigger. Told me he was getting real lucky this time, had some money coming and was gonna get us out of this place." Donna gestured around at the trailer.

"You have a lovely home," said Martha automatically.

Donna snorted in disgust. "Are you kidding me? This place is a craphole. It's not what I ever wanted for Curtis. Who would want their grandson to grow up like this? But it's the best I could do to have a roof over his head, and me and him got along here just fine. But he wanted to get us out of here. Thought he'd finally be able to do it this time." Donna shook her head as tears welled up. "He'd been bringing home these electronic things"—and here she gestured at the TV—"to help me pass the time, and just the other day he brought home a bag of Florida oranges for me. Can you imagine that? Real oranges from Florida. Said he was getting money in the bank and it wasn't gonna be long now till we got outta this dump and lived somewhere sunny with a beach. Go figure. And now he's dead."

"Do you mind if I ask about Curtis's parents or other family and friends?" Martha asked sympathetically.

"Honey, I was pretty much it except for his no-account *girlfriend*," said Donna, making air quotes with her yellowing fingers when she referenced the female in Curtis's life. "His mama—my oldest—took off about five minutes after she had him and I ain't heard from her since. Never knew his daddy. It's been just me and him. I worked down at the Piggly Wiggly and barely made ends meet. Had to stop working a few years ago due to my emphysema." Here she patted her chest with the hand holding her e-cigarette. "But you never saw a more gentle boy."

Her voice broke, but she continued. "He did our shopping, brought me my medicines, and made all of our meals since I got to feeling poorly. Growing up, that boy always said he was going to strike it rich and get us outta here." Martha saw the anguish on the older lady's face. "And that *girlfriend*"—air quotes again—"wasn't gonna be helping him, I can tell you that." Donna gave Martha a knowing look, acknowledging that surely *she* knew the no-good ways of women. Then Donna shook her head regretfully.

"Guess that little boy finally did get outta here. And now I have to leave my home and go live with my no-good son in Missouri." Tears now spilling down her cheeks in earnest, she pulled a crumpled tissue out of the cup holder on her chair and dabbed at her eyes. "And I can't even bring my cats."

Suddenly, she looked up, a spark of a smile making her eyelids crinkle. "But, do you know? I think he was onto something this time. The money really had started coming in for once."

She gestured at the television and the gaming console, and then reached over to locate and hold up a brand-new iPhone. "Each month, he was bringing home more and more, and he was making plans to open a body shop like he always wanted. He was always so good with cars and engines, even as a kid. I hadn't seen him that excited in a good long time. Some sumbitch must have found out what Curtis was onto and decided he wanted it for himself."

Donna was quiet for a moment, and then said more softly, "Lady, do you know what happened to my Curtis? Them police came around, but I know them. They've been after him for one thing and another over the years, and now act like they care about him when all they wanna do is drag his name through the mud and back. I got nothing to say to them."

"Donna, you'll probably have to talk to them at some point," Martha replied softly. "They really are trying to figure out what happened, and I am too. Since he was found on my aunt's property, I need to clear her name before I head back north. Is there anything at all that you can tell me that might help? Anything?"

The older woman shook her head. "I've been going over it and over it in my head. Curtis didn't always tell me the details of things. He got wrapped up with the wrong people all his life, hoping one of them would help him get rich quick, and he always forgot to ask questions about how the money was gonna come. I suspect that girl had something to do with it, though I couldn't say what. All I can tell you is that this time, he said it was just him; that he was the only person he could depend on to get us a different life. And something about always being able to bank on people's secrets. Don't know what that meant, but he said it a coupla times these last months."

Martha felt a chill run over her for reasons she could not explain. Something Donna had just said made a connection in her brain that she couldn't quite put her finger on.

Martha reached over and squeezed the yellowing hand that still lay on the Holy Bible. "Thank you, Donna. I appreciate all you've told me about Curtis. He sounds like a young man who took good care of you, and I am going to do all I can to figure out who killed him. If I do, I promise to tell you. Now can you tell me Curtis's girlfriend's name? She might be able to help me with some information too."

Donna served up the name with a sneer. "Cherry Marshall."

After giving Donna her phone number in case the older woman remembered anything else, Martha left the trailer, not with the rush of relief she'd expected, but with a sense that something awful had happened in Riley Creek. And it had ended in her aunt's backyard.

She needed to talk to Cherry.

Chapter Twelve

The next morning, Martha caught up on some Berry College work. *I could get used to this*, she thought. *No fighting traffic; no expensive parking fees to pay; no interruptions from someone tapping on my office door needing help. Sign me up.* If only she didn't feel such pressure to get back to Boston. She was nearly at the end of the one week she had thought she'd need and still had no idea how soon she'd be able to wrap things up in Riley Creek. Gazing around the homey cottage, she wondered if there was a part of her that didn't really want to hurry back.

Having checked off some items from her to-do list, Martha called Margaret and they agreed to meet at the shop to go over Lorna's papers. From the little Margaret had said on the phone, or maybe from what she *didn't* say, Martha could tell the news would not be good. She arrived just in time to see PJ prepping the burlap bags of green coffee beans for the antique Royal roaster. Her aunt had found this 1905 peanut roaster for sale on the internet a few years ago and had gotten Jimmy to drive her to South Carolina to pick it up. Then she'd hired Frank Elder, the owner of the hardware store, to restore it and convert it to a bean roaster. Now it was the source of all Birds 'n' Beans bags of premium whole-roasted beans and ground coffee.

"Don't worry," said PJ, smiling. "I won't be firing this up till after hours. Just getting things ready to roll so I can start roasting once we close." Martha knew from watching the process in visits past that the machine, while upgraded not to spew the smell of engine oil into the enclosed shop, did make quite a racket once the beans and chaff started cracking and separating.

"You know," Martha said, "since I'm going to be around for a while, I wouldn't mind you teaching me how to run that thing." She looked apprehensively at the large mechanical contraption, partly in fear and partly in admiration. "In fact, you and Helen have pretty much been running this place all on your own since Aunt Lorna's passing and we haven't really talked much about the business."

"Madame Royal is a fickle mistress," said PJ, nodding his head toward the roaster. "But I'd be happy for you two to become better acquainted. And as far as the shop goes, Helen and I are doing just fine. We're here when you are ready to talk more. We both know you have a lot going on at the moment, but we can teach you everything we know. Which between the two of us is half of what your aunt Lorna knew," he added with a laugh.

"Thanks a ton, PJ. You are both lifesavers. I'd love to start my roasting lessons tonight, but Jimmy and Delores have invited me over for dinner. Another evening soon?"

"Sure. I fire up Her Majesty once a week and I'll be sure to get you here to learn the tricks of the trade. Meantime, I think Margaret is waiting for you in the shop."

PJ turned to continue his roasting preparations and Martha looked toward the back of the shop. Spotting Margaret clad in black corduroy pants and black turtleneck with tea in hand, she approached the table.

"Do you want anything to go with your tea?" she asked. When Margaret answered in the negative, Martha went to the coffee self-serve station, poured herself a Bright Breakfast Blend, added some skim milk and raw sugar, and returned to sit. She spotted Mavis perched at the counter, sipping coffee and reading *Yoga News*, and waved a greeting.

"Well, how bad is it, Margaret?" Martha asked, taking a sip of coffee and giggling, both actions betraying her nervousness.

Margaret mirrored Martha, picking up her delicate cup of tea and taking a strong swig. Then she pulled Lorna's portfolio out of her briefcase and rested a hand on top of it.

"I've only ever done the books for the church and I don't have any formal training, but something very strange was going on with your late aunt's accounts. Was she by any chance taking out money and sending it to you in cash? Or do you have any idea of accounts that she might have had at other banks besides our own Mountain State Bank?" She peered at Martha over the rims of her glasses, the line of her bifocals causing a distortion across the horizontal of her upper cheek.

Martha was confused by Margaret's question. "She definitely was not sending me cash. As far as other accounts, not that I know of. I think Aunt Lorna liked to conduct all of her business locally and keep her money here in Riley Creek. Why do you ask?"

"Well," Margaret said, "best I can tell, she started taking out large amounts of cash from her personal and business checking accounts about a year ago—to the tune of a thousand dollars here and a thousand dollars there. But it's all added up to almost twenty-five thousand dollars in total."

"Twenty-five thousand dollars? In cash?" Martha asked, her mouth hanging open.

"Yes. And that's not all. She stopped paying on her life insurance policy months ago so it lapsed and is no longer payable. She missed the last several payments on both the house and the shop loan, and she's got notices from the bank as the mortgage lender and the loan servicer for a home-equity line of credit. She'd gotten quite behind on her finances and is now upside down on both properties." Margaret nodded almost imperceptibly, as if she had practiced these lines and found her recitation satisfactory. "Or, rather, *you* are upside down."

Martha looked at Margaret, willing her to make sense. "What do you mean I'm upside down?"

Margaret looked up at the ceiling in thought for a moment, as if contemplating how to explain a complex concept to a child. Then she said, slowly and with exaggerated enunciation, "You owe more money than either property is currently worth."

Martha leaned back against her chair, stunned. Having been raised under Aunt Lorna's careful financial influence, she'd lived a frugal lifestyle, never spending more than she should, rarely traveling, and only buying what she needed. Living in Boston made that easy, since her rent took a significant chunk of her pay. But the little she had left, she saved carefully and she was never in the red with her savings or checking. By contrast, Lorna had apparently blown through her savings and what equity she'd created in the house and shop, leaving Martha holding the proverbial financial bag. How was that possible?

"Margaret, thank you for figuring all of that out, but what does it mean? Do I owe all of that money now?" Martha asked. She thought about what Albert Jeremiah had explained: her aunt's estate documents were all in proper shape and would require minimal time in the probate court before everything Lorna had owned would convert to Martha's name. What had been relieving news days earlier was now terrifying.

"Well, Shakespeare said, 'He that dies pays all debts,'" Margaret replied. "I guess that was true for Lorna, except that she passed her debts on to you. I'm sure she had plans to make everything right long before she passed away. She would never have wanted you to bear the burden of her bills. That said, I'm afraid you are responsible. You'll have to ask Albert Jeremiah for sure, but when my brother-in-law died and his bait shop was in debt, everything went to my sister Janice and she had to sell the shop in order to pay the remaining debt. She felt terrible having to tell his long-time employees they were out of work."

Martha turned to glance at PJ. He was working away diligently at the roaster, opening and closing valves and reading various gauges to make sure everything was right in preparation for the evening's roasting. Looking satisfied, he threw his hand towel over his shoulder and headed to the hallway that connected Birds 'n' Beans to Silent Sisters.

"Or," Margaret continued, "you could discuss the situation with the bank. They might accept the proceeds from the sale of the cottage and shop and their contents as sufficient payment of the debt."

"Their contents?" exclaimed Martha, sick at the thought of all of Aunt Lorna's beautiful things being sold to strangers.

"Yes, I'm afraid so," answered Margaret sympathetically, looking out at the finches popping around on the feeders. "The current value of the cottage alone is not enough to pay off the rest of the mortgage as well as the home equity loan and late fees that have added up." Here, she paused as if summoning courage to speak her next sentence. "I hesitate to say this, but I believe your aunt has several antiques and family heirlooms that might be of significant value..."

Martha felt a wave of nausea pass over her. "Oh, Margaret, I couldn't. Please, you must keep this information between us while I sort things out. This is worse than I ever expected, but I'm not ready to give up just yet. Can you please figure out what the minimum amount is that I have to pay this month to cover everything? Maybe I could pay it from my own savings while I figure everything else out."

"Another idea," Margaret ventured hesitantly, "might be for me to see if there's a real estate agent who specializes in business sales. Perhaps you could think about selling the business, but not the cottage."

Martha was not sure about this, but what did she have to lose with things in such bad shape?

"Sure, I guess that's something to explore. Thank you, Margaret," she replied.

Just then, a man entered the shop and caught the attention of everyone in the place. He was tall with a dark two- or three-day beard covering his cheeks and a Fu Manchu mustache. His hair was slicked back like he'd just walked off the stage of *West Side Story*, and he wore a blue pinstripe suit with the jacket hanging over his shoulder from one hooked finger. He sauntered into the middle of the shop and looked around, taking a visual inventory of everything and scoffing as his eyes traveled over the stacks of seed and rows of feeders, resting momentarily on the locked case of birding binoculars.

As he turned, Martha saw the flash of a gold cross on a chain against a thick mat of chest hair. All this was visible thanks to his shirt being undone one more button than was necessary.

Riley Creek, a small town that many never even knew existed, was home to all kinds of folks who didn't fit anywhere else, and its residents practiced "live and let live" as a motto. It was part of the town's lifeblood and why Martha had always felt so at home here, so the three black crows tattooed along the visitor's neck would not in themselves have raised her hackles. Rather, it was the man's surly expression as he surveyed the shop.

Mavis, who had been standing at the counter chatting with another customer, to-go cup in her hand, slid carefully into a seat, not taking her eyes off of the man. Martha even noticed some birders who had been browsing field guides casually move away from him and toward the door. Helen, who had been stocking shelves with nuthatch mugs, took notice of the man and moved as if to approach him, but Martha, with a slight shake of her head, warned her off and rose out of her chair.

This place is mine now, for better or for worse, and this guy looks like trouble with a capital T. Martha sensed Margaret fold into herself at the table as she moved toward the man.

"Can I help you, sir?" she asked in a voice that was not quite as steady as she would have wished.

"Yeah. I wanna see the owner of this... establishment," he said, looking beyond her and into the hall connecting to Silent Sisters.

"*I* am the owner," she said in reply. "What can I help you with?"

"The old broad who owned this place and I were doing some business together. I'm here to take that business up with her niece, the girl she probably left the place to." He set Martha on edge with the "old broad" moniker. There was enough Boston in her to rise to the occasion.

"Look, sir, that's my aunt you're talking about, and she only died just over a week ago. I *do* own this place now, but I don't know anything about any business that she'd been involved in with you. Now, if there's nothing else I can do for you…" She held her arm up in the direction of the door, inviting him to leave.

"Yeah… I don't think so," he said, taking his time with each syllable. He slid slowly over to the coffee counter and sat down on one of the swiveling stools, pulling up his slacks to preserve their crease. As he did so, a chunky gold bracelet peeked out from the cuff of his shirt. "I have unfinished business with the owner of this store. As in, the owner owes me some money. And if you're the owner, that means *you*."

Martha felt her anger rise. She had been on the receiving end of men telling her what to do before, ignoring her while expecting her to follow their instructions, and had had plenty of opportunities in her professional life to tell those men what to do with their condescension. But here she felt out of her element. This man had an edge of danger and, much as she hated it, Martha felt she had to keep him talking in order to get him out of the store.

She sat down on a stool next to him, trying to act casual for the sake of the other patrons. It was then that she noticed the crudely tattooed letters on four fingers of each of his hands: G-O-O-D on his left hand and E-V-I-L on his right.

"Name's Imbroglio. But you can call me Cenzo," he said in a lowered voice, using the Italian "ch" pronunciation of the C. "My late partner, a Mr. Sentrich, had established a certain… arrangement with your aunt, and I received regular payments through him. That arrangement has not come to an end, so you and I need to draw up the terms of your payment schedule." He took a moment to look her up and down, clasping his hands on the counter as if intending to stay for a while.

"Look, Mr. Imbroglio, I don't know anything about any business arrangement my aunt and Curtis Sentrich had with you. Best I can tell, he only did odd jobs around her house for her. If there was some kind of arrangement, that is not between you and me. Now, I think it's time for you to leave."

She stood and once again made her body into an arrow that pointed in the direction of the door.

"This is not a very friendly business establishment. But I do see you serve coffee. Since we are going to be partners, why not give me a double shot of espresso on the house?" he asked, peering down at his manicured nails, not moving from his seat.

As if on cue, PJ strode in from the hallway to Silent Sisters, holding in his hand what Martha could only guess was an antique bowling pin. Slender and made from light-colored wood, it was about two feet long with a round knob capping the tip. A faded stripe of red paint went around its center. PJ held the tapered end and let the bottom rest in his other meaty hand, making his intent clear.

The bejeweled barista had transformed into a bouncer.

"Sir," said PJ, his bass tone far deeper than the one Martha was accustomed to hearing, "Ms. Sloane asked you to leave. Now I'm going to ask you just one more time."

Martha made herself close her gaping mouth. She had never seen nurturing PJ transform into a fierce mother bear before.

Imbroglio sized PJ up, sneered dismissively, and then spoke to Martha from the side of his mouth.

"I don't know what kind of place you're running here, but I've got other business to attend to. You and I will meet again," he said, looking Martha up and down suggestively as he rose. "I *will* collect what you owe me, one way or the other."

He looked over at Mavis and sneered. Then he put a hand on the back of the stool he had just vacated and pulled on it hard, causing it to careen back and forth on its post. Flipping his jacket over his shoulder, he walked slowly out the door, ignoring the stares of everyone around him.

Once he'd gone, Martha sat back down on her stool, her heart pounding, and gazed at PJ, who was now leaning against the counter on the hand that didn't hold the bowling pin.

"What the—?"

Suddenly, Ethel Jean rushed into the shop from the back hall, a hunting rifle held hip-high at the ready. All eyes swung toward her.

"Where is he?" she asked, her head turning quickly right to left. "Where is he?"

"Down, girl," said PJ, placing a red-lacquered finger on the barrel of the gun and gently lowering it. "All the action's over."

"Crap," said Ethel Jean. "PJ came over to talk about his roasting schedule since we usually close when he does it. When Margaret called over to tell PJ that some creep was here and refused to leave, I ran down to Fins to Fur to borrow this." She nodded at the rifle. "It's not loaded... I think." She looked at her feet, almost bashfully, then ratcheted things back up to her usual cranky, as if this were just another day in the rough and tumble antique industry. "Anyway, I'll run it back now."

Martha glanced over at Margaret, who had made herself so small in her chair, she was almost child-size. She brought up a hand to show a flip phone that she waggled back and forth with a shy grin.

PJ placed a hand on Ethel Jean's arm just as she turned to head back to Silent Sisters. "Thank you, honey," he said softly. "I know you had my back." He handed her the wooden weapon. "And I should give you this back, too."

"Wow, PJ, I can't believe it!" said Martha. "Coming to my aid with an antique bowling pin."

"Bowling pin, my ass," Ethel Jean yelled over her shoulder. "It was a juggling pin and it's so old, it would have crumbled if it had so much as bumped into something."

PJ looked around at the small crowd of onlookers and shrugged his muscly shoulders, grinning.

"Well, I don't care what you had," Martha said, "I just appreciate you arriving when you did. That guy was getting scary and I didn't sense he was going to leave anytime soon. Who is he, anyway?"

Before anyone could reply, Cat from Early Riser walked in. "What was Cenzo Imbroglio doing coming out of the shop?" she asked, sounding equal parts concerned and angry. "He's not someone I expected to bump into here in town."

"I have no idea. He came into the store demanding some kind of payment from me. What's his story?"

Mavis had gone to stand by Margaret, who was stuffing Lorna's portfolio into Martha's backpack for safekeeping. Both women looked as pale as mugs of steamed milk.

"All I know—and it's not much—is that he owns a used car lot out toward the campground," said Cat. "Word is he fixes the mileage on his junkers to be much less than it really is, and he works with some unsavory 'loan officers'"—she added air quotes with the first two fingers of both hands—"to arrange financing. We only know him because I went out there to shop for a starter car for Lewis a few years back and it turned into a nightmare. We tried to return the car, and Imbroglio and Carl had words. He kind of gives me the creeps and I'd hoped never to see him again. He tends to keep to himself—never normally comes into town. Carl will go crazy if he sees him around here."

"He said something about being Sentrich's business partner and wanting to collect money Lorna owed. We should probably tell the police just to be on the safe side. I'll phone Allison as soon as I settle my nerves." Martha looked around the store at the remaining customers who were still stealing furtive glances toward her. She raised her voice a bit. "It's OK, folks. Go about your coffee drinking. That guy is not coming back."

As a belted kingfisher chirped out the eleven o'clock hour, she *hoped* he wouldn't come back.

Chapter Thirteen

Returning home, Martha thought about the rest of her day. She'd ended up at the shop far longer than she'd intended when she had left the cottage that morning.

Penny is not going to be happy with me, she reflected, picking up her walking pace.

But, like the true friend she was, Penny was happy to see Martha and all slights were forgiven. As Martha entered the unlocked front door, Penny ran to the glass door leading to the back porch. Letting her out, Martha then slid the glass door closed and thought about what she needed to do next.

She realized that the cottage was still looking clean from the gals' ministrations several days ago, but the big wooden farm table was missing something...

Flowers! Martha could recall any number of gorgeous bouquets that Lorna had placed there over the years. Sometimes, she purchased an exotic display from the farmers' market; sometimes a simple floral arrangement from the Piggly Wiggly; and sometimes she'd collected interesting weeds from the riverside to place in a mason jar in the center of the old hickory table. Martha hadn't had time to think about things like flowers with all that had transpired since her arrival, but now that she was going to be spending more time here, she decided to bring back her aunt's tradition. Maybe it would warm the place up a bit. Plus, she needed to pick up a small gift for Delores and Jimmy to thank them for tonight's dinner, and flowers might be just the thing.

Luck was in her favor because today was Monday and that meant the farmers' market was open. Martha had heard some leaf peepers in the shop mention that October was the last month for the fall market and it wouldn't open again until May. Idly, she wondered where she would be in May and whether she would ever again get to enjoy a lazy stroll through the open stalls.

Clipping on Penny's leash, she threw on a baseball cap, put her wallet in her pocket, and headed out the door with a canvas bag from the pantry over her arm. Her walk carried her in a direction that paralleled the river, not taking her far enough west to enter the square, but rather staying along its east edge and meandering north on the Arrowhead Path. Gusts of wind came at her from the left, carrying just enough cool to make her happy she was wearing her long-sleeve waffle-weave shirt.

Martha looked down and smiled to see Penny pointing her head directly into the wind, picking up the out-of-town news. Briefly, Martha wondered at the genesis of the Arrowhead Path name, assuming it was an homage to the Native American presence in this area many years ago. She really didn't know a lot about the history of Riley Creek and wondered how she might find out more.

Why haven't I thought about this before? she wondered. She'd been coming here for years and only now wanted to know more—her brain was doing strange things to her, bringing on odd curiosities. Was this some phase of grief? How many stages were there again? Seven? Seventeen? She should research that too.

After a leisurely thirty-minute ramble, she began to hear the unmistakable sounds of a gathering. The hum of generators and buzz of voices, the squeal of delighted children—they all carried on the wind. Though just a fraction of the size of its summer equivalent, the fall market was special in its own way. Set up in the parking lot of the Green Maples Flea Market, it hosted stalls of various sizes and configurations. Many of the "stalls" were actually pickup trucks full of produce with canopy tents covering their open tailgates. Some sported makeshift tables displaying vendors' offerings, and others had larger, more sturdy tables with substantial tenting protecting their tenants from the elements.

Everywhere, there were splashes of color from the flowers and plants that were on offer, and flashes of brilliance shone from jars of honey, salsa and other preserved goodies. People milled around happily, shopping bags over arms. Some had dogs along, like Martha, and she even spied a few water stations for canine companions. Martha hadn't been here in recent years with Lorna since her visits had been brief, but she knew Lorna had come here to get fresh ingredients for dinner or to pick up a loaf of newly baked bread.

As soon as the memory of fresh bread hit Martha's brain, her eyes spied Early Riser's market stall, which was really three folding tables shaped into a U. An easel held a dry erase board listing the day's offerings and prices (a few gaps showing that some items had already run out and been erased), and there were delectable-looking baked goods piled in bakers' boxes along the length of all three tables. Looking through the gaps between customers, Martha spied focaccia with golden brown cheese and dark red roasted tomato bits, as well as the shop's signature *apfelstrudel*, which she knew was made using Carl's mother's recipe.

Open boxes of cookies, muffins and assorted cupcakes were—if the line of people was any indication—going fast. Lewis was bagging items for customers while Carl handled the cash and restocked items as they ran low. Since she'd seen Cat earlier, Martha guessed she was covering the bakery's customers while her husband and son worked the farmers' market.

Strolling with Penny past offerings of fresh cheese and eggs, homemade oatmeal soaps, and pungent fall herbs, Martha came to a setup she had never seen before, even in the sprawling farmers' markets in the suburbs of Boston. A cornflower-blue vintage Volkswagen van with its side doors swung open had been fitted with a counter and a wide awning, under which sat four bistro tables with chairs. "Love Potion #9" was written in large bubble letters on one of the awning flaps, accompanied by a chubby white daisy with a round yellow center. Artfully arranged flowers decorated the pavement on either side of the van's counter, from small bunches in jars to dramatic bundles of sunflowers in milk churns. The "potion" was being pressed from a large contraption and the van's owners were passing it out in small cups to customers at the counter.

When Martha was next in line, a dreadlocked young lady working the counter asked, "Would you like a raw juice? Boosts your immunity, cleanses toxins. We've got plain beet, carrot, or apple, or I can make you a Super Boost with all three, plus lemon and ginger. Great for your energy."

Feeling unsure, Martha began to explain that she just wanted some flowers, but was interrupted by a deep voice behind her.

"Two Super Boosts, please."

She turned to look at Detective Perry whom she'd last met at the police station. Best she could recall, her last words to him as she'd left had not been very pleasant—something along the lines of him not knowing how to run an investigation and maybe something else about him trying to damage a dead old lady's reputation.

Before she could snap at him for butting in front of her, he gestured to one of the small tables and said, "Join me?" She was *not* going to be rude to him in front of all of these people, so she plastered on a fake smile.

"All right," she said. "But just for a bit."

He retrieved their juices and met her at a far table. Once they were seated, he leaned down to tousle Penny's fur. She responded by flopping over on her back for a tummy rub.

Cheap little tart, thought Martha. *Have you no shame?*

"Cheers," he said, lifting his opaque plastic cup to her. Martha raised her own cup, but eyed its contents suspiciously. It might be good for her, but its reddish-brown color was... off-putting.

"I know, I know. Looks kind of awful, doesn't it?" he said, but drank the entire contents down in one gulp. "I tell myself that one of these each week will counter all of the junk I eat when I'm on a big case. Not sure it does, but it definitely makes me feel less guilty." He smiled. She hadn't noticed what nice teeth he had when she'd seen him last. They were nestled in what appeared to be a day's growth of beard that made him look a little rough around the edges, perhaps recently out of bed. Certainly more approachable than he'd been in his slacks and tie in the police station.

"And is my aunt's case what you would consider a 'big case'?" she asked, tasting the concoction. She was not sure she could recognize the flavor of any of the individual fruits or vegetables that were supposedly in the drink. It wasn't bad, but it wasn't exactly good, either.

"Of course," he said, wiping his mouth. "We don't get many murders in this one-horse town." Again, he flashed a smile at her, but she was not biting.

"Look," she said, "I don't mean to be rude, but the last time we talked, you all but accused my aunt of murder. That didn't go over well with me."

Holding his hands up, Perry said, "Now, hold on a second. I said that we'd determined your aunt was deceased prior to Sentrich's death, but her fingerprints were on the murder weapon. That's not quite the same as accusing her of murder. Look, your aunt is officially off the list of suspects. Given her health condition, the coroner says no way could she have planned to kill Sentrich. But we do have to investigate his apparent connection to your aunt."

Martha continued listening to him, her arms crossed and her eyes narrowed. "So in other words, you still think my aunt was mixed up in something illegal. And what do you mean, 'health condition'?"

He held up his hands again, this time in resignation. "Do you think we could start again? We're here at the farmers' market, it's a beautiful day, and I'm just asking to talk. What do you say?"

Since he had officially taken her aunt out of his list of suspects, Martha felt herself relax. A bit. But she still didn't like his implication that Aunt Lorna was involved in something underhanded.

"OK. That seems fair," she said.

"May I call you Martha?" he asked.

"Yes. Sure."

"Martha, you may or may not be aware that your aunt had begun suffering from a mild form of dementia. It was detected during the postmortem and confirmed with her family doctor." He paused, clearly realizing from her reaction that this was new information for Martha. "According to her doctor, though she functioned at a high level, the kind of organized planning necessary to carry out a murder was something your aunt could no longer manage."

"I... I hardly know what to say. I didn't know. Why wouldn't she have told me?"

"Well, according to her doctor, she didn't plan to share it with anyone until she needed help. Like so many older people with health problems, she probably didn't want to inconvenience anyone." Looking around the market, the detective asked, "Been here before?"

Martha snapped out of her momentary shock. "Not in a long while. It's much bigger than I remember. But that's great for the area, I guess," she said, trying to take small sips of her detox drink. He had bought it for her, after all, and it would be rude not to finish it.

"Yeah, it's a lifeline for some of our local small businesses and farmers. Some actually count on the market as a place to sell the majority of their yearly goods from late spring through fall. So, I gather you've spent lots of time in Riley Creek?"

"I think of it as the place I grew up," Martha replied, "since I more or less did. My mom was Lorna's sister, and my folks sent me here for the summers when I was a kid. It was easier than trying to find good summer camps and I loved being in the mountains with Lorna. I stayed in Boston for school, and then work, but always came home to visit as often as I could, which hasn't been that often these past few years. And since my folks died, it's really just been the two of us."

"Oh, I'm really sorry. I didn't mean to—"

"It's OK. Really. I don't mind talking about it. In many ways, I was closer to Aunt Lorna than either of my parents. I think I was more like her than them; I always preferred slipping around the riverbank hunting crayfish to fancy schools and city life. I mean, don't get me wrong, my parents were wonderful people. We were just... different. And then, once they passed, Aunt Lorna and I became even closer because we knew we were it for each other. And now..."

Here she became a bit wistful, speaking aloud the sense of loneliness that she wasn't sure she'd comprehended before.

"How about you?" she asked, needing to deflect attention from herself before she lost control of her emotions in front of the detective.

"Well, I guess compared to you, I'm a late arrival to Riley Creek. I grew up outside of Raleigh, North Carolina, and when I finished up at the police academy there, I worked in Charlotte for several years. Eventually I wanted to get away from the city, so applied here. Been here for the last three years, which, best I can tell, makes me still a newbie in these parts."

Out of habit, Martha glanced at his finger and saw no ring there. He caught her looking and she casually cast her eyes down to his feet, noticing for the first time a string bag bursting with fresh produce, a wrapped package she guessed was meat, and a long, thin baguette.

"What's for dinner?" she asked.

"Oh, nothing special. I fancy myself a semi-serious cook, but since I mainly cook for myself, I guess I've managed to keep the critics to a minimum." He studied her. "Since you're just visiting, I'm betting a home-cooked meal sometime wouldn't be unwelcome?"

"Um, sure, that could be fun." Martha felt the need to change the topic. Was this the second man to ask her to dinner in the past week? "So, do you have any suspects yet? While I'm glad you took Aunt Lorna out of your line of sight, it is a little unnerving to think a murderer is walking around free."

"Not as many as I'd like, but I do have a few leads. In fact, today is the first time I've taken a half day off since we found the body, so I should probably think about heading home and back to the station." He picked up their plastic cups and carried them to a nearby recycling barrel.

When he came back, Martha said, "To be honest, I've been asking around a bit to see what I can find out." She flushed, embarrassed to be comparing her novice efforts with those of a professional detective.

Perry looked a bit taken aback. "I understand you want to know why a body was found in your aunt's backyard," he said, "but this really is a police matter and you shouldn't get involved in it."

"I know," she said, feeling a bit irritated, "but are you aware of a guy named Cenzo Imbroglio?"

Detective Perry looked confused. "Of course I know of him, but not in connection with Sentrich's murder."

"Well, you might want to look into him. He came into my aunt's shop—*my* shop—today and all but threatened me. He said that my aunt owed him money and that he was Sentrich's business partner and was there to collect. Super creepy guy." Recalling Imbroglio's discomforting presence, she shivered. "Maybe you guys oughta take a look at him."

Whatever peace had settled on them seemed to have broken and she wondered what in the heck she was doing here with him. Perry seemed impacted by what she'd shared with him as he picked up his string bag ready to go. She roused Penny, and together, the three of them walked a few feet away from the camper.

"Oh, I still have to buy the flowers I came here for," she said. But as she turned to go, the detective gently grasped her upper arm.

"There's something I really shouldn't tell you, but I'm going to so you'll be sure to steer clear," he said, looking around to make sure they could not be overheard. "We are looking at one more suspect, someone who was seen arguing with Sentrich in the days prior to you finding the body. I understand from Allison he's an old friend of yours. Jason Turngate. Just give him a wide berth if you see him, OK?"

Martha swallowed, wondering whether to tell him to keep his warnings to himself and settling for a breezy, "OK. Sure." She felt strangely protective of Jason based on their long-ago friendship. But if he was willing to trap small animals in torturous steel traps, was it such a stretch to think he'd bash a human on the back of the head?

"And let's plan for that dinner sometime, OK?" Detective Perry asked her more softly as she was turning back toward Love Potion #9. For reasons she could not have explained, she pretended not to have heard him and kept walking.

Martha had purchased a large bunch of sunflowers for the kitchen table at the cottage and a pot of light purple hardy mums for Delores and Jimmy. She nestled the pot down deep in her canvas shopping bag and tucked the sunflowers alongside, their brilliant golden heads peeking from the top. There was plenty of time for her to get home, shower and enjoy a few chapters of her Fyfield mystery before heading to the Ritzenwallers'.

As she turned toward the parking area and home, her ear caught sounds incongruous with the cheery milling of the farmers' market crowd.

"Oh, screw you," a woman's voice shrieked.

Wow, thought Martha, *that sounds more like Boston than Riley Creek.* She looked ahead and saw a navy blue convertible Mustang pulled into one of the few spots for disabled drivers along the edge of the lot closest to the walkway. The same young policeman she'd seen at the station days ago had pulled his patrol car up behind the illegally parked Mustang and was now issuing its owner a ticket.

"Miss Marshall, you can't just park in a disabled parking space. It's against the law." The young officer, neck blanching, tried to calm the thin blond woman in front of him. Martha noted equal amounts of cleavage bulging from the top of her tight V-neck t-shirt and cheek spilling from the bottom of her even tighter running shorts.

"But I keep telling you, I twisted my ankle at the gym this morning and I *need* to park closer to the market." Both hands were planted on her waist, as if through sheer force of will she could get the young officer to see things her way. Far from nervous in the presence of police, the blond checked her watch impatiently and heaved a sigh.

"Sorry, ma'am. You'll need to move your vehicle now," he said, pasting the ticket to the Mustang's windshield when it became clear she had no intention of allowing him to hand it to her. He tipped his hat to her politely, and then moved back toward his patrol car.

Martha cupped her hand by her mouth and yelled, "Excuse me, are you Cherry Marshall?" She stated the name the way Donna Riggs had pronounced it, like the fruit.

"That's *Sherry*, like the old-fashioned drink. Who's askin'?" The blond eyed Martha with suspicion.

Drawing closer, Martha said, "You don't know me. I'm Martha Sloane, from out of town. I wondered if you'd be able to talk to me a bit about Curtis Sentrich."

Without missing a beat, Cherry said, "Well, right now, honey, I've got to move my car because this so-called *po*-liceman says I can't be here, even though this was a free country last time I checked." She nodded her head derisively at the patrol car, as if indicating a pile of dog doo someone had neglected to clean up. "But sure, for a six pack of root beer, I'd be glad to chat with you if you want to pop out to my place tomorrow. It's my day off, though, so I don't want to chat all day. I'm out at the Vacancy. Lucky number seven." She reached over to pull the citation from her windshield, then jotted something on it before handing it to Martha. "There's my cell number in case ya get lost."

This was not quite the reaction Martha had expected from someone whose boyfriend had recently been found murdered, but she knew from her own experience that grief expressed itself in many different ways and she should not judge someone she didn't know. But Martha did know the Vacancy, so they agreed on a time. As Martha and Penny turned to walk back to the cottage, Cherry (as in the drink, not the fruit) fired the Mustang's V8 engine and screeched out of the parking lot.

All the way back to the cottage, Martha's thoughts kept running from Perry and his invitation to dinner to his mention of Jason Turngate arguing with Sentrich. Arguing about what? The detective was handsome. And employed. But did she want to get involved when she had to start thinking of her return to Boston soon?

Her head spun. This rookie sleuthing was for the birds.

Chapter Fourteen

After Jimmy had served a delicious dinner of fresh river trout, homemade rolls and a delicate salad of cold green beans with mint and lemon, Delores invited Martha out to the back to have coffee and dessert. They sat in Adirondack chairs that faced into a yard giving way to an open field beyond, where three deer were standing at the edge of the bordering woods. Jimmy had started a fire in the pit in front of the chairs, and Fritz and Penny lay in the grass a safe distance away, but not so far that they didn't feel a bit of its warmth.

"I didn't know Jimmy had such a talent for cooking," said Martha. "If I had, I would have come over much sooner!" She sipped her mug of rich Birds 'n' Beans Rufous Blend. *Central American/African blend—Medium/dark roast—Full body—Smooth finish.* PJ's daily lessons on coffee were already paying off.

"He relegates me to dish washing and table setting," Delores said with a companionable roll of her eyes. "When he retired, I kept working and he started making dinner every night. One thing led to another, and next thing I knew, he won a cooking lesson from a bistro in Knoxville at one of the church raffles and that was all she wrote. Now I'm volunteering just a few hours a week at the library and he'll barely allow me past the threshold of the kitchen."

Just then, Jimmy came out holding a small tray with three dishes of light brown custard with a solid sugar top, three delicate silver spoons and napkins decorated with goldfinches.

"*Bon appétit*," he said quietly, passing dishes and spoons around. Martha dug into the sugary brown crust atop the dessert and rich explosions of sweet vanilla went off in her mouth.

"Delicious!" she moaned.

"I think he makes crème brûlée just so he can use his butane torch to crystalize the sugar on top," said Delores, shooting a quick wink at her husband. Jimmy, in his usual way, merely nodded with a small smile as he sipped his coffee, but it was clear that he was pleased at Martha's reaction to the decadent dessert.

"Martha dear, we haven't wanted to interfere, but how are you getting on? With... things?" asked Delores. Jimmy looked down, clearly a bit uncomfortable with his wife prying.

"Oh, I don't mind you asking," said Martha. "Just don't be surprised if I don't have lots of answers." She went on to explain that she was planning to stay a bit longer than she'd intended; how she'd made arrangements to telecommute for as long as the College President would allow and was taking it day by day, trying to figure out Lorna's finances and hoping to clear up the mystery of the body in the backyard. "I can't leave here without getting answers. Not only for my peace of mind, but to lift any cloud of suspicion that maybe Aunt Lorna was involved in something she shouldn't have been. I know she wasn't and so do you, but she's not here to speak for herself and there are some very weird things going on that I can't answer."

She went on to tell them of the missing money, the arrival of Cenzo Imbroglio at the shop, and the strange warning from Detective Perry about Jason Turngate. She held back the information about Lorna's dementia, not wanting to betray her aunt's privacy unnecessarily. It felt good to share all that had been on her mind, and answering the Ritzenwallers' questions helped her order things in her own head.

"Aunt Lorna was not a secretive person, so none of this makes sense." Martha couldn't miss the look that passed between Jimmy and Delores. "What?" she asked, looking pleadingly from one to the other. "Is there something you want to tell me? Please, if there's anything you know that might help me figure all of this out... I hope you'll explain that look the two of you just shared."

Delores looked at Jimmy. "James," she said—Martha had never heard Delores use her husband's given name before, "I know you think we ought not get involved, but we have to tell her."

"What?" asked Martha. "Tell me *what*?" She felt her irritation rise, even at this kind old couple.

"Very well." Jimmy put his empty dessert dish down on a small side table and took up his mug of coffee again. Holding it in his lap between his two massive hands, he said, "Martha, your aunt had a secret. It was an old secret and we don't know the details, but if it's important you know and it can somehow help you, we'll tell you." He took a sip of coffee, looked up at the darkening sky, and then continued. "For many years, we traveled to New Orleans once a year with your aunt, sometimes more than once a year."

"Oh, that's not a secret," said Martha, sitting back and relaxing. She realized she had been clenching her jaw, waiting for some terrible revelation. "When I was younger, my parents talked about how you and she went down for the Southern Book

Festival. You two would go to scope out new books for the library's collection and she came along for the birding."

"That's right, dear," said Delores. "Your aunt would spend the first few days with us, eating out, hearing authors—she usually frequented the naturalist authors' talks—and seeing the city. But what you likely don't know is that she would not spend the rest of the week with us. She would rent a car and go off to visit someone, then meet back up with us at the end of the week for the trip home. We never asked questions and she never told us who she was with. But she did ask in so many words that we keep her side trips to ourselves."

Jimmy added quietly, "At first, we thought she must be birding, trying to find some species or another that she could only see in that part of the country. But you know your aunt: when she went birding, she had her binoculars, hiking shoes, the works. She had none of those things along. When she came back, she seemed somehow sad in a resigned way... It's hard to explain."

"Was she still taking these trips with you when she died?" asked Martha, struggling to make sense of this added layer of intrigue about her beloved aunt.

"Oh no," Delores said quickly with a shake of her head. "Perhaps we've told this all wrong. You see, she only started going with us after your Uncle Tommy died—around 1982—and she stopped in 1989, the year your parents died. We haven't thought about this for many years, because Lorna never explained the trips; she just started telling us that she couldn't go anymore, so we stopped asking. It always puzzled us, but she never explained and we never probed."

"I'm not even sure it's right to mention it now that she has passed on, but with all that's happened, I guess it's OK to tell you," added Jimmy. "Recent events have caused us to revisit those times."

"I appreciate you telling me," said Martha, "but I'm afraid it only makes everything about my aunt more mysterious. I'm beginning to wonder if I ever knew her at all."

Suddenly feeling tired, Martha prepared to leave, claiming to have an early start the next day. Jimmy and Delores predictably would not allow her to help with the dishes, and Delores insisted on Jimmy walking her and Penny the small distance down the street to her cottage. As they reached the bottom step of the porch, Jimmy handed over Penny's leash. As he turned to go, he stopped and looked back at Martha.

"Martha, there are some mysteries that are best left unsolved. But if you are determined to follow this trail to its end, we ask only that you *please* use caution. Your aunt valued her privacy as much as Delores and I do." Pausing before his next sentence, he nodded almost imperceptibly. "And you might visit with Carl one of these days and tell him about Imbroglio coming into the shop. I think you would find him quite informative."

Without a further word, Jimmy made his way home to Delores.

The next morning, Martha slept in and awoke refreshed. Penny was still dozing at the foot of the bed, so Martha lay listening to the river and thinking over the previous day. It was hard to take in the mysteries swirling around her aunt. And how might the many threads come together to explain a dead body and Lorna's money troubles? Did the missing lithograph figure somehow? Not to mention Imbroglio's arrival on the scene and Detective Perry's warning about Jason.

She had been careful to lock the doors and check all the windows before climbing the stairs to bed last night. Martha noticed how flimsy the locks on Aunt Lorna's doors were, but of course, this was Riley Creek and not Boston, where she had triple locks, a chain, and an alarm system guarding her apartment. Her mind went briefly to the idea of having an alarm system installed in the cottage, but she reminded herself that would be something for the next owners to take on. It wasn't an expense she needed right now.

Once she'd managed to wiggle her feet enough to wake the schnauzer, she put the coffee on and let Penny out. By the time the terrier sprinted back up the steps of the deck, Martha was adding fresh cream to her Birder's Blend.

Rich and nutty, but not as intense as a dark roast, she thought as she padded back upstairs for her shower, dressing warmly for the day. Perhaps tonight would be the night for that fire.

After feeding Penny and getting her settled on her doggie bed, Martha headed for the square. Even though the day was overcast and she felt the tiny pinprick of an occasional raindrop, she still appreciated that she could walk most everywhere she needed to here in Riley Creek. Sure, she walked in Boston, but only when she was emerging from the T and rushing along in commuter mode. Today's walking was relaxing: taking in the fresh air, feeling the cold wind on her face, and crunching through the leaves underfoot. Wishing she'd brought a hat or earmuffs, she flipped up the collar on her fleece jacket and scrunched her ears down into it for warmth.

Crossing the square, she took in the usual morning hubbub. Delivery trucks driving up and driving away; newspapers bundled on the ground in front of Toad in a Hole; the waste management company emptying the public trash cans. There was an order to the activity that was faster than normal, but far from the chaos of a morning in downtown Boston. Again she reflected on how easy it would be to grow used to this.

Most of the square was business as usual—people shopping, some kids in the grass with dogs, a few older folks on the benches. But she also spotted Margaret come from behind Toad in a Hole. Back pressed against the white stucco wall, she was walking toward the front of the shop in a way that Martha could only call *stealthy*. As soon as she reached the front sidewalk, Margaret straightened up, jaw high, and walked purposefully across the square toward Birds 'n' Beans.

That's strange, thought Martha. Of course, Margaret *was* a little bit odd, so was this really that out of character? Shaking her head, Martha kept on walking.

Reaching An Early Riser, she ducked out of the way of a delivery van just pulling away. She spotted Lewis behind the wheel and gave a wave. Walking into the shop, she smelled the heavenly scent of baking bread and other sweet goods.

Cat was busy behind the counter. "Something wrong with the order for the shop?" she asked, concerned.

"As far as I know, no. I was actually wondering if you could spare Carl for a few minutes," Martha said. "And I'd love one of those blueberry muffins to go."

After serving Martha her muffin, Cat popped into the back room. A few minutes later, Carl appeared in his white chef's coat. Coming out from behind the counter, he shook Martha's hand.

"Cat said you were asking after me?"

"Hi, Carl. Thanks for seeing me. I had dinner with Jimmy and Delores last night, and Jimmy suggested I come see you to talk about a strange visitor to the shop yesterday. Cat probably mentioned him. Name's Cenzo Imbroglio..."

The reaction Martha got was as swift as it was surprising. Carl's gentle smile fell from his face, replaced by a seriousness bordering on anger.

"I don't want to talk about that here. Meet me at your shop in ten minutes." He turned quickly and disappeared into the back of the shop.

Martha left with her bagged muffin in hand, not without noting the unsettled look on Cat's face. Several minutes later, she was seated at one of the back tables in Birds 'n' Beans, watching the birds and picking at her muffin. She'd helped herself to a fill-up of Breakfast Blend, which tasted like it had been made just to accompany her buttery muffin. Carl entered the shop wearing a warm jacket in place of his chef's coat, nodding at Helen and PJ, but heading in a beeline toward Martha.

She got up as he approached the table. "Can I get you a cup—"

He cut her off with a motion of his hand and placed his tremendous bulk into the small chair next to her. Leaning forward, he almost towered over her from a sitting position.

"Why was Cenzo Imbroglio in your shop?" he hissed.

"Whoa, wait a minute." Martha held up her hands in surrender, taken aback by his tone and direct questioning. "He came in here making all kinds of demands, saying that I owed him money that Aunt Lorna was supposed to give to the guy I found dead in her backyard. He wouldn't leave until PJ almost picked him up and carried him out, but he gave me the creeps. I mentioned it to Jimmy last night and he said that you might know something more. I didn't mean to upset you or anything."

"Sorry," Carl said, letting his shoulders drop and sitting back, but not removing his jacket. "I'm sorry. Tell me exactly what happened and I will tell you what I know."

Martha recounted the conversation—if you could call it that—that had taken place here in the shop, ending with Imbroglio walking out and disappearing when PJ saved the day.

"That guy is trouble. Capital T trouble." Carl kneaded one fist into the palm of his other hand, calmer now, but still agitated. "Catrin did not tell me she had seen him."

And I can see why, Martha thought. *I wouldn't have mentioned it either if I'd known you'd get this upset.*

"Look, Carl," she said in an even tone, "I need to know what you know. If this guy is trouble, he could mean trouble for anyone in the shop, Ethel Jean and Mary Jane next door, or an innocent customer. And for now, that's my responsibility. Who is this guy and why are you so worried about him coming around? Surely it can't be that serious." *After all, this is Riley Creek, not rough and tough New York City.*

Carl seemed to consider her words for a moment, and then, looking down at his huge baker's hands, he exhaled. "I will tell you this, but it's my story and I am not proud. If others in Riley Creek know, they may not come to the bakery. You cannot share this." His blue eyes drilled into hers, as if assessing her trustworthiness.

Martha looked back evenly. "Carl, I know how important your shop and your good reputation are. Please believe me that I'd never do anything to jeopardize either. Whatever you tell me, I won't repeat it unless I have to."

Seeming satisfied, Carl told his story in a low voice, glancing around occasionally to make sure no one could hear him. He told Martha how he had come from a small farming village in Germany to attend culinary school in Atlanta. How proud his parents were that he had completed a prestigious degree at an American cooking school. How he'd been hired as a saucier by an elite restaurant in Atlanta, rising quickly to become the sous chef. How, unbeknown to him, the head chef and many of the other kitchen staff were involved in a narcotics ring, and he'd unwittingly gotten swept up in it. And how, five years after graduating from culinary school, he'd ended up in a federal penitentiary for distributing narcotics. Both of his parents had died while he served his sentence.

The sad story contained the most words Martha had ever heard from the quiet giant. At the end of its telling, he looked physically depleted. Sharing this with her had clearly come at a price.

"But what does that have to do with this guy Imbroglio?" she asked, not wanting to sound unsympathetic, but not making the connection between Carl's story and the creep that had come to Birds 'n' Beans, demanding money.

Carl slowly reached down with his left hand and slid up the sleeve of his jacket to reveal a meaty forearm tattooed with three flying crows. The same crows that were on Cenzo Imbroglio's neck. She looked up at him, confused.

"Prison tattoo," Carl said. "Shows we belonged to the same gang. The difference is, I joined for protection, so I have this tattoo on my arm. I provided small favors in prison to stay alive—extra food from the kitchen, that kind of thing. Tattoo on the neck means you are an enforcer. Killer. Means you have killed for your gang. One bird, one kill."

The implications of the three crows made Martha's head swim.

"But what does he want with me? With the shop?" she asked.

"Curtis Sentrich was involved with him," said Carl. "Sentrich was a small-time crook from what I know of him, trying to get rich quick through one scheme or another. But if he became a partner to someone like Imbroglio, he was moving into something bigger. Something you don't want to be involved in. Not so surprising he ended up dead."

Carl got up.

"Are you leaving so soon? Can't you tell me a little more?" asked Martha, rising with him.

Looking around the shop and toward the door, Carl said, "I've told you all I know. Please keep me out of this and don't ask me any more questions. That life is behind me now and I won't let it get close to my family. Leave it alone, I beg you. It can bring nothing good to you."

He turned and exited the shop, barely acknowledging the goodbyes from PJ and Helen.

Martha was stunned. And she knew she didn't want to be the fourth crow.

Chapter Fifteen

Martha walked back to the cottage, greeted Penny, then grabbed her keys to head to the address Cherry had given her. She thought for a moment about taking Penny with her, but had a sneaking suspicion that Cherry was not a dog person. Her first impression was that Cherry was more a *Cherry* person.

She brushed Penny and played tug with her rope toy for a few minutes, enough to get the little dog good and tired and not as grumpy about not being taken along for the ride. Once the fur ball got drowsy, Martha grabbed her keys and bag and headed out.

The Vacancy Hotel was well-known to anyone who'd spent any time in Riley Creek. Situated on a winding road that climbed its way deep into the Paris Mountains, it was the place for those who *had* no other place. Just a mention that someone was staying at the Vacancy was enough to signal that they had fallen on hard times. When she'd stayed up late one summer and watched Janet Leigh get the chop in *Psycho*, Martha had somehow blended the two locations—the Bates Motel and the Vacancy—so a proverbial black cloud hung over the place in her mind's eye.

Riley Creek gave way to the Little Paris River, which rose and fell to the beat of the Pickens Dam several miles upstream. She knew that old-timers in the area, though they enjoyed having electricity and heat and air conditioning, still spoke of the dam with mixed emotions since its arrival flooded many of their homeplaces. The resultant lakes had created a recreation mecca that attracted the tourists who kept Riley Creek alive in the cold winter months, but Aunt Lorna had always cautioned Martha not to mention the dam in mixed company.

As she drove along the river, broad vistas occasionally opened up and she took in as many as she could while keeping the car between the curvy lines. Feeling the higher elevation in her ears, Martha noticed the kudzu that smothered everything like a deep green blanket. Even the tallest trees were covered with the stuff. She remembered as a little girl feeling a bit of a thrill at its towering walls of green, but when she was older, Aunt Lorna explained to her that kudzu was actually a tree-smothering plant, brought to the United States from China and Japan in the late 1800s and used all around the south for erosion control. Little did those early farmers know how the plant would take over and decimate so many acres of beautiful forest.

True to her last memory of the place, the Vacancy was just an older version of the same run-down heap with red siding. Truth be told, the place had been called something else once upon a time, but the top half of its sign had snapped off long ago, leaving "Vacancy" running vertically along the left side of a white pole, and "Hotel" jutting out horizontally at the bottom. Vintage lightbulbs outlined a cosmic arrow eternally pointing the way.

Martha reflected that the retro arrow signaled what the Vacancy once must have been back in the fifties; a thriving "motor hotel" for tourists to the region. While tourists still came to the area, they now spent their nights at some of the quainter B&Bs that had cropped up over the years, while the Vacancy had become an efficiency apartment building for the down-and-out. At best, it was a landmark for out-of-towners on their way to the state park.

Kudzu threatened all angles, vines dripping onto the building's sloping roof and fingering up the sides and front. Here and there, sumac plants approaching small tree status broke through what was left of the asphalt parking lot. Without intervention, the Vacancy was probably ten years away from being completely absorbed into the forest.

Amazingly, just as Martha remembered from her childhood, there was still so much *stuff* around the Vacancy. Tire planters painted white were scattered here and there, enclosing two or three bunches of plastic geraniums. What doubled as a front yard and parking lot to the left held an ancient red Chevette up on blocks and a junked Ford pickup almost completely covered by kudzu. A parallel area on the right side of the hotel seemed reserved for imports, including an ancient Mercedes whose windows, while intact, were a solid brown from years of piled up dirt. The front half of a gold Volvo took up residence alongside the Mercedes. Bikes, plastic bags, and the odd discarded suitcase dotted the weeds here and there.

A soiled comforter and a faded American flag hung from the white wrought-iron railing that ran along the second floor. Two matching chairs that might have been used in a hotel conference room once upon a time sat next to an upright charcoal grill. Child Martha had found the Vacancy fascinating. Adult Martha found it overwhelmingly sad.

I'm not staying here any longer than I have to, she thought as she parked and carefully locked her Subaru.

Close to the building, amid a row of several inexpensive compact cars, sat Cherry's bright blue Mustang. Putting a hand up to block the sun, Martha spotted room seven at the far end of the first floor. A rattan welcome mat on the threshold read *Stop and Smell the Roses.* A small plant stand stood to the left holding a pot of bright yellow plastic mums. Martha registered that these few decorative touches stood in stark contrast to the rest of the entryways she'd passed on the way to Cherry's. Glancing back toward the row of doors behind her, she saw an industrial-sized plastic garbage can, a rusty playpen, and a few broken folding chairs. Cherry got an A for effort.

The door opened just after Martha knocked, and there was Cherry in all of her glory. She had a towel around her neck and her hair was wrapped in what looked like flat silver tentacles. A vision of Medusa flashed in Martha's mind.

"Doing my highlights, sorry. Be right back. Make yourself comfortable."

Martha was taken aback by the young woman's polite manner, so different than what she'd experienced in the farmers' market parking lot. Cherry turned and walked back into the room and, from there, into what Martha guessed was the bathroom. While Martha had anticipated a typical pair of hotel double beds and a TV sitting on a chest of drawers, she was pleasantly surprised. The room was painted an airy lemon yellow, and a simple daybed with clean white linens was pushed up against the wall. A few serviceable chairs and a coffee table completed the seating area, and everywhere tasteful framed prints lined the walls. Healthy-looking spider plants sat atop the heat and air unit just under the curtained window.

The open sink common to so many hotels of this era had been converted into a small kitchen area, the storage beneath hidden by a floral curtain pulled across a laundry line. Placing the root beer she'd brought on the coffee table, Martha realized that she had misjudged this book by its cover.

When Cherry emerged with a towel over her head and wearing a fresh pair of jeans and a bright yellow t-shirt, Martha began to speak, but was quickly cut off.

"Look, before we get started, just so you know, I don't want any trouble. If you're looking for a news story or digging up dirt on Curtis, you came to the wrong place. Like I told the police, we were going our separate ways anyway and I really don't know anything about what happened to him. I liked him and I'm sorry he's dead, but I didn't want to go where he was going." Her eyes filled up and she sniffed. It was clear to Martha that Curtis *had* meant something to Cherry once upon a time.

Martha explained who she was and why she was trying to piece together more information about Curtis and Lorna's relationship. She decided to leave out the mystery of the missing money and stick to Curtis ending up dead in the pile of leaves. Cherry seemed reluctant to say much, sharing only that she and Curtis had had a difficult breakup.

"At first, it seemed like he had really changed, like he wanted to get out of here and try a fresh start somewhere. He was even saving up money to move us along with his grandma to somewhere better. But a few months ago, I was driving back in from some work out at the campgrounds and passed that used car lot... The Car Man? There he was, right out in front, talking with that creepy loser that owns the place. Everyone knows that guy is trouble. I'm really making a change this time and I wasn't going to let Curtis mess it up for me. I cared about him, but at my age, if you don't make a run for it, you end up in a dump like this forever..." She gestured around the room. "I told him we were done."

"If you don't mind me saying so, you've made it really homey here," said Martha politely. "And you... you seem a little different than I first thought."

"Thanks," Cherry said, dabbing at her eyes with a Kleenex. "But it doesn't stop the roaches from coming out at night. When I turn the light on in the morning, they all run for cover. That's the thing I hate the most."

She shivered at the thought of it, and it was all Martha could do not to shiver in sympathy.

"That whole scene you saw at the parking lot? That's the version of Cherry"—here she pronounced it like the fruit—"I put on to make sure no one around here messes with me. You can't be soft and live in a place like the Vacancy or you're asking for trouble. Plus, to be honest, I did that to get out of getting a ticket. I'm trying to save every cent I earn right now to get out of here." She laughed, the first real laugh Martha had heard from her.

"Cherry, what was your plan? What were you and Curtis going to do?" Martha asked.

"Well it doesn't matter now if you know, I guess. I have to figure it out on my own, but for a while, we were planning to save up enough for Curtis to open a body shop in Nashville, or maybe Florida. He'd been picking up odd jobs here and there—including the ones for your aunt—and I was picking up extra houses to clean. See, my plan was—is—to go into business on my own." She laughed, a sad, desperate laugh. "That's a reason I changed how I pronounce my name. I want to start my own cleaning business called 'Ship Shape with Sherry.' If there's one thing I know how to do, it's clean, and I've read about how women can hire other women to clean houses, but the owner runs the office. That's what I'm going to do."

"But why don't you just start that business here?" asked Martha.

"Because everyone knows me as the old Cherry, the ditzy blond who barely finished high school. I can't even go to the grocery store without someone I know calling me 'Cherry on Top' like they did in school. I want to go where people will take me seriously as a businesswoman. I need a fresh start."

"But why does Donna Riggs talk about you as if you were trouble for Curtis? It sounds as if you must have been a good influence on him."

"She doesn't like me because Curtis spent his money on me, even though I told him not to. I told him we really needed to save, but he said I wouldn't be able to get more houses to clean without having a fancy car to drive like a real businesswoman. He gave me that Mustang and his grandma has been mad at me ever since. She thinks I talked him into buying it for me, but that couldn't be further from the truth."

"Do you mind me asking how Curtis could afford to buy you a car like that?" Martha inquired.

"Well, that was the weirdest thing," Cherry said, shaking her head and tearing up a bit again. "I explained this all to the police when they came to talk to me. Curtis drove it over here a few months ago. I think he thought the car would distract me from being mad at him for not saving, and I did get over it eventually. But, well, once I saw Curtis at The Car Man, I put two and two together and realized the car probably came from there. With my luck, it might even be stolen. That was the last straw for me. I broke up with him."

"But why?"

"First off, there's no way he could afford it if he was doing legit work. Second, if we were really going to have a new start, that included not hanging around with people that are bad news. I tried to get him to take the car back, but he refused. He said things were starting to look up, that he had money coming in and was expecting more where that came from. I asked him where the money was coming from, but he didn't want to tell me.

"When we broke up, I tried again to get him to take the car back, but he told me to keep it for when I start my new business. So I've carried on cleaning the houses he found for me and I'm going to keep cleaning them until I save enough to head out of here for good."

"Houses he found for you?" asked Martha.

"Yeah. Your aunt had all these friends who need help here and there with their house cleaning. Some need a regular cleaner, others just need help with spot cleaning before and after family come to visit. I've actually added quite a few houses to my rounds. See?"

She walked across the room to the far side of the daybed and pulled out a large corkboard from behind what doubled as a headboard. Attached to the corkboard were small hooks, each holding a key with a round label. Each label listed a first name and address.

"Those are all of my clients. I've memorized each person, their address, and how often they want me to clean. It's worked out great. I'll miss lots of the old folks I clean for when I get out of here. Some of them are so sweet and just enjoy the company I think."

"Did you clean for Lorna?" Martha asked. "I guess I should take her key back if you did. To be honest, I can't afford any extra expenses at the moment."

"No need. I only cleaned for her once in a while, and the house was always unlocked. I just came and went as I liked. I think everyone did."

Chapter Sixteen

The next few days were busy ones. Martha was on the phone much of the time, talking through a presentation to the Board of Trustees with the University President. She had expected him to bring up the topic of her return to Boston, and was relieved when he didn't.

She also spent more time with PJ, Helen and Margaret, trying to understand the shop and the way money flowed in and out of the business. She'd had no idea how much money it took to buy supplies, or how narrow the margin was on food and beverages. The bird merchandise actually created more profit for Birds 'n' Beans, which made attracting the birding public so important. But the majority of Lorna's regular income had come from local businesses that bought her hand-roasted Birds 'n' Beans coffee brand.

There was no doubt about it, though; Aunt Lorna had taken money out of the shop's account and cashed in on the equity she'd built up in the building, leaving the whole enterprise on very shaky ground. Margaret had helped Martha figure out that she had enough, between her own savings and the shop's regular sales, to cover the rent and make payroll for the next month. That would give her a little more time to think. Now, after working nonstop on the Board presentation and the shop's finances, she figured she was due for a day off.

After coffee and breakfast on the back deck, watching Penny buzz along the riverbank checking for messages, Martha dressed, and then brushed the little terrier.

"We're going on an outing, girl, and you've gotta look your best."

She packed up a leash and water dish, and they headed out to the car. Martha had written down the directions that Allison had given her over the phone and reviewed them once more before pulling out of the drive. Delores was working in her front yard, and she shot Martha a wave as she drove by.

After heading out of town and driving about twenty minutes of lefts and rights and one unplanned U-turn, Martha came to the small community of Riverton. It boasted a modest shopping mall, a couple of gas stations and a commercial seed company. But what really put it on the map was its Harley Davidson dealership. Riders from all over the country came to the area to drive the winding mountain roads, and sooner or later, they all stopped at the dealership for a t-shirt, a Harley poker chip, or a barbecue sandwich hot off the smoker in the parking lot. As she passed the dealership, she spotted a small number of riders taking a driving course in the adjoining parking lot, orange cones lined up in ordered rows and motorcycles of various sizes and styles weaving between them.

Following Allison's directions, she eventually found what she was looking for; a sprawling single-floor beige brick building with a tasteful sign reading "Meadowlands Memory Center" in front. She pulled into a visitor spot and clipped Penny's leash on before setting the small dog down on the ground. After signing in with the receptionist just inside the front door, she was directed down a quiet hallway with rooms on either side. Each door had the name of a resident in a nameplate next to it, and some doors had fall decorations on them. She spotted Indian corn, a construction paper pumpkin with a lopsided green stem, and a small knitted cornucopia as she walked. She tried not to be nosey, but glimpsed a few residents here and there.

She arrived at the large common room and found it brightly lit from a series of skylights overhead. Martha sensed that this room was in the center of the building, the adjoining hallways extending like spokes on a bicycle wheel. Chairs had been stacked to the side and tables pushed along the wall to make room for the special visitors in the center; about fifteen golden retrievers and their handlers.

The beautiful dogs, in various sizes and shades of caramel, were soaking up the attention they were getting from (and giving to) the elderly residents. Each golden was accompanied by a calm and smiling handler as they traveled from person to person, plopping their big heads in laps and happily accepting pats, strokes and belly rubs. Where Martha had expected vacant gazes and strange smells from the residents, she observed smiling eyes and laughter.

Allison looked up, spotted Martha and waved her over.

"Hey, you, welcome!" Allison said. Penny, to Martha's relief, retained her composure and didn't strain on her leash as Martha had expected. She seemed to realize that this was not *her* show, and instantly dropped down and showed her belly to Allison's huge golden.

"Oh brother, what a pushover," said Martha, surprised to see her dog not even attempting alpha status.

"What a cutie," said Allison, dropping down to greet the terrier. Holding on to the leash of her own dog, she cocked her head toward him and said, "This is Chip. I'm really glad you two could join us here. We have a big crowd today, so if Penny is up for it, it would be great to have one more helper." She introduced Martha to the other handlers and the group of residents, then showed her the ropes. She taught Martha how to introduce Penny to a new person, how to help them stroke her and, in some cases, hold her on their laps. Martha felt her heart swell as the men and women, regardless of their age and physical limitations, connected with the animals and enjoyed the simple pleasure of petting soft fur and getting warm doggie kisses. The smiles and tears that came forth made her grateful that she'd agree to meet Allison here. And she was so proud of Penny's good behavior. It was as if Penny knew instantly that these people were new friends who would never hurt her, but needed her to be her most gentle version of herself.

A tall order for a schnauzer, Martha thought. But Penny behaved perfectly.

After about an hour, the staff announced that they were pulling the tables back in so that they could serve an afternoon snack. They also announced that a slide presentation of the castles of Ireland would begin in thirty minutes. The dog handlers bid many of the residents goodbye by name with promises to return in a few weeks. Martha and Allison walked toward the entrance, Penny and Chip beside them.

"Want to sit and catch up a bit?" asked Allison as they emerged into the cool afternoon sun.

"I thought you'd never ask," replied Martha. Truth be told, she had been on high alert monitoring Penny's behavior and felt a bit tired.

"Follow me," said Allison, and led them around the side to the rear of the building. They emerged onto a large fenced-in garden, flowerbeds running along the sides and a water feature at the center. A few residents sat in wheelchairs or on benches, visiting with what Martha assumed to be family.

Allison reached over the gate to open a fairly complicated locking mechanism. "They have a safety lock on here so that some of their more energetic patients don't accidentally wander off," she explained, leading Martha and the dogs to a bench under a small reddish-purple dogwood tree. Both dogs flopped down in the shade, exhausted from giving and getting so much attention.

"Wow, what an amazing afternoon," Martha said. "Thank you so much for inviting me. To be honest, I wasn't sure what to expect, but it was really moving to see the dogs and residents together. Like a match made in heaven."

Allison nodded. "That's exactly how I feel. Our Golden Tennessee Rescue Team has been coming here for a little over a year and it's been really rewarding. Not only does it help us to socialize some of our rescue dogs, but it seems to bring out something special in these folks. Some here are struggling with mild dementia and others more advanced Alzheimer's, and there are some who are doing rehab from mild strokes. Being around a dog, they seem to tap into something primal, reaching beyond any physical ailment they have to something kind and happy and hopeful."

"Selfishly, I also really appreciate the chance to escape my own problems at the moment," said Martha, shaking her head. "It put lots of things into perspective for an hour or so. Being here today made me realize how long it's been since I did something that was just... about creating simple happiness." She gazed off into the field beyond the fence.

Allison eyed her. "But don't you feel you do that in your work in Boston?" she asked.

Martha reflected for a moment. "Well, to be honest, I've not really thought about it like that before. My life in Boston has been like a machine, first to college, then to grad school, then into a job, then moving through one promotion to the next. Don't get me wrong: I love my work and the people I work with, but I'm not altruistic enough to say that I do it because it is good for other people. I do it because... it's what I do and it pays the rent. The very, very expensive rent." The two women shared a laugh and a knowing nod of the head.

"My boss has been great about me telecommuting, but I know at some point, I'll have to head back to the city. And to be honest, I'm beginning to dread that. I've only ever come here as a visitor, but now, without Aunt Lorna, I'm having the chance to be here as an adult and... I feel more at home here than I ever have in Boston, or even back home in Ohio where I grew up with my parents. Boston is a great city, but the longer I'm here, the harder it is to think about going back." Martha trailed off, watching swallows swoop over the fields, chasing their lunches of small insects.

"So what's the alternative?" asked Allison.

"To what?" asked Martha.

"Going back to Boston."

"Well, I'm not sure there is one, which is pretty depressing now that I've had time to reflect on it. I feel like I'm so far down the path, there's no off ramp."

Allison's brow wrinkled. "Oh please, don't give me that. A woman with a graduate degree and a head on her shoulders? There are always options. Look at me. I was on the fast track to move up in the Bureau—they even had a big push on back then to promote women into leadership positions, but I realized I'd had enough and left to come to Riley Creek. The reasons why are a story for another day, but my point is that the only one forcing you to stay on a certain path is you. Don't get me wrong; it's hard to start again in a new place, but you'll survive. You strike me as a pretty tough customer."

Martha blushed a bit at the compliment. "Well, thanks for your encouragement. But let's say I'm not a born risk-taker." *Risks and dreams and journeys are for those with a safety net that I've never really had.*

Martha felt the need to lighten things up a bit. She reached over and elbowed Allison in the arm.

"Hey, I'll be sure to send you a check for the therapy session. But what about you? How did you end up in Riley Creek? I don't remember ever seeing you here when I visited Aunt Lorna. Of course, I've also made a point of avoiding the police whenever I've been in town," she said, laughing.

"Oh, that's a long story." The breeze ruffled the police officer's spiked hair as she gazed out into the distance. "But I can give you the short version. Girl goes to University of Tennessee for college, just to watch Pat Summitt coach basketball. Girl graduates with a forensic science degree, moves back home to Nashville and joins the Nashville Metro Police. Has visions of living real life CSI. Spends ten years in Nashville, gets major dose of reality, then joins the FBI somewhere around 2007. Spends ten years there, until it all comes crashing down. Girl comes to

Riley Creek about five years ago to live out a quiet, peaceful life in a small Tennessee town. End of story."

She smiled at Martha, her eyes suggesting that there was a lot more to her story than she'd revealed. Martha wasn't quite sure how to respond. She wanted to ask what came crashing down, but didn't want to pry.

"So, coming to Riley Creek… has that been a good chapter in your story?" she asked instead.

"Best move I ever made," said Allison. "And your aunt was one of the first friends I made here. We never had the time to become *close* friends, mind you. My first few years here, I wasn't in very good shape, and having a quiet coffee in the shop and watching the birds became an escape for me when I wasn't on the job. Lorna never asked questions. When we finally began to talk, she told me that for some people, Riley Creek is the place they come when they have no other place in the world. And she was so right. She also told me about the birds. In fact, she turned this city girl into a bit of a bird nerd." She shook her head, then gestured at the birds over the field. "See those purple martins?"

"I thought they were swallows," said Martha, squinting to get a better look at the speedy missiles swooping down low over the grass and back up into the sky.

"They are a swallow species for sure, but these have purple heads and bellies. Tree swallows would have bright patches of white you would be able to see. And look," Allison pointed to the far side of the garden in the direction of the memory center's roof, "your aunt donated that."

Close to the building was a tall pole with what looked like a miniature dollhouse on the top. Shaped like a barn, it was a martin house with two rows of three openings and, Martha presumed, another six openings on the other side. Tiny railings ran the length of each row, creating a "porch" for each front door. A few martins darted in and out of the house, rarely staying still for more than a few moments.

"They'll start winter migration soon, but when they come back in the spring, the residents will get a kick out of watching them build nests and raise their young," Allison said.

They watched the busy birds in silence for a few minutes, then Martha reluctantly brought them both back to the moment.

"Allison, I know it's your job, and Detective Perry's, to solve what happened to Sentrich, but the more I learn, the more I feel the need to figure it out if I'm to get closure before I go back to Boston. I've discovered some... discrepancies related to my aunt's last months and I want to clear everything up. Since she and Sentrich seemed to be friendly, I think solving his murder may help me understand whatever was going on with her."

"You know I can't talk about the case officially, but I will say the police agree with you on it being a complicated matter."

Martha turned sideways on the bench to look at Allison. "Tell you what," she said, "why don't we talk about this hypothetically, so *you* won't feel like you're discussing the case and *I* can sort through some of the things I'm thinking about?"

"Oh-kaaay..." said Allison, clearly not feeling totally comfortable. "Let's try that. But if it gets too close to the actual case, we stop talking about it."

"Deal," said Martha. She went first. "So let's say *hypothetically* that a scary ex-con comes into Birds 'n' Beans, suggesting he had something going on with Aunt Lorna and she'd been paying him through Sentrich on a regular basis. Now he wants to continue that arrangement with me, but I have no idea what she'd been paying him for. And let's say I know enough to realize he is a seriously bad guy and I want nothing to do with him. And I know he has a violent history."

"How do you know his background?" asked Allison, clearly taken aback.

"Maybe the proverbial little bird told me he'd been in prison and was involved in some pretty shady stuff."

Allison nodded, but her brow wrinkled. "Let's say—hypothetically, of course—the police are aware of this bad guy. But it doesn't make sense that he would kill the man who was helping him get money out of your aunt on a regular basis."

"Well, maybe they had a falling out. The bad guy killed his partner, and the whole scene at the shop was designed to make the money keep coming."

"Martha, in my experience, crooks and ex-cons are not usually that smart. They don't really go in for elaborate ruses and cover stories, and they stay as far away from police investigations as possible. I think if the bad guy had killed his partner, he would have done it and gotten out of Dodge."

"Fair enough. But the little bird who told me about the bad guy may himself be a suspect."

Without naming names or specifics, Martha went on to relay to Allison a general sketch of the surprise visit she'd had a few days ago. After her conversation with Carl, Martha had headed home to the cottage and decided to spend some time in the backyard; she'd not yet cleaned up from when the police and lab techs had crawled all over the murder scene. Many of the grasses around Bird Paradise had been trampled and the pile of leaves was strewn all around.

She'd just started building a second pile when she felt a hand on her shoulder and nearly jumped out of her skin.

"Lewis!" she'd said, swinging round to confront Cat and Carl's son and putting a gloved hand to her chest. "You nearly gave me a heart attack!" She and Lewis blushed together at the unfortunate turn of phrase.

"I, um, know you don't really know me that well, but I want you to know my dad had nothing to do with that guy getting killed in your backyard." Lewis glanced around. "I know my dad was talking to you at your shop today, and he was really grumpy when he came back. That guy Sentrich would hardly leave Dad alone, but I'm telling you, there's no way he would kill anyone." He'd angrily wiped tears away. "You need to talk to Mr. Bennett at Toad in a Hole. Sentrich was in and out of that place all the time, mostly at night. I saw him lots of times when I was locking up the bakery."

Allison nodded when Martha had finished. "Yep, that could be someone trying to cast suspicion in another direction, or possibly describing a guilty party."

"At least we know Cherry Marshall is in the clear," said Martha, absentmindedly.

"Are you actually talking to witnesses?" asked Allison, raising her brows. "Martha, I understand that you're interested in clearing your aunt's name, but this is not a game. You've got to be careful. Perry will have a stroke if he finds out you're nosing around."

Martha put her hands up in a sign of surrender. "No, no, I'm not interviewing people. I just bumped into her and we had a conversation. Totally innocent, I assure you."

The policewoman scrutinized her. "Since you had this 'conversation,' tell me what makes you think Marshall's in the clear?"

"Well, she explained that she'd parted ways with Sentrich—"

"Uh-huh. The Sentrich who had given her an expensive almost-new Mustang? She just parted ways with him, no questions asked?"

"I don't follow," said Martha, confused.

"Did you really buy her story that she offered the car back to Sentrich and he refused? Isn't it equally possible that he demanded the car back—her one ticket out of this town—and she killed him?"

"Ohhhhh... I hadn't thought of that." Martha felt like a sucker; Cherry had seemed so sincere!

"It's OK. In my profession, you learn not to believe anything a witness tells you unless they can prove it. And in Cherry's case, it's her word against a dead man's."

As the hypothetical seemed to be morphing into the real, Martha decided to share something else with Allison. "Let me tell you a strange thread that I've uncovered, and it's totally thrown me for a loop. It's about Aunt Lorna." She went on to tell Allison the story that the Ritzenwallers had told her about her aunt's mysterious side trips to who-knows-where to visit who-knows-what-or-whom.

"Bizarre," said Allison, shaking her head. "I didn't know your aunt for very long, but she certainly didn't seem like the type who would have led a secret double life. What do you make of that?"

"I have no idea," Martha replied, "but I'd say there is a lot more going on in Riley Creek than meets the eye." She suddenly felt the need to change the subject. "Allison, there's another lead the police are following that I just don't understand." Instantly, she saw a defensiveness creep into her new friend's eyes. "Detective Perry told me to watch out for Jason Turngate."

Allison was clearly uncomfortable with this line of conversation. She shifted her muscled frame.

"Martha, I shouldn't tell you this, but I'm going to for your own safety. Apparently, Sentrich had been setting illegal animal traps on the lower part of Talisman Trail, and Turngate and he got into an argument in the middle of town. Seems it isn't a big help to Turngate's business if he's guiding naturalists and one of his customers sticks their foot into a fox trap. But believe me, Turngate's background has mysteries in it. We're still looking into him."

As she tried to take in Allison's warning, all Martha could think about was what an ass she'd made of herself by assuming Jason had set the trap she found on Talisman Trail.

Chapter Seventeen

The next morning arrived too early, even for Martha who had been a morning person all of her life. She'd left the memory center late the previous afternoon and gone over to Birds 'n' Beans, wanting to learn the roasting process from PJ, including how to bag the signature coffee for the local restaurants they sold to and how to restock the selection they kept on the counter for sale to customers. They'd started after the last customer left so they'd have the store to themselves.

She'd learned about the various still-green beans the shop purchased in bulk, and how the roasting process was different for each type of coffee they produced: less time for light roast (*Colombian Wingbar*) and a longer time to release the coffee bean oils for the darker roasts (*Sumatran Migration*). She had to admit to feeling a certain sense of pride as she came to understand how to check the "doneness" of the beans as they roasted, how long to run them through the cooling drum, and how to stamp the brown bags with the Birds 'n' Beans logo and mark the coffee flavor before arranging them in a display. There was something primal in the way the machine belts whirred and drum vibrated when the green beans were poured in; a mysterious alchemy transforming them into aromatic pebbles pouring out into the drying pan.

They had heaved and labeled heavy bags and roasted beans until long past midnight. As PJ had explained, it was most efficient to roast large batches, minimizing the times the heat and chaff filled the air in the shop.

At one point during the process, PJ had sent Martha up to the second floor to get another package of bags. She'd remembered coming up here with her aunt a few times, but now surveyed the space with new eyes. There were two modestly sized rooms and a bathroom that looked as if it had not been used in some time. One room held shelves of bird-themed inventory and all of the extras needed to run the shop. The other held some random pieces of furniture, a vacuum cleaner, and a few odds and ends. Martha reflected how in need of a thorough cleaning this whole floor was and spied a few cloudy spots on the ceiling.

How much would a new roof cost? How much less attractive would the shop be to a potential buyer if it needed a new roof?

When she'd come back into the shop, she'd asked PJ about the upstairs. PJ had shaken his head slowly.

"Well, honey, to be honest, I haven't been up there much recently. Last time Lorna and I were up there together was probably, oh, about six months ago, or even a year. We talked about cleaning the whole space out and using it in some different way, but just never got around to it. That was right before things started getting a bit odd, and she became less and less herself. It was as if she forgot all about it. I guess the rest of us forgot all about it too."

While she had enjoyed the quiet time with PJ (quiet except for the thrum of the roaster), Martha woke this morning feeling sore and bleary-eyed. Looking at her clock, she wondered why she had woken up so early. But just as she was about to turn over for a few more Zs, she heard someone knocking on the front door.

Penny leapt down from the bed and headed for the stairs, barking in her customary high pitch. With a jolt, Martha remembered that she and Mary Jane were heading over to Adair together for the annual Yoga Fest.

With a refrain of "Crap-crap-crap," Martha threw on a robe, stumbled down the stairs and opened the door to find Mary Jane, fresh and pink and tightly packaged in spandex.

"Namaste!" she said, pushing lightly past Martha and walking straight to the kitchen. "Get dressed and I'll make you some coffee!" she hollered perkily. Seeing Mary Jane open the French doors for Penny's morning outing, Martha headed up the stairs to dress before the offer of coffee was revoked. Donning loose shorts, a sleeveless t-shirt and some sport sandals, she then returned downstairs to find coffee and a chocolate croissant laid out on the kitchen table.

"Wow, thanks, that looks delish! Aren't you having one?"

"Oh, I've had two, thanks," Mary Jane replied, patting her stomach. "Frank came over early this morning with a bag of them, fresh out of Carl's ovens. He knows they are my kryptonite."

"So, what's the story between you two? You and Frank?"

"Ah, Frank's a sweetie. He really is. He'd do anything for you, give you the shirt off his back." Mary Jane looked away, shaking her head slightly.

"Do I detect a 'but' in there somewhere? PJ said you two are dating."

"I guess you could call it that," answered Mary Jane, examining her nails as if something fascinating was written on them. "But it's not serious."

"Hmmm. Anyone that gets up at the crack of dawn to bring you your favorite food right out of the oven can't be all that bad," Martha said, giving Mary Jane a wink.

"Oh, he's not bad at all. But I suppose in some ways, I'm still figuring out life after Paul and don't want to be too quick about anything. If it were up to Frank, we'd be headed down the aisle next Saturday. I won't say there's not something appealing about that, but I'm not there yet."

What little Martha knew about Mary Jane's deceased husband was what PJ had shared with her the night before: the two had been very happily married for years, and Mary Jane had retired from nursing to see Paul through the conclusion of a five-year battle with terminal cancer.

"Well, if you and Frank enjoy spending time together and you're both OK with where things are, I guess that's good too. But for the record, he sounds like quite a catch."

"And you sound just like your aunt," Mary Jane said with a laugh. "Lorna was always telling me that I should be careful about deciding to be alone. She said I might work so hard at enjoying my own company that someday I'll come to prefer it."

Martha's jaw dropped open. "Can you believe she told me the *exact same thing*? She'd say, 'Martha, you've got to know the difference between keeping your eye on the ball and making yourself cross-eyed.'"

Mary Jane looked at Martha tentatively. "Honey, I know it's none of my business, but do you have someone special up in Boston?"

"Nope, sure don't. With my work, there's just not time."

Mary Jane looked down at her hands, then back up at Martha. "I know your aunt worried about you after your... experience up there some years ago."

Oh, Aunt Lorna, you didn't... Martha was stunned when she realized Mary Jane knew about what had happened.

"Oh, that's ancient history," she said in an attempt at breeziness.

"I'm not so sure Lorna saw it that way," Mary Jane ventured, her eyes questioning.

"How about that?" Martha shook her head, trying to change the subject. "My long-widowed aunt passing out romantic advice, but staying single all this time."

"The only person less qualified to give romantic advice would be my sister, the confirmed bachelorette!" said Mary Jane and they both giggled.

"I'm guessing Ethel Jean's not coming with us today?" asked Martha, knowing the answer.

"Bwah!" Mary Jane barked a laugh. "She'd rather drop dead than be seen at a yoga festival. Speaking of which, let's scoot. I've got to work these croissants off." She slapped her own backside with another laugh and made to leave. Martha leaned down to kiss Penny, and then they were out the door.

Mary Jane drove them in her red Volkswagen Beetle to Adair, about thirty miles from Riley Creek. Adair had grown up along the railroad tracks that cut into the mountains, once upon a time delivering timber down to the river for transport far and wide. The railroad had long stopped running and the rail bed had been converted years ago to a twenty-five-mile greenway. Small specialty shops and farm-to-table restaurants had popped up all over; the area brought in bikers and families of tourists almost all year long and was now known as *the* place to come for a weekend of trail riding, shopping and dining out. It was also where Mavis, Aunt Lorna's old high-school friend, had set up her Ohm Mama yoga studio.

Unlike Riley Creek, which was situated around an historic town green, Adair embraced a cobblestone road. Martha guessed the original cobblestone had been replaced some years ago, because the new road was laid out in artful designs, with huge pots of fall plants lining sidewalks all the way down the main street. Every now and then, a white-striped pedestrian crossing indicated the way for walkers to cross the street. Solid wooden benches sat outside many of the shops, providing resting spots for husbands babysitting purses and purchases.

Mary Jane parked in a diagonal spot outside of the Oak and Vine Bistro, and she and Martha picked up their bags and water bottles to head to the festival. Mary Jane also retrieved her yoga mat from the trunk and assured Martha that there would be plenty of extras at the Yoga Fest for her to borrow. Heading south down the main street, they spotted some fellow yoga aficionados, dead giveaways in their spandex with rolled-up mats slung over their shoulders.

As they arrived at the end of the main street, it opened onto a small town square. Nothing near as large as Riley Creek's village green, but large enough to hold a rustic bandstand and a large swath of grass. A vinyl banner hanging over the bandstand steps declared "Welcome to Yoga Fest" and every spare patch of grass was filling with yoga pads of every color.

It was clear to Martha that the festivalgoers covered the span of yoga ability. Some looked like ballet dancers and were limbering up with impossible bends and stretches. Others, like herself, had on shirts or t-shirts and looked like they'd wandered into the festival by accident. Martha felt a bit more relaxed when she saw she was not the only beginner there.

Mary Jane was looking around excitedly, taking it all in. "I'm happy to see so many people have turned out," she said quietly, almost to herself. Leaning closer, she added, "Between us, I've heard that the studio has been struggling and Mavis is really counting on this event to bring in new business."

At the front of the bandstand, Martha spotted Mavis Settler. She was dressed in black tights and a purple tie-dye crop top with a gauzy long-sleeve shirt over the top. The look was finished off by another pair of Birkenstocks festooned with silver sequins. While Mavis was perfecting the sound on a large speaker and looking harried, about six feet from her on the deck of the bandstand, a young woman with a body that was little more than skin pulled over solid muscle adjusted a microphone headset. Martha guessed this would be their instructor.

While Mary Jane unfurled her mat, Martha went to retrieve a loaner from the pile at the side of the bandstand. She returned and set up next to Mary Jane. Then haunting willowy music began and everyone quieted down.

The instructor told them all her name was Alexis and gave a peppy introduction, then led them through various stretches and breathing techniques. Martha felt a bit self-conscious at the beginning, particularly when Alexis guided them to close their eyes and become conscious of their breathing. But she was happily surprised to find that she could master the various beginner poses Alexis taught them, laughing silently during something Alexis called "Child's Pose." No wonder she could master *that* one.

Martha was impressed with Mary Jane's limberness and ability to transition quickly from one pose to the next. She was pleased with her own dexterity and thought that her recent running and hiking were partly to thank. By the end of the session, she was sweating but feeling good. Maybe she should find time for yoga when she got back to Boston? She dismissed the thought almost as soon as it registered, remembering that in Boston, she never had time for anything other than work.

As the music faded and the beginner session ended, Alexis placed her hands together in front of her chest as if praying and said to them all, "Namaste." Most of the group, including Mary Jane, did the same back to Alexis. Martha leaned over to Mary Jane, who still had her hands pressed together and her eyes closed.

"What does 'namaste' mean?" she whispered.

Mary Jane dropped her hands and opened her eyes. "The divine in me bows to the divine in you."

The groups of people around them clapped, then began to get up, gathering their mats and water bottles. Amidst the hubbub, a voice sounded through the microphone. It was Mavis, using Alexis's headset to project her voice.

"Thanks so much for that wonderful introductory session, Alexis! Everyone, please remember to stop over at the table near the bandstand to learn more about yoga, sign up for lessons at our studio, and pick up a Namaste t-shirt." Mavis pointed over to a large table laden with every color t-shirt imaginable. Alexis and a man-bunned twenty-something were frantically exchanging t-shirts for cash.

Mavis waved to Mary Jane and Martha through the crowd and made her way over to them, shaking hands and again reminding festivalgoers to stop at the table before they left. She got to them and, after hugging Mary Jane and thanking them both for attending the morning's demonstration, focused her attention on Martha.

"It means so much to me to have you here," she said, holding both of Martha's hands in hers and looking at her intently. "Your aunt and I shared so many memories, and something will always be missing with her gone. I hope you'll consider joining the studio so I'll see you more often?"

Martha was slightly thrown off. "Uh... I'm so sorry, but I don't think I'll be around long enough. But I'd really like to hear more about Aunt Lorna's younger years, if you ever have time to chat."

Mary Jane chimed in. "I know! Mavis, what time is your next demonstration? Do you have time for a bite? My treat."

Mavis hesitated, looking back at the bandstand area that was quickly clearing. "Well, we are pretty busy today, booking lessons and so on—"

"Nonsense," said Mary Jane. "I'll just boogie over and ask Alexis to cover you for thirty minutes or so. I'm sure she won't object." Before Mavis could respond, Mary Jane, like a freight train of optimism, was making a beeline for Alexis. She was back before long, confirming that Alexis was only too happy to cover things for a bit.

"Is there a good place for a quick bite?" asked Mary Jane, shading her eyes with her hand and looking up the street.

"I suppose we could pop into The Greenery," replied Mavis, still not exactly sounding enthusiastic.

They walked the short block to a small establishment, which featured a back patio clustered with bistro tables and chairs, and ordered sandwiches—all vegetarian, much to the disappointment of Martha, who'd worked up an appetite. Mary Jane paid, and then the three women sat at one of the tables in the shade. They talked about the festival first, and Mavis told the other two how she was trying to get more interest generated in yoga practice in the local area. She had bought the building about two years ago after returning from twenty years in India.

"It was time to come home," she explained.

"What took you to India?" Martha asked, intrigued and impressed.

"Well, you know, the usual," said Mavis, shrugging.

"Come on, Mavis," said Mary Jane. "You may be humble about the whole thing, but to everyone else, it's a grand adventure and we want to hear more."

"Well, as you may know, part of yoga practice is the betterment of oneself. When my husband died, I felt the need to explore my spiritual side so I sold everything I owned, left for Mumbai, and never looked back. I spent twenty years in an ashram in study, but once my teacher died, I felt called to come back to the States, and then head home to Riley Creek."

"Wow, that is amazing. What a brave way to live your life. I don't know that I'd ever have the courage to leave behind everything I know." Martha wondered what kind of person would do something like that. "But tell me more about you and Aunt Lorna. Were you friends in school? Had you always stayed in touch? I'm sorry to say I was not aware of your friendship."

"Well, truth be told, when I left for India, I severed most ties. It was important for me to begin anew, to build my spirituality from the ground up. That included walking away from those that were part of my old life. It was one of the hardest things I ever had to do, but my teacher explained that it was necessary. But when I came back to Riley Creek, your aunt was one of the first people I contacted, and we picked up where we'd left off. I guess some friendships are like that."

Martha caught an odd look cross Mary Jane's face, but it disappeared as quickly as it had come. She was too interested to hear more about her aunt to ask what the look had been about.

"What was she like in high school, Mavis?" she asked.

"Oh, she was wild, so much different than she was later in life. She liked the boys, dated lots of them, and was really a bit on the shallow side. To be honest, in some ways, I'm surprised we were friends because we were so different. I had always been what you might call an 'old soul.' Not quite one for parties or dances; much happier with a few true friends who looked beyond such trivial things. But your aunt and I balanced each other. I was a little too serious, and she was a little too flighty. Somehow, opposites attracted and we were great pals."

Martha was taken aback. This did not sound like her aunt at all, and Martha couldn't imagine her that way, even as a teenager. Before she could express her confusion, Mary Jane got them back to Mavis's narrative.

"But after you and she graduated in... what, about 1965 or so? What happened then?" she asked.

"It was 1970," said Mavis. "I couldn't wait to leave Riley Creek and did so as soon as I could. Lorna stayed here, as I understand, and married one of those high school boys sometime after we graduated. I went to college, traveled around the country quite a bit, and had a successful professional life in the entertainment industry. We just lost touch as people do..." She waved a hand, as if she no longer wanted to discuss details, and then frowned, looking off into the distance. Then she glanced down at her watch. "Oh gosh, the time! I've got to get back to the studio before our next demonstration."

She stood up as if to leave without them, but paused long enough for the others to rise. Together, they exited the front of the restaurant, and Mary Jane gestured across the street.

"That's Mavis's yoga studio right there." Martha looked at the modestly adorned brownstone building with "Ohm Mama" written in exotic script in purple letters. Then Mary Jane said, "Say, Mavis, I need to use the ladies' room before Martha and I visit some shops. Any chance I might pop into the studio with you for a pit stop?"

Martha thought she registered a slight pursing of Mavis's mouth, but the older woman replied in the affirmative. The three ducked across the street and into the studio. Mary Jane headed toward the rear, where Martha could make out a small hallway slightly hidden by a folding screen. She thanked Mavis, who was already going to talk to one of three women who were practicing various poses on mats on the shiny wooden floor, then waited on a bench by the window. Martha took in the scent of sandalwood and the sound of gentle New-Age music. Was it a Celtic tune? An Andean lute? Martha hadn't a clue.

The inside of the studio was all brickwork with exposed beams and ducts. It seemed modern, but in a way that held in the historic elements of the architecture. Near the front of the studio, next to a young man who seemed to be the teacher, stood a rack of exercise balls, Styrofoam blocks, rolled up mats, and a basket of canvas straps.

Modern torture devices? Martha mused.

Mary Jane came out from behind the folding screen. "Your turn," she said. Martha realized she did indeed need to use the facilities, so she traded spots with Mary Jane and headed to the hallway.

After using the bathroom, she came out and peered down the rest of the hallway. Tastefully framed black-and-white art photos lined the walls, lit from above by intense bright bulbs strung to a wire that seemed as thin as a filament of a spider's web. Looking further down the hall, Martha spotted a twisting carpeted staircase. Illuminated wrought-iron sconces leading upward seemed to beckon her.

She was taking a few steps forward when a stern voice said, "Martha!" Spinning around, she saw Mavis peeking at her from around the folding screen.

"Oh my gosh, I didn't even hear you!" said Martha with a start, putting her palm to her chest as if to keep her heart from bursting out.

"The curse of the yoga teacher, I guess. We're notoriously light on our feet," said Mavis, her voice returning to singsong. "I was just checking to see if you were all right."

"Oh yes," Martha said, embarrassed. "I'm afraid you caught me being nosey and looking at these beautiful photos."

"They are stunning, aren't they," Mavis stated more than asked. "I think Mary Jane is ready to go."

"Oh, right."

For the next few hours, Martha and Mary Jane strolled around Adair, mostly window shopping. It was only at the end of the afternoon, when they were settled into the VW and heading back toward Riley Creek, that Martha returned to something that had been puzzling her.

"Mary Jane, this may be a weird question, but did something Mavis said at lunch bother you? I could have sworn that at one point, you looked sort of perturbed about something." Martha let her words fall gently, not wanting to go too far in case she'd misinterpreted what she'd seen.

"Was it that obvious?" asked Mary Jane. "Well yes, to tell you the truth, she did say something that seemed strange to me. When she was discussing Lorna, she talked about her as if they'd been the best of friends. If they were, I guess I missed it. Lorna never talked about Mavis like that. I guess I was just reminded that we never really know people as well as we think we do."

Chapter Eighteen

Once again, the morning came too soon for Martha. As she awoke, she registered strange sensations in her calves and shoulders. Putting a sweatshirt on over her flannel pajamas, she felt each sinew in her back. It was clear that doing yoga the previous day had awakened muscles that had been quite happy staying asleep.

Her stomach registered "still full." Padding down the stairs for coffee, Martha recalled the Mexican food she and Mary Jane had stopped for on the way home from Adair the previous evening. The lingering flavors of cilantro and beer led her back up to the bathroom to brush her teeth.

Mouth refreshed, Martha let Penny out the French doors to catch up on the previous evening's doggie updates, then stood sleepily watching the coffee brew. She added a slosh of cream to her coffee when it was done and went out to enjoy the morning sun on the back deck. The chill in the air made it clear that there wouldn't be many more mornings warm enough to sit outside.

Sumatran Migration, she thought, sipping her coffee. The session with PJ had helped her appreciate the roast in a way she never had before.

As she sipped and watched Penny nosing around nooks and crannies she'd checked a thousand times, Martha recalled Mavis's story about Aunt Lorna. Something about it bothered her. She stepped back into the cottage and went to Lorna's two "barrister bookcases," as Martha had always called them. Constructed from deep cherry wood with stained glass front panels, they stood almost seven feet high and were positioned catty-cornered to one another on two walls of the living room.

With her finger, she traced along each row of books before she found what she had been searching for. From four identically tall navy blue books, one for each year Lorna had attended Lewis High, she pulled out one that read "Lewis High 1969." It appeared to be a bit more well-thumbed than the others. She went back out to the deck and sat down with the yearbook.

It fell right open to a page of black-and-white photos of neatly dressed young men and women in the senior class. Since the class wasn't very large, it didn't take Martha long at all to find her mother. She was stunning in a simple off-the-shoulder dress and a string of perfect pearls. The photographer had positioned each girl with shoulders back and head turned just slightly, and the overall effect made her mother look like a young Lauren Bacall.

Martha ran her fingers down the rows of names, looking for Lorna and Mavis. She found Lorna in the class of 1970, but Mavis didn't appear until 1971.

That's odd, Martha thought. *I could have sworn she said she and Aunt Lorna were best friends and in the same class.* She sipped her coffee, thinking back over the conversation she and Mary Jane had had with Mavis at The Greenery. She couldn't recall if Mavis actually *said* she was in the same class as Lorna, but Martha was pretty sure she'd said they both graduated in 1970. Maybe back then, people referred to their graduation years differently than they do now. Maybe they referred to the nearest year ending with a zero for ease of reference.

As she moved the book from her lap to the side table, she noticed one page was dog-eared at the top right corner. Scanning the page of photos, Martha couldn't make out anything of significance. Boys wore bellbottoms and shirts with wide lapels. Girls were in skirts, Mary Janes and homemade sweater vests.

As she closed the book, Martha caught sight of a small photo. In it, a young man stood next to a piano on a stage, one hand on his cheek and his eyes turned skyward from a tilted head. He held a microphone with a wire trailing away behind the piano, and he wore heavy horn-rimmed glasses. But his eyes were unmistakable. She read the tiny print below the picture, then turned back to the rows and rows of class photos. When she reached the junior class again, there he was; Lincoln Settler.

That's odd, she thought. *I don't remember Mavis mentioning that she had an older brother, or that he'd been in Aunt Lorna's class.* On the other hand, Martha had been asking about Aunt Lorna, so why would Mavis have mentioned him? Ah, well. High school was a long time ago, and there were far more pressing matters right now.

Martha closed the book. *How much longer can I stay in Riley Creek?* she asked herself. She had a high-paying job that others would envy. The College President had assured her that he had big things in mind for her future. She was living a vibrant city life. *Well, if you call working all hours and not even knowing my neighbors a vibrant life.* But what was the alternative? What was her brain struggling so hard to figure out? After all, the shop and the house might be hers, but they were riddled with debt. What was she contemplating? Living here? Taking over the shop?

She sat up straight, realizing that's exactly what had been percolating in her brain for the last few days. Spending time with

PJ, Mary Jane, Allison, the Ritzenwallers, Margaret, and all the others—even Ethel Jean, for heaven's sake!—felt so natural and right, and as each day slipped by, she had a harder time imagining driving back to Boston, completely stripped of her family roots, to resume her regular life. When she imagined that drive, it filled her with a feeling of emptiness; not the sense of resolution and closure she had intended.

She set her empty mug on the table, the sharp crack of it making her jump. It was time to take control of these jumbled thoughts, and the best way she knew how to do that was through something physical.

Fifteen minutes later, she was heading for Compass Trail, water, map and protein bar in her hip pack, binoculars secured to her chest by a solid harness strap. She hiked along the trail's familiar lower section, taking in the sight of beautiful yellow buckeyes losing the last of their leaves. Aunt Lorna had reminded her that they were the only trees in the area with five leaves coming together to form a compound, and that early settlers to the area thought the nut looked like the eye of a deer.

How many of those nuts did I carry back to the cottage when I was a kid? she wondered. *Had Aunt Lorna just taken them back up the trail on one of her own hikes?*

Today, she felt like taking a more strenuous trail, hoping a rigorous hike would shake out the disquieting questions of the morning. She cut across a familiar quarter-mile pass that came out at the start of Ernie's Ear, a notoriously steep and little-traveled trail. Adjusting her hip pack tightly, she extended the telescoping walking poles she'd strapped to her pack, knowing that two more legs would help her on the way up *and* down. The elevation changed by almost a thousand feet over the four-mile trail, but she felt energized and ready for the challenge.

Fifty yards in, the way turned rocky and steep. To the left of the narrow trail, a slim stream trickled down the mountain. The sun had yet to peek over the mountain, and Martha spied a jagged edge of ice on the parts of the stream that were still in the shadow of laurel and rhododendron. Her nose and ears registered the chill as her elevation increased, but her growing body heat equaled things out. She carefully placed her walking sticks as the rocks grew slippery with dew that had been flash-frozen overnight.

About twenty minutes in, she reached a plateau where the trail widened and an overturned tree trunk formed a natural resting spot. She had not spotted a single person on the trail, but realized most casual walkers would not attempt a steep and slippery hike when there were so many other options. She helped herself to a few swigs of water and a couple bites of granola bar; even though she was not really hungry, she knew the shot of sugar would help get her up the remaining length of the vertical trail.

Getting her breathing under control, she heard what she thought was a Carolina wren calling "Teakettle, teakettle, teakettle!" If she spent more time here, she would need to improve her birding skills. Aunt Lorna could identify tens of birds just by their calls. How had she ever learned that? They all sounded the same to Martha, except for the handful that were as familiar to her as the sound of Penny's bark.

I guess I could learn, she thought. After all, she knew the wren had just sounded. *That's a place to start, right?*

She peeled herself off of the log and started up the mountain once again. She and Aunt Lorna had done this trail a handful of times, but she'd balked at joining her aunt once she hit her teens. What was it that happened to teenagers? One minute, she'd loved clambering up this trail, and the next, she'd preferred to stay in her room. She felt another pang of guilt as she imagined how her sudden disinterest might have felt to her aunt.

A large bird riding the air currents overhead caught her eye and Martha pulled up sharply, reaching for her binoculars. Was that a flash of reddish brown she'd noticed on the hawk's breast? Anxious to reacquaint herself with her old friend, she brought her binoculars to her eyes and adjusted the focus at the same moment as the hawk went into a dive toward the ground. Unable to track the speed of the bird's descent, Martha contented herself with being ninety-nine percent sure this had been the magnificent Cooper's Hawk. Smiling wryly, she forgave the bird for being too focused on its prey to doff its cap to her right at this moment.

Still smiling, Martha secured her binoculars to her chest again and continued her hike. After another half hour of steady climbing, picking out each step carefully to avoid slipping or twisting her ankle, Martha came to the top of the trail. Catching her breath, she slipped her pack off and took in the vista. From this elevation, she could see over the mountains almost as far as North Carolina. Looking through her binoculars, she spotted some dark scarring on the hillsides far away, evidence of a recent burn that must have been extinguished before it could develop into a full-fledged forest fire.

Continuing to turn in a circle, she spotted the namesake of this trail, Ernie's Ear. It was an exposed cliff where softer rock had eroded under a solid sandstone cap. In some parts of these mountains, the erosion had continued until a hole opened up and an arch formed. Here, while the erosion had taken place, no hole had formed, but it had left something resembling a human ear.

There are so many strange names in this area, Martha reflected. *Why don't I know more about them?*

Martha sat down to rest, but knew she couldn't stay long. Her sweat was already causing a chill, though the welcome sun provided at least a bit of warmth. As she put her pack on and stood up to head back down the trail toward home, she detected movement about a hundred yards into the trees. Peering closely, she made out Helen tromping in her direction, cheeks pinked, brow furrowed and clearly not happy.

"Hey, Helen!" Martha yelled, waving to get the other woman's attention. Helen looked up and gave a half-hearted wave in response. As she got close, Martha said, "What's up?"

Helen nodded as she sat down and peeled off her pack. "You caught me at a frustrating moment. I've been following what I thought was a magnolia warbler for over an hour. Turns out it was a yellow-rumped warbler. I thought I was really onto something, but I guess I was foiled again." She removed her ball cap and the binoculars that had been harnessed to her chest and took a long pull from her water bottle.

"Well, that beats anything I've seen today. So far, I've seen a Carolina wren, and I think I saw a Cooper's Hawk, but it dived before I could get a focus on it, so a definite identification of a yellow-rumped warbler sounds pretty amazing to me."

Helen gave a small smile. "It was a great little bird, don't get me wrong, but the magnolia would really have gotten me on the map. It hasn't been spotted in this county since 2014."

Martha struggled to keep up. "Gotten you on the map?"

Helen's neck reddened. "Oh, I was just excited that maybe I'd spotted something rare and could have reported it on myBird. That's a website where birders can share sightings in various locations." She gazed off, shaking her head at herself. "I've always wanted to find something special, something that sets me apart from being 'Don's wife who works at the bird shop.' Silly, I know."

"Not really," said Martha. "Even adults want to have a special talent—a superpower of some kind. Don't worry,

I don't have one either."

"Oh, I'm not so sure about that. The gals and I were just talking about you the other day and how effortlessly you're becoming part of the gang. And PJ agreed you are getting the gist of the coffee business with the greatest of ease."

"Well, everyone sure has made me feel at home here. I'm a bit out of place, trying to learn all that Aunt Lorna knew and figure what to do about the house and the shop." She trailed off for a few moments. "Speaking of the house, Helen, would you mind helping me with something?"

"Anything," said Helen. "What is it?"

"Well, it's a bit awkward to ask, but the police are done testing Aunt Lorna's birding scope and are returning it to me soon. They say they've cleaned it up, but I don't know a thing about it. I'm not sure if I want to keep it, considering..." Here, she veered off, not wanting to state the obvious about the skull-crushing scope. "But knowing how valuable it is and how much Aunt Lorna treasured it, I at least want to see if it is still in working order. Could you stop by sometime and take a look?"

"Be happy to," replied Helen. "Are you still leaving the doors unlocked like Lorna did?"

"Well, to be honest, I've been locking up, but just give me a ring and I'll be sure to be there when you come over. Shall we head down?"

"After you," replied Helen, gesturing down the trail. "And thanks," she said, looking shyly at Martha. Pleased to have lightened Helen's burden, Martha felt happier herself as the two of them hit the trail for home.

Chapter Nineteen

Feeling refreshed by the tough hike, Martha headed home to shower and pay some bills online before she tackled any other shop or cottage-related business. She'd spotted the phone and cable bills in Lorna's mail the other day and wanted to stay current with the utilities at least, even if everything else was in arrears.

Her eyes fell on the two lithographs on the floor, leaning against the sofa. After bringing them home from the shop following Ethel Jean's outburst, she'd simply left them there to deal with later. She realized she'd been putting off trying to figure out where they fit in the grand scheme of the puzzle her aunt had left behind. If they were worth so much, why hadn't Aunt Lorna sold them to help pay her debts?

Maybe Aunt Lorna didn't know what she had, Martha thought. She emptied the portfolio of its other documents and slipped the prints inside.

The next five minutes were spent on the daily put-a-leash-on-Penny routine, which meant chasing her to her favorite play-hiding spots. Leash finally on the little schnauzer, Martha headed downtown with a lightness of step, feeling more hopeful after her hike. Penny was just happy to be out of the house. The smell of wood smoke was in the air, and Martha remembered again that she'd planned to make a fire.

Maybe tonight? She didn't recall seeing any wood in Aunt Lorna's firewood rack, so decided to stop at the hardware store on the way home to see about getting a load delivered.

By the time they got to the square, Penny had sniffed every tree trunk, curb, and pile of leaves she could get her nose on. But at last they reached their destination; Toad in a Hole Bookshop. The sandwich board Martha had helped Mr. Bennett with was out in front of the shop again. Having been thoroughly cleaned, it now advertised the shop name and hours, albeit in handwriting that was less than welcoming. She guessed it had been written by Mr. Bennett himself.

Martha situated Penny by a nearby flowerpot, telling her to stay in a voice that said she meant it. Penny chuffed her disagreement, shifting from paw to paw, but staying as Martha walked away. As she approached the compact limestone building, she recalled what her Aunt Lorna had said years ago about the unusual bookstore owner.

"He's different, all right. But aren't we all? Just wish he'd come down off of his high horse a bit and let people get to know him. He thinks we all need a little culturing. We'll see how that goes."

Martha was curious to see what she could learn about the lithographs, but she had to admit, she was also curious about Mr. Bennett. She pushed the glass door open, and in doing so jangled a small brass bell that hung from it.

Is there an independent bookstore on the planet that doesn't have one of those bells? she thought. *Do they pass them out at indie bookstore owner meetings, complete with tarnish and a worn yarn hanger?* The first thing that struck her was that the shop smelled like an old bank. That gluey post-officey smell of officialdom must have permeated the very fiber of the place. But that was where the similarity ended.

Her eye was immediately drawn to the floor-to-ceiling stained glass that made up most of the back wall of the shop. In the shape of a sail, it contained swirls of every blue Martha had ever seen. The shop was ringed with tall shelves, and tasteful display tables of books were sprinkled evenly around the middle. The worn wooden floor, which from the looks of it must have been the original, matched the ladders attached to tracks running the length of the bookshelves on either side of the store. Martha felt she was entering the hush of an ancient library. The only item out of place (in that it was not a book) was a tall, slender vase containing two sunflowers. They were a bit worse for wear, but still added rustic charm to the space.

When she spotted an overstuffed chair near the window, Martha promised herself she'd come back one day to spend some time there, reading. Now, though, she approached the counter and greeted the owner.

"Hello, Mr. Bennett. Great to see you again," she said with a small laugh. "And I love your sunflowers." She nodded at the droopy gold faces.

"Oh, Mrs. Ritzenwaller from the library dropped those off a few days ago. Aren't they lovely?" Martha smiled in agreement, guessing she knew the sunflowers' provenance quite well.

"I haven't forgotten my promise to oil those squeaky hinges on your sign, by the way, but today, I was hoping to get your thoughts on something. I know you run a bookstore and not an art museum, but I was hoping you might be able to help me with these." She opened her pack and removed the lithographs from the portfolio. Handing them over, she briefly explained how she came to have them and that she wanted to understand their value better.

Mr. Bennett admired the prints, turning them this way and that, looking at the backs of the pictures and examining the artist's signature so closely, his nose nearly touched the plastic cover.

"Well, young lady, this is your lucky day. It just so happens I studied Art History at Cambridge and have some ideas about how we might find out more about them. Do you have time to wait while I make a few calls?"

Martha thought again about the sandwich board. "Sure. Do you mind if I pop over to the hardware store and come back?" she asked.

"Perfect," he said. "See you again shortly."

Martha put her nearly empty pack on and cut across the square. Penny came along and lay down in the shade outside of the store when Martha went in. She quickly found the spray lubricant she was looking for and took it to the checkout counter.

"Why, hi there, Martha! Nice to have you around town for a while," said Frank Elder, the shop owner.

"I've heard all about you and your chocolate croissant deliveries," Martha replied, giving him a conspiratorial wink.

Frank reddened a bit, then laughed. "Well, they say the way to the heart is through the stomach. And I'm not sure if you know this, but Mary Jane has a soft spot for chocolate." He gestured at her purchase. "Got a nasty squeak somewhere?"

"Naw," said Martha. "I'm just buying this stuff to help Mr. Bennett with his creaky old sandwich board. It must be as old as the actual bookstore building."

"Indeed," said Frank. "But we sure were happy someone came along to fix the old place up. I haven't been in many times, but it is a beautiful renovation. I've never been one for 'literature'"—he lifted his hand to air quote the exotic word—"so I really only pop over to get a newspaper now and again, but still, glad he's here. He must be relieved about the Sentrich kid."

"Relieved?" Martha asked.

"Well, yeah." Frank shifted foot to foot, looking like he'd said too much. "I just mean Bennett must be happy not to have the kid hanging around anymore."

"He hung around A Toad in a Hole?" Martha asked. This backed up what Lewis Shipman had told her a few days ago. "From what I've heard about him, it doesn't quite seem like his kind of place."

"You can say that again. From what I saw, he mostly came around to argue with the old guy."

Martha took this in for a second. It was hard to comprehend what Sentrich and Bennett could have had to talk about, much less argue.

After arranging for a supply of wood to be dropped off at the cottage, she went back to the bookshop. Bending, she sprayed the oil onto the old brass hinges, then opened and closed the sign until it operated smoothly with no audible complaint.

She re-entered the bookshop, calling, "Mr. Bennett, I oiled your sandwich—" and stopping when she spotted Margaret just beyond the counter, sitting on the floor next to an open box of books. The books were navy blue with swirling white letters. Margaret had removed one and was now absorbed in it.

"Hello, Margaret, I didn't know you were here," Martha called. Margaret made a high-pitched squeak before slamming her book closed and throwing it in the box with the others.

"Oh, ah, h-hello, Martha. I was giving Mr. Bennett a hand, but am heading out..." She jumped up from the floor and hurriedly picked the box up and moved it to a corner of a nearby table, in the process spilling some of its contents onto the floor. Martha couldn't miss the heaving bosoms and gauzy lace splayed across the covers. She couldn't quite make out the title, but was pretty sure "Bitter" was one of the words.

Margaret moved like lightning to gather the books up, shove them back into the box, and run in the direction of the shop's back room. She disappeared with the box, and moments later, Mr. Bennett emerged from the same doorway.

"I didn't know Margaret worked here," said Martha pleasantly, disguising her nosiness as friendly banter.

"Oh, she helps me now and again," he said, not looking up from the legal pad in his hand. "I found a bit of information on your lithographs. They are not as valuable, say, as an authentic Audubon would be, but their artist was a middle-tier expert of the same general time period, making them quite valuable and certainly collectible." He showed her his notes, pointing to a sum at the bottom with his pen.

"Wow! That is amazing. No wonder Ethel Jean was upset with Mary Jane." She went on to explain to Mr. Bennett the exchange she'd had with the two sisters.

"A mockingbird print would certainly fetch a high price, particularly among collectors and regional museums here in Tennessee. Any idea where the third print might be?"

"Not a clue," answered Martha, shaking her head. "But hey! On the up side, I oiled the hinges on your sandwich board so it should be a bit easier to handle. May I ask you another question?" Mr. Bennett nodded. "Frank Elder at the hardware store mentioned that you and Curtis Sentrich, the man found dead at my Aunt Lorna's cottage, had words from time to time. May I ask why?"

Mr. Bennett was visibly uncomfortable. "I barely knew the young man. He came in a few times, but was quite irritated that I didn't carry the book he was looking for. Now, I really must get back to my work. Thank you for taking care of the sandwich board, and it was so nice to speak with you."

He came out from behind the counter and walked her to the door. Martha was taken aback by the change in his demeanor, but got the message. She walked out to Penny and picked up the end of her leash, considering Mr. Bennett's claim that he barely knew the dead man. Based on what she'd heard of Sentrich, she was a long way from believing that he and Bennett had had words over a piece of fine literature.

Chapter Twenty

Martha spent much of the next morning on her university work (or, as she'd come to call it, her *paying job*.) Firing up her laptop, she was startled to see that the large neighboring university had finally gotten serious about a merger and had sent an executive proposal. Martha read through the high-level vision it had shared and was pleasantly surprised. While the university proposed to purchase the college outright, its price was generous and included a restructuring with no layoffs. Further, it offered to keep Berry's President on the Board of Trustees for the next five years, which would coincide with the timeline of his anticipated retirement. It even offered to incorporate "Berry" into the name of the new entity.

Martha sat back and whistled. This was a sweeter deal than anything she and her colleagues had expected. These people meant business. She scheduled a call with the President for early that afternoon to discuss the proposal. Right now, it was time for her to eat some crow.

She closed her laptop and moved to the kitchen to make coffee. She ground some Colombian Wingbar (*Light/medium roast—Light body—Crisp finish*) and ran upstairs to change clothes while it brewed. Once it was done, she poured some into a to-go cup, added a splash of cream, and headed out the door with Penny in tow.

The walk downtown was fast and a bit warmer than it had been the day before. Reaching Fins to Fur, she was putting out her hand to push open the door when a card hanging in its window caught her eye: *Gone fishin. Back at 2.* She rolled her eyes, thinking irrationally but irritably, *He did this on purpose. As if this wasn't already going to be hard enough.* But she was pretty sure she knew where the "fishin" would take place, if Jason was the creature of habit she suspected he was.

She walked briskly all the way back to the cottage, got her keys and backpack, and loaded Penny into the Subaru. Driving out of town, she followed the river road about four miles until she reached the turnoff to what had been Jason's favorite fishing spot. Pulling over to park on the side of the gravel road, she helped Penny out of the station wagon, and together they walked down a trail that led through the trees and into a glade before stopping at a pebbly bank by a wide spot in the river. And there, true to form, was Jason, gracefully casting his trout line back and forth, the fly just staying on top of the water for a few moments before he flicked it out and back into a fluid rhythm.

"Anything biting?" she called out, emerging from the trees and onto the rocky shore next to him.

"Well, hey there," Jason replied, pushing his sunglasses onto his ball cap and looking at her tentatively. "What brings a city girl like you out here to the woods?"

She refused to take the bait. After all, the purpose of this sojourn was to make an apology. It really wouldn't do to take his head off.

"Here you go. Hope you like it with just cream," she said. Jason accepted the cup, took a swig, and closed his eyes.

"Mmmmmm…. Wingbar?" he asked. Martha gawked, shocked that he'd guessed the coffee flavor.

"How—?"

"Lorna and PJ invited me over for roasting night every once in a while. Took me some time to convince her to put me to work, but I'm pretty sure I've roasted over a hundred batches of that stuff." He nodded at the cup. "I think I enjoy drinking it way more than I do roasting it. Thanks. But what's the occasion? I thought you'd already turned me in to PETA and thrown away the key." He wiggled his eyebrows up and down and flashed a million-dollar smile.

"About that…" Martha said sheepishly. "Look, I was wrong. So sue me. I found a trap up on Talisman Trail, you're running a hunting store; I put two and two together and—"

"And came up with five," Jason responded acidly. "And for the record, I run a store for those who love the outdoors and want to enjoy it responsibly. *Including* hunters, who have to be licensed, dispatch animals quickly and humanely, and never bag anything over their legal limit."

Martha held her tongue, hating to take this retort from Jason, of all people. Yet she realized he was absolutely right. She had been quick to assign blame to him and deserved everything he was dishing out.

Just as she reached the point where she couldn't take any more and would soon tell him off and leave, he ended his lecture. She tuned back in just in time to hear him say, "No wonder you and the rest of the village have their eye on me for Sentrich's murder."

"What did you say?" she said, focusing her eyes back on him. He thrust the coffee cup into her grasp and expertly pulled in his slack line with his left hand. Martha could see the tip of the rod bending down toward the black water, and within a few moments, something wet and shiny came up, causing a bubbling froth where the line met the water. Jason netted the fish, and then proudly held it up for Martha's inspection.

"Rainbow! How about that?" he said, boyish pride showing on his face.

Martha marveled at the speckled pink scales shining in the sun. "Beautiful fish! Will you eat him for supper?" she asked.

"Oh, no. Strictly catch and release for me. I caught my fill back in the spring when they were really running, so this is just for fun." He gingerly removed the small barbless fly from the fish's lip, careful not to tear it, and then bent down to ease it back into the water. It stayed suspended near the surface a half second, and then fluttered into the blackness of the river.

"Now, what were you saying about Sentrich?" asked Martha.

"Just that I know everyone considers me a 'person of interest' in his death because of my troubles out West."

"I don't know anything about your troubles out West," Martha said.

"Let's just say I got involved with the wrong people, started drinking and drugging pretty heavily, and did some time in jail. I'm not proud of it, but it's something I'll carry around for the rest of my life. I know I was one of the first on the police's list when Sentrich turned up dead because they came and grilled me after you found him in the backyard. It didn't help that I'd argued with him a million times about his stupid traps."

Martha felt the sting of this remark, even more ashamed now that she'd blamed Jason.

"They talked to you first?" she asked, surprised.

"Oh yeah. The morning after you found him," Jason answered.

"And?" Martha persisted.

"And I told them he was a lowlife jerk that I'd never waste my time murdering. I have a life here and I'm in absolutely no hurry to do any more prison time."

"And did they believe you?" Martha asked.

"I have no clue if they did or not, but my only alibi for that night was that I was home in bed, so they probably didn't."

"I'm sure you're exaggerating their interest in you. There are a few others around this area who have done hard time, so at least you're not alone."

"*Hard time?*" parroted Jason. "Are you Nancy Drew all of a sudden? Or should I say Miss Marple? Weren't those the books you were always reading when we were kids?"

"Laugh all you want," Martha replied shortly. "I'm trying to figure out what Sentrich's body was doing in my aunt's backyard so I can clear her name. There were definitely some strange things going on with my aunt and I'm going to get to the bottom of them."

"Yep, there's the old Martha. Or maybe the new, improved, even more Teflon Martha."

"What's that supposed to mean?" she demanded, placing her hands on her hips. *What is it with this guy? Why does he get under my skin so much?*

"Nothing, nothing," he said, holding his hands up in mock defense. "Don't be mad. It's just that... well, you always did tend to see a mystery around every corner when we were kids."

"In what way?" Martha asked, hands still on hips.

"Remember the case of the missing bicycle? You called 911, claiming your bike had been stolen when your aunt had taken it in for a tune up."

"Yes, but it was an easy mistake to make—"

"Or the time you were sure Jimmy Ritzenwaller was a Russian spy?" said Jason, laughing at the memory.

"Well, he did tend to travel a lot and he knew so much about airplanes," said Martha, a tad defensively. "Anyway, I should be going."

She'd let Penny off the leash to explore the surrounding beach, but now whistled for her to come back. After she'd put the leash on the little dog, she took her leave.

"Hope you have a good rest of the day," she said, wanting to get out of there as soon as she could.

"Hey, Martha, one more thing," said Jason, grasping her gently by the elbow.

"What?" she said, her voice light and breezy, trying her best not to pay attention to the heat of his hand on her arm.

"You're right; there *is* another person in the village who spent time in prison and had issues with Sentrich. But he had nothing to do with the murder. If you are really trying to solve this thing, leave Carl out of it."

After delivering Penny back home and spending time tidying up the cottage following a call with her boss, Martha was again checking work emails when her phone rang. Picking it up, she was surprised to hear Margaret's voice.

"Hello, Margaret. How are you? Is everything all right?" Martha asked. "Do I hear voices in the background?"

"Oh yes, indeed. Everything is all right. I'm in the bookstore and Mavis and some of the other gals are here for their book club, so that might be what you can hear. I just wanted to tell you I was going back through some of my notes about Lorna's statements, and I came across something rather odd. It may mean nothing, but..."

"Please tell me what you found," Martha responded encouragingly.

"Well, it's the strangest thing. Back in 1982, she began giving donations to an entity called the Carville Foundation, one per year. Then, in 1989, the checks stopped."

Just like the trips with Jimmy and Delores, she thought. *Starting the year Uncle Tommy died and ending the year my parents died.* Martha shook the thought away to tune back into what Margaret was saying.

"I have no idea what the foundation is, but it must have been important to her. Some of the amounts were sizeable. I've been able to look up the old checks, and they each say 'Linc' in the memo line."

Something buzzed in Martha's memory, a thread of recognition that she couldn't quite grasp. She was just getting ready to hang up when Margaret cleared her throat.

"Oh, and I wanted to add that I'm sorry I was not more agreeable when you saw me here the other day. I was simply... surprised. I had just opened that box of books—I have no idea what the title even was—and you startled me. That was all." Martha told Margaret that it was fine and not to think a thing about it, and once again thanked her for the information about Lorna's finances. She ended the conversation by asking Margaret to please see if she could find any more information about the Carville Foundation. *Such an odd bird,* Martha thought as she hung up.

Martha spent the evening working at the shop, stocking shelves and practicing her hand at the espresso machine. She much preferred the simplicity of the basic roasts, filling the large push-top coffee urns at the to-go station with that day's featured flavor. But PJ and Helen had taught her that offering a variety of coffee, along with other drinks, food, and bird merchandise, was important for the shop's profit margin, and as the (at least temporary) owner, she needed to understand how all of it worked. And she had begun to enjoy putting the many pieces of business ownership together. It stretched her brain in ways she hadn't realized she'd been missing.

At closing time, as the last of the customers dawdled out the door and Martha locked up behind them, she peered hard out into the darkness. Running a hand through her hair and over her face, she looked up to see PJ gazing at her from behind the coffee counter.

"Everything OK?" he asked, his brow wrinkled with concern.

"Oh yes, for sure," she replied breezily. "It's silly, really. I'm still ruffled by Imbroglio's visit the other day. I'll shake it soon."

"Don't shake it too soon," said PJ. "That guy is bad news. The real deal. I think it's good for us all to be a little extra vigilant until we're sure he's going to leave us alone."

"I wish the police could get to the bottom of Sentrich's murder. It's like it's hanging over my head. Imbroglio just increased the creep factor in an already creepy situation."

PJ sat down in one of the swiveling stools at the counter.

"In my opinion, one less Sentrich on the planet is addition by subtraction." Martha looked at him, surprised. PJ never had a bad word to say about anyone, even Ethel Jean. "Lorna knew this, but I'll tell you too. About a year ago, Sentrich tried to threaten me. He followed me home one night after closing, and told me that if I didn't pay him five thousand dollars, he would contact my parents and tell them that I dressed, as he put it, 'like a two-bit hooker.'"

Martha's mouth opened in horror.

"Oh, don't worry about it. He didn't bother me. First, I gave him my classic Dolly line: *'Honey, it costs a lot of money to look this cheap!'* But that just seemed to agitate him. So then I told him the reason I hadn't even *talked* to my parents in over thirty years was because they *already knew* I dressed this way, and so threatening to tell them wasn't worth a cent to me." He shook his head. "Believe me, him following me home caught me off guard, but he didn't have anything on me. Plus, just because I wear the odd dress doesn't mean I couldn't flatten him in five seconds. Once he realized I wasn't afraid of him and he couldn't cash in on any of my secrets, he left pretty quickly."

Cashing in on secrets, Martha repeated to herself. *Cashing in.* Some gear in her mind was clicking. If only she could fuel the engine behind it to really get it moving.

PJ spoke again. "And some of us have secrets that need to see the light of day so that we can get past them." He looked at Martha. She blinked.

Does he mean me? she wondered.

PJ threw his apron in a bin and was out the back door with a "G'night!" thrown over his shoulder before she could respond. A few minutes later, Martha turned her attention to refilling the feeders in the back courtyard so the others didn't have to do it in the morning. Seeing the deep darkness outside the windows, she clicked on the single floodlight, walked out the door and began the process of filling the feeders from a pitcher of seed.

"Well, here we are, together again at last," an oily voice said behind her. Turning quickly, she faced Cenzo Imbroglio. He loomed out of the dark alley that ran from the courtyard along the back of her store and Silent Sisters. This time in jeans, turtleneck and leather jacket, he had the same slicked-back hair and, of course, the chilling crow tattoos. Martha held the almost-empty plastic pitcher of seed in front of her, her heart pounding so hard she could feel it in her grip. This time, there was no PJ around to rescue her. She was on her own.

"I appreciate your aunt's down payment. But now it's time for you and me to come to an arrangement for the rest." He drew back one flap of his jacket to show a gun holstered just under his armpit.

I'm going to die and I have no clue why, Martha thought. Wind chimes hanging from one of the small trees continued their tinkling as if all was right with the world.

"Down payment for what?" she said. She was trying to sound calm, but her voice came out an octave too high.

"Don't play dumb with me. Your aunt may not have filled you in on our little arrangement, but let's just say she was more than happy to pay on time and in full every month. But now it's time to pay the balance. Unless you wanna pay it off in other more... *creative* ways?" He looked her up and down as he'd done the first time they'd met. Clearly seeing the disgust behind the expression on her face, he became serious again. "I'm expecting twenty grand and I mean to get it. From you." Imbroglio moved closer, yanking her by the top of her arm.

Thinking fast, Martha mustered all her professional communication powers. She forced herself to adopt an irritated tone.

"All right, all right. Just hold on. I'm already in the process of gathering the money, but if you keep barging in with your demands, making things more public than they need to be, we're both going to have problems. My aunt didn't leave things in great shape, you know. I just need more time."

"Well, I ain't got a lotta time. Having my former partner outta commission has put a serious crimp in my cash flow, you might say," Imbroglio sneered.

"Did you kill him?" Martha blurted.

"HA! What are you, stupid? You think I'd say so out loud if I did? You're probably wearing a wire from the police or something. Not a chance." Did he mean "not a chance" did he kill Sentrich or "not a chance" was he going to admit that he did? Either way, Martha was pretty sure it wasn't the time to request clarification. She needed to get away from him.

"Look, Imbroglio, I just need... say... a week?"

"You got one week. No more. I want twenty thousand. And don't think I won't be watching you and your little dog. If I even think you are snitching to the cops, your dog and the sweet little oldies down the street with the German Shepherd will have a bad day. A. Very. Bad. Day."

He turned and stalked back down the alley. Martha slumped onto one of the benches, feeling queasy now that the immediate threat had passed. How did he know about Penny? And the Ritzenwallers? Had he been following her? And now she'd committed to giving him money. What was she going to do?

Chapter Twenty-One

Martha passed a fitful night, only sleeping after she'd checked and rechecked the cottage doors and windows, read several chapters of her mystery and taken a mega-dose of some "this product may make you drowsy" cold medicine. Her run-in with Imbroglio had left her shaky and she wanted nothing more than to go straight to the police station to tell Detective Perry and Allison about him showing up at the store with a gun. But she'd read enough police procedurals to know that if they arrested him, he'd clam up and ask for an attorney. Then she'd likely never find out her aunt's connection to him, nor what had happened to Sentrich. Frightened as she was, she was determined to have that closure before she left Riley Creek.

She spent the next morning at the shop with PJ and Helen, stocking shelves and stacking extra to-go cups for the evening's owl prowl. The Hot Spotters—a Riley Creek birding group that Lorna had belonged to—organized regular nighttime walks to hear owls over on the Tarberry Nature Center grounds, and tonight was the night of their monthly jaunt. It was tradition, especially on cold evenings like this one was sure to be, for the group to stop at Birds 'n' Beans first for hot drinks and snacks to take along. Helen and Don were leading that evening's walk, so Helen would be leaving the shop early to head home and get ready.

Late morning, Martha popped over to An Early Riser to pick up an extra order of assorted cookies. Cat handed the boxes to her, saying quietly that Carl had been irritable since he'd visited with Martha at the shop and asking if anything was wrong. Still uneasy about what Carl had told her—that Imbroglio had killed at least three people while a member of the same prison gang as Cat's husband—Martha thought it better if she played dumb.

"No idea why he's grumpy," she said lightheartedly, shrugging her shoulders and feeling guilty about not being totally truthful with Cat. "He just told me about the car salesman guy and what a bad experience you all had had with him. Maybe it brought up some bad memories for him."

Birds 'n' Beans was relatively quiet when she returned, so Martha checked with PJ and Helen to see if she could be away for a few hours before Helen had to leave.

"Honey, the 'Beans' side of this shop can practically run itself once the bakery goods and coffee urns are filled," PJ replied. "As for the 'Birds,' unless we know there's a tour group on the way, that side can be pretty self-sufficient too. You go on."

The clock's belted kingfisher sounded eleven o'clock as if to send her on her way. Martha needed some time alone to process last night's events. The one-week timeclock with Imbroglio meant she had to be quick about figuring out why he'd been expecting twenty thousand dollars from Aunt Lorna—and now from her—and what to do about it. What had she been thinking to say she'd have it in a week?

She walked home to pick up her trusty Subaru, and then drove out to Burnt Ends, a small barbecue joint on the edge of Adair that she and Lorna had visited a few times over the years. She didn't want to bump into anyone she knew, nor did she want to drive so far out it would take her a long time to get back to the shop; she simply wanted to escape into her mystery for a while and let her mind work on the problem.

When she was a few miles out of Riley Creek, her phone beeped to indicate she had a voicemail message. It was from Donna, Sentrich's grandmother.

"Don't know if it'll amount to much, but thought I'd tell you. That no-account girl left town. Word is she left in the middle of the night without telling anyone and hardly took anything with her. Good riddance, I say."

Donna had then hung up without a goodbye. Martha reflected that leaving town abruptly hardly sounded like the Cherry she'd met. That girl had a carefully considered plan for her exit from Riley Creek.

Martha smelled the hickory smoke before she saw the actual restaurant and immediately realized how hungry she was. Parking her car and entering the small dining room, she selected the barbecue plate with slaw and hush puppies and decided to splurge on a banana pudding.

I'm going to need some more yoga and *some more running if I keep eating like this*, she thought.

After making herself an Arnold Palmer at the self-serve drink station, Martha heard a voice call, "Why, hello there, Ms. Sloane. Care to join me?" Mr. Bennett was seated in a small booth along the front windows, sporting his usual argyle sweater, tan slacks and New Balance tennis shoes. His reading glasses hung from a string around his neck and he had a book in his hand. An empty tray of food lay at his side. Given the tiny size of the dining room, Martha couldn't see how she could decline his invitation politely, so she nodded her thanks and slid in across from him.

He smoothed down his comb-over and folded his hands on the table. "Ah, the barbecue plate. A wise selection." Mr. Bennett smiled his approval.

Nodding at the book he'd just laid on the table as she began to eat, Martha asked, "What's your literary poison?"

"Oh, just about anything, really," he said, drawing out the last word. "Biography, historical dramas, modern literature." Martha thought she detected a note of pride in his voice. "And you?"

"Usually mysteries. They're easy to pick up and put down, which works well for me at the moment." Martha was still absorbed in a Frances Fyfield mystery that made her curl her toes at the thought of ever visiting a dentist again. But for reasons she couldn't explain even to herself, she didn't want to admit it to Mr. Bennett.

"I'm told you're fitting right into our little village," he said kindly. "And are adept at both the bird and bean aspects of Lorna's fine establishment."

"Oh, I'm not sure I'd say that," she replied modestly.

"I have it on the highest authority; the Silent Sisters."

"Ethel Jean and Mary Jane? I didn't know you all were friends," said Martha.

"To be clear, I heard it repeated by Margaret, who heard it mentioned between the sisters."

Who aren't really that silent, reflected Martha.

Looking around and gesturing at the dining room, Mr. Bennett continued, "I venture out of Riley Creek every so often to immerse myself in local flavor." He grinned at his own clever pun. "When I first moved here from the UK, I could not understand the draw of barbecue. I must say, though, that over time, I've become quite an aficionado. In fact, I judge Burnt Ends as top of class."

"May I ask how you came to live in Riley Creek, Mr. Bennett? It seems a rather... random place to relocate from the UK."

"Indeed." He nodded, straightening his book so that its pages lined up with the table edge. "And please call me Octavius. My elderly mother would certainly agree with you about Riley Creek's, as you say, 'randomness.' She insists I come back to London, to what she calls 'the bosom of the family.' It's been over five years now, and I don't have the heart to tell her that it was the bosom I was fleeing."

"Oh my. That must be difficult," Martha said sympathetically.

"It is, but time has lessened the blow. But back to why I came here. Well, my dear, it seems far-fetched as I recall it now, but Riley Creek is where my finger landed on the map. Literally." He sat back, a sparkle in his eye.

"My gosh!" said Martha as she realized that he was serious. "I could never be that adventurous."

Octavius laughed. "Well, the truth is that one can afford to be adventurous when one is financially well off. I was educated at Cambridge, then moved home to care for my mother and our ancestral home. But I finally realized that I needed to make a change before I was too old to do so. I was determined to bring culture to Small Town USA, so I started the bookshop in Riley Creek. And the rest, as they say, is history."

Martha had read her fair share of British mysteries, so knew a reasonable amount about titles and landed gentry.

"So are you an earl or something?"

"No, no, nothing of the sort. Just the beneficiary of a long line of prudent investors. Real estate and energy interests and such. Actually, my dear, when you stopped in the bookshop the other day, I assumed you were there to discuss my business arrangement with your aunt."

"What arrangement?" asked Martha, confused and just a bit alarmed. "I've been trying to learn as much as I can about the shop from Helen and PJ, but I don't recall them saying anything about a business arrangement with you."

Octavius raised his eyebrows a bit. "Indeed. Well, your aunt and I decided years ago to have what you might call a 'profit-sharing' arrangement. She doesn't sell bird books and I don't sell coffee. And my agreement with your aunt has proved to be mutually beneficial. She sends birders to me and I send thirsty customers to her. I suppose I should say... sent. Of course, now that you are here, you may decide to maximize your potential literary profits."

"Oh my goodness, not at all," answered Martha. "In fact, I admit I found it odd that there were no bird books in the shop, but I've been so busy with other things, I haven't had time to ask Helen about it." She wrinkled her brow as she reflected on the other "things" that had been taking up her time, in particular the tall tattooed one currently trying to extort money from her.

"I've gathered from Margaret that something distasteful is afoot, though I confess I am sorely lacking in detail," the little man said.

"Mr.... Octavius, it's probably better you don't know. It has to do with Curtis Sentrich and an awful man named Cenzo Imbroglio and something my aunt had gotten mixed up in. I don't want anyone else involved, but I am going to get to the bottom of it and clear my aunt's name."

"My dear, you are not alone in finding Mr. Sentrich a mental distraction. Though one should never speak ill of the dead, I feel I can share that Margaret found him utterly reprehensible as well." Octavius reflected for a moment, seemingly caught up in his own recollections, then said, "I certainly hope you are not involved in anything dangerous?"

"I'm working with Officer Tomlinson and Detective Perry while doing some digging of my own," Martha replied, not quite lying.

"Very good. I am pleased to know that. As I mentioned to you, I really did not know young Master Sentrich well, but my sense was that the young man did not have an illustrious future ahead of him. But your aunt, my dear, was a perceptive and purposeful woman. If she had brought him into her circle, he was there for a reason. And I've no doubt you will find out what it was."

Chapter Twenty-Two

After her illuminating lunch with Mr. Bennett (*Octavius*, she remembered), Martha had gone home to gather her things for the evening's owl prowl, tie up a few loose ends at work, and do some thinking. Closing the lid of her laptop having completed her work, she picked up a pad of paper and pen from the secretary and sat back down at the farmhouse table, feeling a bit of a chill in the late afternoon air.

I've got to figure out what Imbroglio and Sentrich were up to and how Aunt Lorna was involved. But how? She began jotting thoughts on the pad, trying to put the bits and pieces she'd learned into some logical whole, but was interrupted a few moments later by a knock on the door. When she nearly jumped out of her chair, Martha realized just how edgy she'd become after Imbroglio's threats.

Martha found Mary Jane on the stoop with a large bubble-wrapped object cradled in her arms.

"I nearly opened the door and came right in," she said, walking through the living room and setting her bundle on the large dining table. "I still have to remind myself that someone else is living here; that civilized people respect privacy and actually knock first." Her laughter held a bittersweet ring. Martha was sure Mary Jane felt the reminder of Lorna's loss as keenly as she did.

Mary Jane pulled a Swiss army knife from the pocket of her pants and cut through the packaging tape holding the bubble wrap in place. When the wrap was pulled back, there lay Lorna's beloved Swarovski scope.

"Detective Perry brought this by the shop for you today," she said, giving Martha a sideways look as she fitted the scope onto the tripod, turning a lever to lock it firmly into place. Then she fiddled with the scope, looking through the eyepiece and turning the knobs this way and that. Finally, she stood up straight, raising her eyebrows to Martha as if waiting for a reply.

"What?" asked Martha, pretty sure she knew what the look was about. "He brought the scope by. It was his job to return it. So what?"

"So, he also informed me that he'd paid one of his lab techs on the side to completely clean it and recondition the optics for you. It's as good as new, maybe better. Seems like he really went above and beyond for you."

"I'll admit, that was very nice of him. But he didn't have to do it. I'm not even sure I *want* this scope around now that I know what it was used for."

"First of all, of course you'll keep it. It was your aunt's pride and joy. Second, I think the poor man *likes* you. You could at *least* give him the time of day."

"Mary Jane, I'm not in Riley Creek to be liked. I'm here to… to…" Martha hesitated, no longer sure how to end this sentence and feeling the stress of the past twenty-four hours catching up to her.

"Martha, why won't you let your hair down a little? This man obviously likes you and he's perfectly decent. You know, just because Brian—"

Mary Jane pressed her hand to her mouth, as if realizing she'd crossed a very big line when Martha's face clouded over. Then Martha cracked wide open. The strain of trying to figure out her aunt's finances; the fear of Imbroglio and his threats; the stress of her job back home... whatever the reason, it all came flooding out and she hurled it right at Mary Jane.

"Just because Brian *what*, Mary Jane? Did my aunt tell *everyone* my business? I fell head over heels with Brian, we put a down payment on a house using *my* money, were planning to get married, and then a month later, he died from a massive heart attack. Oh, and that little detail about him already being married with two kids that I only found out when they came to the funeral. That I paid for. So, you think I shouldn't be so paranoid about dating again? Yeah, right. I'll keep that in mind. I appreciate your sage advice, especially seeing how you've done so well on the dating scene since your husband's death."

The last sentence was flung like a knife and hit dead center. Tears sprung to Mary Jane's eyes as if Martha had physically hit her.

"Oh, Mary Jane, I didn't mean that. That was my hot head speaking. Can you forgive me? I know you were just being nice, and I'm so sorry." Martha stumbled over her words, wishing she could take back what she'd said to this sweet soul.

Mary Jane shook her head, smiling through her tears. "No, no. It's fine, dear. You know, the thing is, you're right. I'd rather talk about your love life than mine. And I don't want you to think Lorna told the whole village your business. She shared with a few of us, mainly out of concern you hadn't ever moved on. But sometimes talking about things takes some of the sting out of them."

Martha blew out a breath. "It was a long time ago, but then sometimes it feels like yesterday. Maybe it's time to rethink my rapid march toward spinsterhood. It's just... it was so messy and embarrassing—not to mention expensive to deal with the aftermath—and it's taken me this long to get over. I'd rather—"

"—be on your own." Mary Jane finished her sentence for her. "Do you know what this calls for?" She reached into her pants pocket and pulled out a Snickers. "I don't know much about men, but I know Snickers really satisfies."

The two broke out in laughter.

Recovering, Martha fanned her red face and said, "Whew! We are a pair, aren't we? What would Aunt Lorna make of us?"

Mary Jane pointed skyward. "She's probably up there, shaking her head and thinking how lucky we two confirmed spinsters are to have each other." This set off another round of laughter.

"Seriously though, Mary Jane, I've been too busy with my career to put much thought into that part of my life," said Martha, recovering.

Mary Jane looked at Martha, and then said in a low voice, "If you don't mind me making an observation, it seems your career has filled in for lots of things in your life."

Martha started to object, but stopped herself, realizing the older woman was right. Work *had* taken the place of almost everything else: her love of the outdoors; romantic interests; and, to her eternal regret, time with Aunt Lorna here in Riley Creek. But there was something about being here in the cottage, away from the rat race of Boston, that was causing her to rethink her priorities.

"I suppose so," said Martha. "It just felt so... *urgent* after my parents died to make sure I never depended completely on anyone, even Aunt Lorna. Then when I finally did let myself trust in someone else, it turned out that the whole thing had been a farce. Work is clean. It's hard, but I only depend on me, and I know what to do to be successful. Relationships? Well, those are another story."

"You're right about that," said Mary Jane. "Relationships can bring great pain, but they can bring great happiness, too. I had that with Paul and I'm not sure there's anyone out there who will ever hold a candle to what we had. So do I really want to invest that much? Or would I rather just enjoy my own company?" Her eyes landed on the notebook that lay on the table. "What's that you're working on?" she asked.

Martha was too emotionally exhausted to lie. "I'm trying to figure out how Aunt Lorna and Sentrich and Imbroglio were all connected and who killed Sentrich in the backyard," she said, feeling a bit embarrassed. Did she really think she could figure that out?

"But shouldn't the police be doing that?" said Mary Jane, wrinkling her forehead.

"Yes, and they are working on Sentrich's murder. But Cenzo Imbroglio is mixed up in it somewhere, and if the police arrest him, I have a feeling I may never be able to clear Aunt Lorna's name and separate her from whatever Sentrich and Imbroglio were up to. On top of that..." She stopped for a moment, not wanting to worry Mary Jane over the previous evening's run in with Imbroglio. But the one-week deadline had put her under such pressure, she'd spilled it all out before she could stop it.

"Martha!" said Mary Jane, concern in her voice. "This is serious! He had a gun? You've got to tell Detective Perry or Officer Tomlinson."

"I will, I will, I promise," said Martha. "But first, I want to see if I can put all of this together." She ran her fingers through her hair.

Mary Jane's brow remained wrinkled. "All right. If you'll promise me you'll tell the police about him coming to the store, I'll help."

"You will? Oh, thank you! And yes, I promise," replied Martha, squeezing Mary Jane's hand while crossing the fingers of her other hand. "Let me put on some coffee while you light the fire."

"So, what do you have so far?" asked Mary Jane, reaching up from the couch once the fire was crackling and accepting the steaming mug of coffee from Martha.

"*Sumatran Migration's always the right choice for a good jaw-bone*," Aunt Lorna would have said.

"Well, the first person the police actually must have considered was Aunt Lorna," said Martha as she joined the older woman on the couch and propped her notebook on her steepled legs.

Mary Jane was already munching on the chocolate chip cookies Martha had placed on the long coffee table in front of the couch. Through her masticating, she managed a garbled, "Nonsense."

Martha nodded. "They had to at least consider her, since Sentrich was found on her property and he was killed with *her* scope that had *her* fingerprints on it. But they quickly discarded that idea because she'd been deceased too long to have had anything to do with it."

"Who else?" asked Mary Jane.

"According to Allison, Jason Turngate is a prime suspect because of his prior record. He did some jail time when he lived out West, and he had been seen arguing with Sentrich."

"He has a *record*? That nice young man?" asked Mary Jane, horrified.

"Sounds like he got mixed up with the wrong people, perhaps did some drugs."

"*Drugs*?" Mary Jane shook her head regretfully. Martha sipped her coffee, and then redirected Mary Jane's reflections, explaining what she had recently learned from Turngate himself; that the arguments had been over Sentrich setting traps in the nearby woods.

"But isn't it possible Jason would take advantage of your old friendship to try to make you doubt he could be a suspect?" Mary Jane asked carefully. Now she knew of Jason's past involvement in *drugs*, she seemed more than willing to entertain him as a suspect.

"It's a good question, but I don't think so. Why would he come all the way back to Riley Creek, start a business, and then murder someone? Plus, I don't think he's changed so much. The real Jason seems like he's still there, ya' know?"

"Uh huh?" Mary Jane replied, her raised eyebrow waiting for more.

"Stay on task," Martha admonished. "I can't handle more than one conversation about romance today. And then, of course, there's Cenzo Imbroglio, the original gangster. Word has it he killed people in prison and he's super creepy. And now he's threatening me over money Aunt Lorna supposedly owed him. Yeah, I would definitely say he could be a murderer."

"I agree, he seems like a troublesome character," Mary Jane said, nodding. "But, Martha, why would he murder his own business partner? Wouldn't it make more sense to keep him alive if Imbroglio thought Sentrich could help him get money?"

"But maybe he wanted to cut out the middleman," said Martha, jotting a note down. She pressed the pen to her mouth, going on to the next suspect. "There's another person we have to look at: Carl."

"Carl Shipman? Never." Mary Jane crossed her arms.

"Mary Jane, how am I going to go through this list with you if you refuse to even consider half of the suspects?"

"I'll try to be open, but not about Carl. It's just not possible. He simply would never put his family in jeopardy in any way."

Martha had to agree. Carl's devotion to Cat and Lewis was well known and it was hard to believe he would do anything illegal to bring harm to their door.

"And besides," Mary Jane said, "why would Carl murder Sentrich?"

"To dry up Imbroglio's cash cow and get him to leave Riley Creek? Carl despises the man."

"No, Carl wouldn't do that." Mary Jane was adamant.

"This next one is *really* weird," said Martha. "Frank told me he'd seen Sentrich arguing with Mr. Bennett. When I asked Mr. Bennett about it, he said they were arguing about books."

"Books? Sentrich?" replied Mary Jane, visibly skeptical.

"I know, that's what I thought. Not likely. But I also don't think it's possible that Mr. Bennett could cave someone's skull in with a scope."

Mary Jane shook her head at the absurd image of tiny Mr. Bennett lifting the scope up to smash it over Sentrich's head.

"But I've also seen Margaret creeping around the outside of his shop," added Martha, "so there's definitely something weird going on over there."

"I had no idea there were so many secrets in the village," said Mary Jane, clearly mystified. "What about Sentrich's girlfriend? Is she in the frame?"

"Funny thing about that. Sentrich's grandma, Donna Riggs, called earlier to tell me Cherry just left town. But Cherry had told *me* when I met with her recently that she was planning to keep working for a while and save up before leaving." Martha went on to explain Cherry's plan to open a business of her own, and the circumstances of her breakup from Sentrich.

Mary Jane pondered this. "Would she have had a motive to kill Sentrich?"

"I don't think so, though someone else wondered if she might have killed him to hold on to the Mustang he'd given her as a gift. She said she tried to give the car back, but he refused and told her to keep it to start her business. Now that I think about it, she didn't seem that broken up about their relationship ending. If anything, she seemed to lack any strong emotion about him, as if she'd already moved on. But she really seemed to be focused on getting out of Riley Creek, so I can't think what she'd be angry enough about to want to kill him."

How do detectives ever figure these things out? Martha wondered.

"But look at that another way, honey." Mary Jane gestured with the hand not holding her coffee mug. "What if it was like that other person you spoke to said: Sentrich demanded the car back, she refused, and he said he was going to take it by force? If that car was her ticket out of town, him threatening to take it away could have been enough to flip some kind of crazy switch in her."

Martha pondered this. Though it didn't seem likely, it certainly was possible. Martha had felt the young woman's desperation to get away from Riley Creek. And desperate people do desperate things. Plus the timing of Cherry leaving town... might she have left because she thought Martha would figure out she'd killed Sentrich?

"You're right, Mary Jane. I need to keep an open mind to all of the people on our list. They all could have had a motive to kill Sentrich, even sweet Mr. Bennett. Maybe Sentrich was bullying him and he got tired of it and killed him." Even as she said it, Martha knew she didn't really believe it. But if she was going to solve this mystery, she needed to consider everything.

The two women sat in silence for a bit, enjoying the last of their coffees and the mesmerizing flickering in the fireplace. Then Martha stood up and stretched.

"Mary Jane, thank you so much for helping me think through this list. And I promise I'll tell Detective Perry about Imbroglio's threat yesterday evening. But now, we'd better get ready for the owl prowl."

Before Mary Jane could answer, Martha's eyes fell on the nearby bookshelf and dredged up a memory.

"Hey, I found another weird thing. Apparently, Mavis and my aunt weren't in the same class in high school, but Mavis's brother and Aunt Lorna were. I was leafing through her yearbook the other evening and noticed that."

"Odd," said Mary Jane. "I thought I heard Mavis say she graduated with Lorna too. Maybe we were both so Zen from the yoga, we misunderstood what she'd said." The older woman laughed, dismissing the topic.

Martha shrugged her shoulders. "You're probably right. And hey, if we are going to be on time to owl prowl, we'd better get a move on."

Chapter Twenty-Three

With the sun going down, Martha drove north toward the DLT, technically the Doris Lee Tarberry Nature Center. Doris, who had grown up on the land and was described as a force of nature herself, had left her family's four hundred plus acres to the residents of Riley Creek in the early 1900s. Local lore held that the town council quickly designated the area a protected birding and wildlife preserve for fear of the strong-willed Doris coming back to haunt them.

During Martha's summer visits to Riley Creek, Lorna had taken her to the DLT for stargazing, tadpole dipping, and to learn about local geology. While she didn't remember much about the geology of Riley Creek except that there were lots of caves in the vicinity, Martha definitely remembered the owl prowls that she'd been on with Aunt Lorna, who had frequented and sometimes co-led them. She recalled them as slightly creepy affairs with adults tromping around in the dark, listening for distant owls calling. When the owl calls came closer, the adults got excited. Martha got scared.

Today's owl prowl participants, she'd learned from Helen, would meet in front of the DLT at dusk, and then walk together along the Belt Buckle Trail. Belt Buckle was a rigorous trail that made a series of switchbacks until it reached the top of a ridge. From there, the trail meandered along the ridge and deeper into the mountains, with occasional views across the tops. The tall pines found at that elevation made great perches from which the nighttime feeders could swoop down on unsuspecting mice and other small mammals not fast enough to escape.

Penny had not appreciated being left behind. But Martha was not sure if 1) dogs were allowed on Belt Buckle Trail and 2) the presence of a dog, no matter how adorable, would help in the attraction of owls.

There were not many businesses on the way out to the DLT, only a few sprinkled here and there. If they had once been thriving, they were now closed down or saw very little custom. One of them, sitting on the same lot that used to be owned by Jason's father, was The Car Man.

Aka Cenzo Imbroglio, Martha thought with a shudder.

In her youth, it had been a bustling business with neat rows of sparkling American cars lined up. Jason's father was known to sell a dependable car at a good price.

When he wasn't drinking too much, Martha reminded herself. OK, so it hadn't been perfect. But it was a far cry from what sat there now.

The showroom building, which had been a crisp, clean and sparkling white, was now a faded corn yellow. Vinyl stickers on the windows proclaimed "WE SELL 4 LESS" and "$0DOWN/$0FIN." The twenty or so cars on offer had two things in common: they were flashy and outdated. An eighties Fox-body Ford Mustang and a Honda coupe with an exceptionally large spoiler were parked nose to nose, making a chevron shape, each with the hood popped and a "SALE!" sign wedged into the engine compartment. An inflatable air dancer crumpled and stood, crumpled and stood, advertising CAR MAN vertically each time it rose to attention.

Martha caught herself accelerating at the thought of being in such close proximity to Imbroglio. She decelerated as she approached the DLT, parking to join her friends. A climbing wall had been erected in the parking lot, along with a food truck looking like its specialty might be pizza by the slice. Kids and families milled about.

Martha saw Helen walking along at the same moment Helen saw her. They joined at the edge of the parking lot.

"Wow! This is a far cry from the owl prowls I remember," Martha said.

Helen laughed. "Oh, I bet! Let's say they've evolved to suit the modern sensibility."

Mary Jane came walking up, outfitted in hiking pants and a fleece jacket, retying her hair in a ponytail.

"Whew!" she said. "That climbing wall is something."

"You tried it?" asked Martha, staring up incredulously at the fiberglass tower. She wasn't sure, but she guessed Mary Jane was in her seventies.

"Heck, yes! I always do the first climb to make sure all the safety equipment is good to go. It's a fundraiser for the nature center, and we partner with Fins to Fur to run it, but I feel better being the first up." Martha scanned over the heads of the kids surrounding the base of the climbing wall. She spotted the back of Jason's head as he fixed a harness onto a small girl whose parents stood by with a camera.

The three women headed over to the group assembling at the trailhead and Helen took her place next to Don as he began the program.

"Good evening, Hot Spotters and birding friends. Welcome to the October owl prowl! I see lots of familiar faces, but also some new. Helen, would you mind covering some of the basics for us?"

Helen talked the group through their intended route, as well as how they would attempt to attract the owls and what types of birds they might hear. The last point she covered was advisory.

"For any of you who don't have a red light option on your flashlight or headlamp, we've got red cellophane and rubber bands to give you. Covering the bright white of your flashlights and headlamps with red will help all of us to establish and maintain our night vision as we walk along."

Don took over. "I know there are different opinions on pishing for owls, and maybe we'll hear so many, we won't need to call any in. But trust me when I tell you we won't do it more than a couple of times, just to see who's around."

An older lady in the crowd raised her hand. "Excuse me, but what's pishing? Isn't that something we're supposed to watch out for on our computers?"

Don nodded to a boy of about eleven with binoculars around his neck and glasses falling down his nose a bit.

"Nathan, would you help us all understand pishing?"

The boy spoke shyly, looking at the ground more than at the adults around him. "It's when you go like this to attract birds. Like wrens or finches, usually." He concentrated for a moment, and then emitted a "Pish-pish-pish" that sounded remarkably like the sparrows that hopped around Lorna's back porch, making a racket. "Lots of people say you shouldn't do it because it could make some birds upset or take them away from their usual stuff like feeding their babies or building their nests. Don uses his phone to play owl calls, which isn't exactly pishing, but pretty close."

Don nodded and took up the explanation. "That's right, Nathan. If you pish or use a recorded call, you should not be excessively loud or do it more than a few times. Tonight, depending on what we hear, I may try some recorded calls from my phone, but I'll keep them brief and make sure to only use calls from eastern screech owls so we don't scare any smaller birds with a great horned owl call."

"Hi there!" Mavis called as she approached Martha. "I have something for you." She pulled a book from the small liver-shaped bag draped across her shoulder, entitled *Birds of the Southeast*, and handed it over. "I happened to stop at Toad in a Hole today and thought this might be nice for you to have."

"Oh, Mavis, how kind of you. I'd been toying with the idea of getting a little more into birding, at least for the remainder of my time here. I always enjoyed learning from Aunt Lorna, and it somehow seems fitting to keep birding in her honor." Martha gently tucked the guide into her backpack as they set off down the trail.

The owl prowl was much more fun than Martha had remembered. Probably thanks to the benefit of age, she was no longer afraid once the owl call-and-response started up. It only took one call from the recording on Don's phone to get the owls calling back and forth to each other from the towering trees along the ridge. Over the ninety minutes, with Don and Helen's patient instruction and Nathan chiming in with interesting facts about each species, they identified the calls from screech owls, barred owls and even (maybe) a great horned owl.

By the time the owl prowlers arrived back at the parking lot, the food truck had left and the climbing wall was being loaded in pieces onto a flatbed truck. The temperature had dropped substantially and the crowd dispersed quickly. Martha went up to Don, who was standing listening to an animated Nathan. While looking down at the ground, the boy was explaining to Don that great horned owls eat a wide variety of prey, including snakes, bugs and even porcupines.

"Yep, that's right!" said Don. "That's partly why they're sometimes called the 'flying tiger' of owls. They know no fear."

When Helen approached the three of them, Nathan peeked up at her.

"I saw you at the Green Maples Flea Market. Four last Thursday afternoon."

"Nah, I don't think so, buddy," said Helen. "I haven't been out there."

"Yes, you were at the book stall. Four—"

Don jumped in. "Hey, buddy, why don't you jump in my truck? I turned it on and it should be nice and warm. I'll swing you home in just a few minutes." As Nathan headed toward Don's truck, which was marked with the symbol of the state park, Don turned to his wife. "That was odd. Were you out at Green Maples?"

"Definitely not," Helen said. "He must have confused me with someone else."

"How do you know Nathan?" asked Martha.

Don explained that he'd met Nathan through Delores Ritzenwaller, who had observed the boy spending hours alone after school in the nature section at the library. She'd learned that Nathan's mom, Dot, helped to manage the Green Maples Flea Market and often worked long hours, picking him up from the library at the end of her shift. One day, Don had been in the library when Dot came by, and Delores made the introductions.

"He's a great kid," said Don. "Spends a lot of time on his own, so he's a bit... unusual for his age. It's just him and his mom at home, so I bring him along to nature programs that might interest him, as long as Dot says it's OK. He's especially into the birding walks and is like a walking field guide. Speaking of Nathan, I'd better get him back home."

It was past 8 p.m. when the little group broke up. After letting her station wagon warm up for a few minutes, Martha hit the road home. Approaching The Car Man, she noticed that the inflatable dancer had fallen to sleep, flat on the ground, though the lights on the lot and in the showroom still shone. On a whim, Martha pulled into the parking lot of the shuttered business next door and turned her car engine off.

What was she doing? Had she lost her mind completely? But it would feel good to have the upper hand on Imbroglio. After all, what could she lose at this point? Apparently, he'd been watching her; now it was her turn to watch him.

A chill seeped into the car after just a few minutes. Much as she wanted to, Martha didn't dare turn the engine back on, afraid the exhaust would give her away if Imbroglio suddenly emerged from the building. Mustering her adrenalin, she slid out of the car (keys in hand and ready to run like heck) and along the side of the cinderblock building. She peeked in through the front window and saw no movement. As far as she could tell, a dark hallway led to some offices at the back. Bright light beamed from one.

She waited a few more minutes at the edge of the glass, but still saw no one inside. Then she crept to the side door and tried it. Some dealers had sensors that dinged anytime a person opened the door. She was ready to bolt if one sounded.

Nothing happened.

Her senses on high alert, Martha made out the low hum of a televised basketball game coming down the hallway. She eased herself past the door and stood behind a shiny Pontiac Grand Prix that bragged "JUST 199K MILES" in white lettering across the windshield. Still hearing no movement, she edged around the car to the hallway. She crept along the wall, keys still in her hand, hearing the squeak of shoes coming from the basketball game. Every step, she paused and listened. Reaching the open office doorway, she craned her trunk forward, her bottom half like an independent entity ready to run like the wind.

She took in a desk with an outdated computer covered in sticky notes. Files and papers were piled haphazardly around it. Moving more fully into the doorway, she saw a credenza with a small black-and-white TV sitting on top, broadcasting the game. Turned to face the credenza was a tall-backed office chair. Imbroglio's wavy hair shone greasily above the headrest and his arms hung limply over the sides.

He must be asleep, Martha thought. But for reasons she couldn't have explained, even to herself, she knew something was wrong.

She took two steps into the office and leaned forward so she could peek around the side of the chair. Imbroglio's bulging eyes stared back at her.

As Martha's brain struggled to translate what she was seeing, a female voice from behind her said, "OH MY GOD!" Martha whirled around to see Mary Jane standing there, looking down at Imbroglio's lifeless form with her hand over her mouth.

"Mary Jane, what are you doing here?" said Martha.

"What are *you* doing here?" Mary Jane echoed. "I left the DLT right behind you and saw you pull in. I parked in the space next to your car when you came in here, deciding I'd better come and get you out of trouble. What in the world are you doing? What happened to *him*?" She gestured at the dead man, then stood up straight. "Did you decide to off him?"

"Do you hear yourself right now? '*Off him*?' Mary Jane, this is serious. I don't know what happened to him, but no, I didn't 'off him.' He could have had a heart attack, for all I know."

"Um, with a little help from whatever was wrapped around his neck," replied Mary Jane, pointing. Looking closely, Martha could see a thick line of blue bruising appearing around the tall man's neck, what looked like a pale O forming in the center of the bruising.

"What are we going to do?" she asked, shock now giving way to panic.

"What do you mean, what are *we* going to do?" said Mary Jane. "*We're* getting out of here. The last thing you need is to be found with another body. And this body belongs to someone who came into the shop a few days ago to extort money from you."

"Mary Jane, do you seriously think we can just leave him here and go about our business as if nothing happened?"

"I don't know about that, but I do know you've already found one body, and adding another to the pile may make you look miiiighty suspicious."

Martha popped her head out the door, ensuring no one happened by to make a late-night used-car purchase. Then she turned back to the other woman.

"Oh, Mary Jane, come on! Do I look like I could strangle a grown man? I don't even have anything I could have strangled him *with*!" Martha held out her hands to prove she hadn't brought along a garrote. "We need to call the police. *Now*."

Mary Jane pulled out her phone and tried to call 911. Realizing she had no reception in the cinderblock room, she walked down the hall to the showroom where Martha could hear her talking excitedly. Martha's eyes moved around the office, trying not to look at Imbroglio sticking his dead purple tongue out at her. They came to rest on the pastel sticky notes pasted around the frame of the computer monitor.

Leaning in, she read one carefully. Hearing Mary Jane coming back down the hall, she unstuck it and shoved it in her pants pocket.

"They're on their way," said Mary Jane. She pulled something from her purse and held the open yellow box out to Martha. "Raisinet?" When Martha shook her head to say no, Mary Jane began popping the chocolate-covered raisins into her mouth by the fistful.

"Oh, and Mary Jane? Don't mention Imbroglio coming to the shop with a gun just yet. I haven't gotten around to telling the police about that."

Just as Mary Jane opened her mouth to protest and probably lecture, cars with sirens blaring swung into the lot.

Small mercy, thought Martha.

Prior to this week, Martha had only ever spoken to the police once, when she'd been pulled over after rolling through a stop sign on campus on her way to an important meeting. Now, she spent her second night in just over two weeks being grilled by Riley Creek's finest. Where had she been? Why was she at the car lot so late at night? How had she known Imbroglio?

Mary Jane, who'd shifted into fragile old lady mode, explained that she'd been watching Martha the whole time and there had not possibly been any opportunity for her to strangle Imbroglio. But the questions she and Martha were asked seemed endless, only coming to a close when Detective Perry and Officer Tomlinson arrived on the scene. Perry indicated to the other officers that it was time to pause the questioning and let the women go home. Allison walked them out to their cars, seeing Mary Jane off first.

"Nice routine. I particularly liked the part about you needing to get home to take your blood thinners on schedule," Allison said. With a wink, Mary Jane hopped in her car and floored it out of the parking lot.

When Allison and Martha reached the Subaru wagon, Martha got in, but rolled down the window.

"How are you holding up?" asked Allison, both hands on the car frame.

"Well, this is my first time finding two bodies in a couple of weeks, so I'm not too sure, but I think I'm hanging in there." Martha was trying to convince herself as much as the other woman.

Allison nodded. "Yeah, this is a little out of our league, too. I mean, back in Nashville, two dead bodies in a week wouldn't be a shock. But here? Perry is talking about calling in reinforcements if we can't find the murderer soon."

"Murderer? As in singular? So you don't think two different people killed Sentrich and Imbroglio?"

"You know I can't discuss it officially, Martha. But they are known associates, so we will likely be treating their deaths as linked and committed by the same person."

Martha shuddered, as much from fear as the chill of the evening. "Well, whoever that 'same person' is, I sure hope you find them soon. The thought of a murderer running around gives me the creeps."

As Martha was pulling out of the lot, she was flagged down by Detective Perry. She rolled her window back down.

"Detective?" she asked.

"Miss Sloane," he said in his deep voice, "I just wanted to remind you that you'll need to come to the station tomorrow to make a statement." She nodded. "And please," he continued, "do not do any more of your amateur sleuthing. Leave it to the police. I don't want you taking any chances before—" He caught himself. "Before you can make that statement."

"I'll be there in the morning," she promised agreeably. The detective waved her out of the parking lot and she saw him in her rearview mirror, watching her headlights fade into the night.

By the time Martha let herself into the cottage, it was spitting cold rain. Penny was shortchanged with a quick pit stop in the backyard, then Martha methodically checked the locks on all the doors and windows while the schnauzer shook the raindrops from her fur coat. Gazing out into the night, her brow furrowed with questions, Martha fingered the note in her pocket. Then terrier and human climbed the stairs and snuggled up in bed. Not many minutes later, both were fast asleep.

Chapter Twenty-Four

Waking up the next morning, Martha had only one thought in her mind; coffee. After getting to sleep in minutes, she had stirred in the early hours and tossed and turned all night. Now, feeling and looking like one of the zombies from *The Walking Dead*, she needed some recovery time before she could even think about going to the police station to make a statement.

Thinking back to her night of roasting with PJ (had that really only been a few days ago?), she remembered something he'd said: "*When you've got bats in your belfry, there's nothing quite like a steaming cup of Italian Roost to clear it out.*" They'd both laughed at the bird reference, deciding that roasting beans past midnight in a shop for birders was bound to cause punchy side effects. But a cup of Roost was just what this morning called for.

After putting the coffee on to brew and letting Penny out for a meander, she lit a fire. She let Penny in and fed her, then sat at the farmhouse table and fired up her laptop. And at last, there it was.

Martha, might you tell me when you think you'll be heading back to Boston?

President Baskin had been nothing but patient and supportive as she had telecommuted from Riley Creek and tried to sort out Lorna's affairs. But if he was asking this question, he needed her back. Soon. He was just too kind to come out and say it.

Martha thought back to a few days ago when she'd finally acknowledged to herself that she'd been contemplating a different life, one here in Riley Creek. Her mind had been quietly working the idea over, nibbling on it, tasting it, trying to imagine what it might be like. Events since that day had been so disorienting, she had not come back to it.

Before she could keep going on this line of thought, her phone rang. Picking it up, she heard Margaret's quiet voice on the other end. Margaret explained that she had found out a bit more about the Carville Foundation. Apparently, it was part of a large medical foundation located in Louisiana.

"The interesting thing is the foundation's history," Margaret said, uncharacteristic enthusiasm creeping into her voice. "Though it now funnels corporate and private funds to a number of worthy medical causes, it was founded in the 1970s to support individuals with Hansen's disease, and did so until the early 2000s."

"Hansen's disease?" asked Martha, feeling lost.

"Yes. It's what you may know as leprosy, but the name of the illness was changed back around 1940."

"So are you saying that Aunt Lorna was donating money to people with Hansen's disease from 1982 to 1989, then suddenly stopped?"

"She was donating to an organization whose origins were in supporting those with Hansen's disease, definitely," said Margaret. "All in all, she gave quite a significant amount over the years."

Martha shook her head, frustrated that instead of getting clearer, her aunt's business affairs kept getting more and more mysterious.

"This is so strange," she said. "But thank you for your research, and for letting me know."

"Oh, and one more thing," said Margaret. "I found a realtor who specializes in business sales. They may have a buyer interested in purchasing Birds 'n' Beans."

"Margaret, I really appreciate all the work you are doing, but I don't think I can deal with this today." Martha paused. "You may not have heard, but I found another body last night."

"*Another one*?" Margaret exclaimed. "Oh my goodness. Indeed, today is not the day to talk about financial matters. Call me anytime." The mousy woman got off of the phone as quickly as she could without asking for any details.

Martha was dreading what she had to do this morning, but she knew she had to face it. She closed the lid of her laptop and Penny looked up from her bed near the warm fireplace.

"Want to come along this time, madam?" The terrier jumped out of her bed, not clear on the details but understanding enough to know they were going on an outing. Dressing warmly herself and slipping a little fleece jacket on Penny, Martha locked up and took her car keys out of her purse. After giving the Subaru a few minutes to warm up, she headed back past the DLT and on to the Paris Mountain State Park campground, where Don and Helen lived in the ranger residence. She hadn't been there before but followed the signs to the small log home up a short driveway near the entrance to the campground.

As she drove up, Don came out the front door, outfitted in his usual state park uniform. Pointing toward the house, he mouthed, "She's in there," and got into his state truck to head off. Martha waved goodbye to him, and then she and Penny walked up the path to the house. She heard Helen's faint "Come in!" in response to her knock, and she and Penny entered.

The small log home was simple but comfortable with a deep scent of wood smoke baked into the walls. It was furnished in large pieces, all dated but comfortable. Throw pillows and afghans adorned almost every surface and peppered throughout the visible space were tricks of the park ranger trade: snake skins, tiny rodent skulls, bird nests, and other show 'n' tell items.

Helen came out of the kitchen smiling, with a mug of coffee in her hand and a towel around her head.

"Get you a cup?" she asked Martha cheerily, holding the mug toward her.

"No thanks. I'm already caffeinated." Martha tried to sound upbeat, but was struggling. Something in her voice must have given her away because Helen's brows furrowed.

"Everything all right?" she asked, setting down her mug and picking up a very happy Penny.

"Can we sit down, Helen?" asked Martha.

"Uh oh. Is she going to say she's just not that into me, girl?" Helen laughed, nuzzling the little dog's neck.

"Actually, I do need to talk to you about something," said Martha, trying to sound more confident than she felt. *If this is a wild goose chase, I could lose a valuable friend and employee.*

The two women sat down, Helen in an easy chair and Martha on the overstuffed futon couch.

"What is it?" asked Helen, seeming to grasp Martha's somber mood and putting Penny down on the floor. She also removed the towel from her hair and ran her fingers through it nervously.

Martha reached into the pocket of her cords and withdrew the sticky note she'd surreptitiously removed from Imbroglio's computer the night before. She un-crumpled it and handed it over to Helen.

"What's this?" Helen asked.

"I'm hoping you'll tell me," replied Martha. "I found it at Cenzo Imbroglio's used car business, stuck to his computer. Last night. When I found him dead in his office. Strangled."

"*What?*" said Helen. Her wide eyes locked on the paper and Martha watched as the color drained from her face. Martha had easily memorized the three short lines of handwriting: HELEN BIRD LADY (top line), $5,000 (middle line), BIRD PAINT-ING (third line).

"Why did Imbroglio have a note about you stuck to his computer, Helen? What's the $5,000 and what's the bird painting?"

"Why do you assume that's me?" asked Helen, smoothing the note down against the thigh of her cargo pants. "It could be some other person... I don't know. Why would you think I even *know* him?"

Martha watched as Helen's neck blushed a deep red, the color rising up into her cheeks.

"I don't know, Helen. But this is a pretty small place and I'm sure there's only one 'bird lady' named Helen in town. After all, you work on the *bird* side of a *bird* lovers' coffee shop and you lead *birding* walks. Kinda makes you a unique Helen." Martha heard an unfamiliar peevishness in her voice that came from sheer exhaustion combined with stress. Still, if Helen knew something, Martha intended to find out what that was. "How did you know Imbroglio?"

Helen struggled for one last moment, then glanced at the window, as if hoping someone would come to the door and stall this conversation. Tears had formed in the rims of her eyes.

"Oh, all right. All right, all right!" Her voice rose as she stood up from her chair and paced the room, giving in to the inevitable. "I didn't actually know him until recently. That man is—was—horrible! He came here after Sentrich died, making demands and threats. You can't tell Don. You just can't!"

Martha shook her head. "Helen, tell me what he wanted. Tell me about the $5,000 and the painting. What *is* this all about?" She was close now. She could feel it.

"It was Sentrich, to begin with," said Helen, slumping back into the chair with tears streaming down her face. "He started all of it."

Martha softened. This was one of her aunt's best friends and she was in crisis. She reached over and squeezed Helen's hand.

"Helen," she said in a much softer voice, "just tell me. It will be OK. Remember what Aunt Lorna always said? A problem shared is a problem halved?"

The tears spilled from the other woman's eyes. "Oh, Martha, if only you were right. What I've done... I can't undo." Helen was quiet for a few moments, trying to calm herself—or brace herself to share her story. "I can never make it right with your aunt."

"Make what right?" Martha gently probed.

"Nothing, directly. When Sentrich first came to me... I don't know how he knew. Well, I guess I know now, but I didn't back then. It was he who found out I had the mockingbird."

Something clicked in Martha's mind. "The mockingbird? You mean the lithograph?"

"Yes. You see, several months back, I offered to pop over to Lorna's cottage to get some work invoices she'd left there. You know she always left her cottage unlocked, so it was no problem getting in. Anyway, this was weeks after the big blowout with

Ethel Jean about the lithographs. We'd all heard it. I drove over and let myself in, and there they were, sitting on her open secretary. They were such a discovery, Martha!

"Heaven help me, but I picked up the mockingbird along with the papers she wanted, and simply put it in the trunk of my car. I said to myself she'd never miss the one print, and she didn't! She never said a word. No one did, until you brought the other two to the store last week and Ethel Jean noticed the missing third print. She told me about it the next day, since she was still upset and she knew *I* could appreciate how valuable they were."

"But in that case, how did Sentrich find out you had it?" Martha asked.

"When he confronted me at the store and said he knew I had it, I connected the dots. It was Cherry." Helen shook her head, the misery on her face showing the heavy weight she'd been carrying.

"Cherry? His ex-girlfriend?" asked Martha.

"Yes," Helen replied. "When Don and I got busy with the leaf-peeping crowds early in the fall, we asked Cherry to help us with a few cleaning chores at the campground and here in the house." She gestured around the room with her head. "Cherry must have seen the print and told Sentrich."

"But how would Sentrich have known that the picture was important?" asked Martha.

"Are you kidding me? Everyone knew, after Ethel Jean went so crazy. For a while, she would rant about it at Silent Sisters so loudly, everyone could hear. She went on and on about the mockingbird, how valuable it could be, and so on. And you have to understand, Sentrich was around the store on and off back then. He'd come in to do some light repairs, wash up, help move bags of beans or run other errands for Lorna. He could be a slacker one minute, a hard worker the next. We were all a little wary of him, but Lorna had taken him on as her pet project and there was no talking her out of it."

"Helen, I really don't understand why you took the print in the first place. You know Lorna would have given it to you had she known you wanted it."

"That's the worst part of it. I *know* you're right. And I can't explain it. But something in me saw this as my opportunity. *Finally*, I had something to contribute to the world of birding, something unique and special of my own. This might be the one chance I would ever have! I know it sounds crazy now, but at the time, it was as if destiny had taken me to Lorna's house and *given* me that print.

"While I was still struggling with what to do, several weeks after I'd taken it, Sentrich confronted me on a quiet day in the store. He said he knew I had it and wanted $5,000 to keep it quiet that I'd stolen it. I told him that was extortion."

"Is that worse than theft?" Martha asked, surprised to hear the words come out of her mouth.

"I know, I know. As soon as I took it home, I knew I'd made a mistake. Don kept asking me what was wrong, but I just told him we were busy at the store and I was stressed—but I couldn't figure out what to do. I mean, Don and I don't have a spare $5,000 just sitting around and I didn't know how to return the print and tell Lorna what I'd done. I was so ashamed.

"I avoided Sentrich at the store and he never came back to me to demand the money. Then, one day, several weeks later, I was in the alley putting trash in the dumpster when he came out to talk to me. I was sure this was the moment he'd say he was going to tell Lorna. But instead, he told me to forget the conversation we'd had as if it had never happened."

"He didn't want the $5,000?" asked Martha.

"Exactly. He seemed... different somehow. Apologetic and embarrassed that he'd ever asked me for it. That clinched it for me. You see, that's when I knew he'd told Lorna I had it. Who else could have talked Sentrich out of blackmailing me? I was determined to put the print back with the others, then somehow find the courage to confess to her and hope that our friendship—never mind my job at the shop—could somehow survive what I'd done."

Martha remembered Helen's name appearing on the list attached to Lorna's fridge and nodded slightly. Was the list linked to Lorna's association with Sentrich? Probably. It would have been so characteristic of Lorna to have known all along what Helen had done, but put friendship above possessions and forgiven Helen for her lapse of reason, whether or not Helen confessed.

Helen went on speaking. "But before I could get back into Lorna's house, she died. The police locked the house up afterwards—I know because I went over one night to put the print back—and then you arrived and have been locking the doors ever since. The whole thing has been a nightmare, and I'll never be able to make up for what I've done. She was one of my best friends and never even confronted me about stealing from her."

Martha was quiet for a few moments, then made up her mind. "Helen, the important thing is that you realized you made a mistake and had planned to make it right. It's over now. I'm sure Aunt Lorna would have forgiven you once the two of you talked it through."

"No, it's not! Can't you see?" Helen got up again and paced the wooden floor. "A few days ago, Imbroglio drove through the campground. He stopped at the camp office, claiming to want to rent a campsite. I happened to be there and helped him at the counter. At one point, he quietly said to me, 'The $5,000 still stands. You need to get it to me. And soon.' Martha, I tell you, I was afraid of that man."

Martha nodded. "You don't have to explain that to me. I've had a few run-ins with him and he scared the heck out of me too. But he's dead now so you don't have anything to worry about."

As soon as the words were out of her mouth, Martha froze, grasping their significance. Helen nodded.

"Exactly. I become a prime suspect in his murder if the police find out he was blackmailing me."

"Nonsense," said Martha, trying to make the woman feel better, at the same time realizing the only way the police would find out about the blackmail was if she was the one to tell them. She blinked that thought away as a new question occurred to her. "Helen, why did Nathan say he'd seen you at the book stall out at the flea market the other day? He seemed pretty certain."

Helen heaved a heavy sigh. "He was right. I was there. I was hoping to slip the lithograph in between some books and leave it there for someone to find, but there were too many people and I ended up just bringing it back home. I guess I'm a pretty pathetic thief."

"You're not a thief," Martha said. "You're just someone who made a big mistake, and then had a terrible time undoing it. You're also someone who was being blackmailed."

Blackmail, she thought. This was the second time she'd heard about Sentrich threatening to blackmail someone. PJ had also mentioned it, but Martha hadn't thought any more about it. But could Sentrich have threatened to blackmail the wrong person and gotten himself killed?

Chapter Twenty-Five

Martha left the campground with the lithograph lying on the backseat. Helen insisted she take it and seemed relieved to be rid of it. Martha briefly admired the workmanship, but her mind was far too focused to spend much time looking at it. There was some link between Sentrich and Imbroglio in life and in death. Allison had said as much last night, and now Helen had confirmed it.

Should I go to the police? she wondered. She briefly toyed with the idea of going straight to the station to feed all of this new information to Allison or Detective Perry while making her statement, but realized in a flash that would likely guarantee Helen would become a suspect in Imbroglio's strangling. But there was one person who might know more, if only Martha could ask the right questions.

Martha pulled off into a clearing next to the river and rummaged in her backpack for a moment before coming up with the neon orange traffic citation with Cherry's number on it. Hoping against hope that she could get a good cell signal, she called the number.

"Hello?" a cautious voice sounded.

"Cherry, it's me, Martha Sloane. We met at the farmers' market and I visited with you last week."

"Oh, yes, hi there. Why are you calling me?"

"Well, I had some more questions for you, but I heard you left town. Are you coming back?"

"No way," said Cherry, sounding close to tears.

"Cherry, are you all right? Has something happened?"

"I'm fine, do you hear me? *Fine.*" Cherry was clearly not fine.

"Listen, Cherry, I don't want to bother you, but the guy you told me about—the car guy that Curtis was hanging around with, Cenzo Imbroglio—well, I found him dead last night. I know there was a connection between them and my aunt and I'm trying to figure out what that connection was."

There was silence on the other end.

"Please, Cherry," Martha went on. "I'm like you. I just want to get out of here and get on with my life. But I can't do it without clearing my aunt's name. Tons of money has gone missing from her accounts over the last months and I need to prove that she wasn't involved in anything illegal. Please. Is there anything you can tell me about Curtis and Imbroglio and my aunt? Anything at all? I just came from Helen's and know about the bird lithograph. Does that have anything to do with this whole thing?" Martha heard the desperation in her own voice, but she was going in circles without more information.

After a pause, Martha heard Cherry let out a long breath. "Your aunt," she said, "was the salt of the earth. You shouldn't let anyone say anything different." She paused. "OK, I lied about some stuff when I talked to you before. I told you I didn't know where the money was coming from. It was coming from her, from your aunt. She was the one giving Curtis all that money he was saving."

"What?" Martha asked, confused. "I mean, I know she was paying him to do odd jobs around the shop and her house..." her voice trailed off. What did a glorified honey-do list have to do with the tens of thousands of dollars that had gone missing?

Cherry's voice was impatient. "Don't you understand? She was giving him money to make him stop *taking* money from people. She found out about the scam Curtis was running. Well, to be honest, the scam I was accidentally helping him run. Look, I could get in big trouble for this." The young woman sounded as if she might hang up the phone. Martha knew she had to keep her talking, no matter what. Cherry held the key to the whole thing.

"Look, Cherry, I'm not interested in anything you did. I just want to know how my aunt was involved. I don't even know where you are and I'm not involving the police. Please, tell me what you know so I can finish this thing and get out of here too."

This seemed to touch a nerve with Cherry. "Fine," she said, "but I'm going to tell you, and then get off the phone. And please don't call me again. I won't answer."

Martha didn't doubt her for a second. "Deal," she said.

"Well, at the beginning, the two of them—Curtis and Imbroglio—had started a scam. Curtis would come over while I was cleaning people's houses and nose around, finding out little embarrassing details, and then contact the people to blackmail them into giving him money.

"It was Imbroglio's idea, so he had been making Curtis give him half of anything he was able to get out of people. It was mostly small stuff, like folks who had dirty movies hidden at the back of their bookshelves. But it paid well, apparently.

"I told Curtis I wanted out of it as soon as I found out what they were up to. He told me to hang on, that they had something really big on your aunt and planned to cash in soon, and then he'd have enough for us to leave town and start our new business-es. He promised we were going to be 100% legit."

Martha took this all in, desperately trying to think what Lorna had to hide that would be worth so much money.

"But when your aunt hired Curtis to do odd jobs for her, something changed," Cherry continued. "He started talking about going straight, setting up his own garage, leaving Riley Creek, and really making something of himself. I could hardly believe it! Somehow, your aunt believed in him, had him thinking he could be somebody else. He talked more and more about getting away from Imbroglio. He actually told your aunt about the whole scam, except for the part that involved her, and she didn't go to the cops. She didn't seem to hold it against him at all."

Martha was not surprised. For the second time that morning, she realized it was exactly like Lorna not to judge someone and, in Sentrich's case, to help them see themselves as she did.

"But why didn't you and he just leave?" she asked. "Tell Imbroglio it was over and head out of town?"

Cherry laughed cynically. "Martha, you obviously don't know what it is like not to have anything, no family you can lean on, nowhere else you can land. Curtis had to save up, think of where to go, figure out how to take his grandma along, all of that. Trust me; it takes a lot to plan out a whole new life. We'd never done it before. But he and Lorna made a deal; if he stopped blackmailing townspeople, she would give him the money to keep Imbroglio off his back, and at the same time pay him to help her out around the shop and house. And give him some more on top of that to save toward his own business."

This must have been around the time that he told Helen to forget about the $5,000, Martha realized.

"But Imbroglio was so angry, threatening Curtis to get more 'business,' as he called it. He'd stopped coming around my clients' houses by this time. Eventually, Lorna started giving Curtis more and more money to satisfy Imbroglio. Nobody ever said, but I got the feeling from Curtis it was starting to get really hard for your aunt financially. Plus, she was getting confused. She wasn't sure how much money she had left and how much she'd given Curtis. It was weird."

You can say that again, thought Martha.

"But where *is* all that money she gave Curtis?" she asked.

"Well, some of it is in this car I'm sitting in," said Cherry, sheepishly. "The rest, I don't know. See, part of what I told you was true. I really thought Curtis was distancing himself from Imbroglio and the whole scene he represented. But when I spotted him at Car Man that last time, I put two and two together and realized he'd paid that creep some of your aunt's hard-earned money to buy me this car. And that they might still be planning to extort money from your aunt. That was the last straw for me."

"But what could they possibly have planned to blackmail my aunt about?" Martha persisted. "And why did you suddenly leave town?"

"Curtis would never tell me. I honestly don't know. But whatever it was, it was tearing him up. Before we broke up, he wasn't sleeping at night and was constantly stressed about it. He did ask me one time what kind of lowlife I thought he was for taking money from the one person who'd ever helped him get ahead. It was weird.

"As for why I left town, a couple nights back, Imbroglio showed up at my room, demanding I start working the blackmail scam with him like I did with Curtis. I said sure, pretended I'd do it, just to get him to leave. That night, I packed up and left town. I knew going into business with him would get me the same thing it got Curtis."

"Are you saying he killed Curtis, Cherry?" asked Martha, holding her breath.

"I don't know if he did or not. But I know being involved with him had something to do with Curtis getting killed."

Martha could hear the young woman's breath catch in a soft sob. She had a million more questions, but before she could ask one, Cherry cleared her throat.

"Look, Martha, I gotta go. I've told you all I know, and I really just want to put as much distance between myself and Riley Creek as I can. I want to help you, but I've probably already said more than I should. Bye."

With a click, the line went dead.

Chapter Twenty-Six

Martha weaved her way back to town, one hand on the steering wheel and the other on the sleeping terrier, the feel of Penny's wiry fur connecting her to the here and now while her mind spun in a thousand directions. She needed to sort this all out, get her head organized somehow. She was beginning to piece together the mystery of her aunt's money and the two murders, but she had to calm down in order to make sense of it all.

Back at the cottage, before making lunch, she lay down on the couch to think through the morning. Her conversation with Helen had been emotionally draining and the phone call with Cherry bewildering. The whole thing seemed so far-fetched. How had Aunt Lorna let things get so bad without telling the police? Or telling Martha? She could have helped if only she'd known that Imbroglio was blackmailing Lorna and she'd gotten in too deep.

She called the police station, claiming she'd not slept well and would need to come in later to give her statement. Then she remained where she was on the couch, certain that if she just focused, like Hercule Poirot, she could pull all of the threads together into a stunning revelation.

Two hours later, she woke up, shocked that she'd fallen asleep on the couch. She let Penny out, and then, after settling the little schnauzer in her bed, snatched up her pack and headed for Birds 'n' Beans. Martha arrived just at the end of what, by Riley Creek standards, was a rush. A gaggle of hikers was making its last purchases of bags of coffee and bird-themed bandanas. As they trickled out, Martha placed her pack in a chair at one of the tables, waved to PJ and Helen, then went to the counter to help herself to an egg salad sandwich with a bag of chips. Dropping her lunch at the table, she went to put her money in the cash register, then poured herself a nice cup of coffee on the way back to her table.

She wolfed the sandwich and chips down in record time, and as she sipped the coffee, she could feel her clarity of mind returning. *Wow*, she thought, looking down into the cup of Sumatran Migration. *PJ is right about this. It is good for ruminating!*

She watched a piggish red-bellied woodpecker make a complete mess of a feeder out in the back, wondering if that was how she'd looked diving into her bag of chips. Not particularly in the mood for company, Martha picked up her coffee and went out to sit at one of the patio benches, watch the birds, and be alone inside her own head to consider what she'd learned from talking to Helen and Cherry.

In partnership with Imbroglio, Sentrich had been running a scam on residents of Riley Creek. He got access to their homes through Cherry's cleaning business, then figured out ways to blackmail them. But Aunt Lorna had convinced him to work for her. Had they met when he'd started to blackmail her? Over time, he'd rethought his life. She gave him money to keep Imbroglio at bay and even helped him with seed money toward his future. Things were looking up for him, but then Aunt Lorna died and he was murdered a few days later.

Now Martha knew where all the money had gone, one thing that was bothering her was how Aunt Lorna—a woman who had managed her own finances most of her adult life—had gotten in so far over her head. But something Cherry had said helped make sense of it; she'd mentioned that Martha's aunt had started getting really confused. This must have been the dementia Detective Perry had told Martha about. Aunt Lorna might have gotten so stressed and confused, she couldn't keep all of the credits and debits straight. Martha thought about the portfolio of statements she'd found. Everything had been in one place, but it had been a mess.

Who had killed Sentrich and Imbroglio? And why? Someone they'd blackmailed who killed them in revenge? Someone who couldn't risk having them around?

Martha did a virtual roll call of her suspects. First up; Jason Turngate. Not really a serious suspect anymore. Jason had fought with Sentrich, but had not even been acquainted with Imbroglio, as far as Martha knew.

Next; Octavius Bennett. While Mr. Bennett was certainly unusual and had been seen arguing with Sentrich, he didn't seem to know Imbroglio. Also, did he have the strength to whack someone over the head or strangle them if he couldn't even handle a sandwich board? Not likely at all.

And she couldn't discount Cherry. *Sherry*, she corrected herself. Was her earnestness just a ruse to cover a darker side? Was she so eager to get out of Riley Creek that she'd kill instead of return the car, her only means of escape? And did Imbroglio's demand for her to be in cahoots with him drive her to the brink? More conceivable than Mr. Bennett, surely, but still iffy. Plus according to Donna, Cherry had been out of town by the time of Imbroglio's murder.

Finally, Carl, the sweet, dedicated family man. He'd done jail time, sure, but why would he risk everything he had to murder Sentrich and Imbroglio? Maybe that old saying about still waters running deep was true and this was a case of an ex-felon who couldn't stay on the right side of the law. But Martha couldn't see it. It would ruin his family's lives.

Martha was frustrated. She wasn't a detective. She had some ideas and some possible motives, but nothing was falling together to make her *sure*. Who would have benefited from killing both Sentrich and Imbroglio?

As she sat pondering, Mary Jane came out of the shop door and plunked down on the bench next to her.

"Phew!" she said, puffing out her cheeks. Looking pink and winded, she held what Martha guessed was an iced mocha in her hand.

"Rough lesson at the yoga studio?" asked Martha.

"Not even close. Still recovering from my morning at An Early Riser. The Adair Scout Troop had a fundraiser to pay for new bat boxes at the DLT and I helped them box up nearly three hundred dozen cookies this morning. Yoga would have been way easier."

"After last night, you had the presence of mind to box cookies?" It was all Martha could do this morning to get out of bed; it wasn't every night you found a dead body. But she took the opportunity to nose around one of her suspects. "How did Carl seem?" she asked casually, checking her cuticles.

"Oh, poor Carl! I guess you haven't heard. He and Lewis spent most of yesterday afternoon and evening in the emergency room at the hospital. Lewis had an accident with their delivery truck right around dinner time and apparently broke his wrist.

He and Carl didn't get home until after midnight, so Cat had to come in early this morning to prep most everything for the scouts."

"But that's great!" said Martha, lighting up for what felt like the first time in forever.

"Great?"

"Don't you *see*?" Martha turned sideways on the bench and gestured excitedly as she explained. "If Carl was at the ER from lunchtime to midnight, he couldn't have been murdering Imbroglio. And as the police are saying the same person killed both him and Sentrich, then Carl is totally off the hook."

"Oh, but that's wonderful!" said Mary Jane. "And speaking of Imbroglio, now you're off the hook, too. No more worries about him creeping around, threatening you."

"I know, Mary Jane, but there's still a murderer creeping around, and my aunt's name is mixed up in it thanks to Sentrich being found dead in her yard. But I'd be lying if I said I didn't feel a *little* relieved."

"Well, I think you should stop worrying about all this and let the professionals handle it," Mary Jane said, slapping her thighs and standing up. "I'm off to get a nap in before going to the library to see Delores and pick up a pile of mysteries she's been holding for me. How about you?"

"I told PJ I'd do the roasting tonight after we close. I need the practice."

"All right," said Mary Jane. "You have a good night and call me if you need me. And no more dead bodies, please!" She added a finger shake and was off.

Martha stood, stretched, and headed into the shop. There she emptied coffee urns, washed dishes, and inventoried binoculars until the last customer left. She walked PJ to the door, promised to call him if she had any problems with the temperamental roaster, locked up and pulled the blinds. The mourning dove on the clock gave eight *oo-oo-oo*s to tell her it was time for her very first solo roast.

A few hours later, Martha was in the thick of it and having the time of her life. The roaster was rattling on full blast, the smell of crackling beans was in the air, and Martha was stripped down to her t-shirt and jeans with a bandana head wrap keeping her hair out of her eyes. She had successfully bagged and labeled an entire fifty pounds of Birder Blend and was quizzing herself on the difference between fish crows and American crows when she heard a loud knock on the backdoor.

That's strange, she thought, going to the door. *Who would knock at this time of night?*

But it was just Mavis.

"Hey, Mavis, what's up?" Martha said, opening the door wide to let the smaller woman in.

"Oh, I was passing through and saw the lights on and thought I'd check in on you. I bumped into Mary Jane a bit ago and she said you'd be here roasting. Can I give you a hand?"

Martha thought quickly. She preferred to work solo to concentrate on PJ's instructions, but it felt unfriendly to turn down Mavis's offer.

"Sure," she said. "I need to carry a few bags of beans over to the roaster if you'd like to help."

Mavis took off the gym bag that had been strapped across her small frame. As she set it on one of the swivel chairs at the counter, a yoga strap with a D-ring like the ones Martha had seen at Ohm Mama flopped out of its top. Mavis tucked it back in and turned to Martha.

Fanning herself with her hand, she said, "Whew! Sure is warm in here."

"Yep," responded Martha. "That's why we only roast after closing. It's too stuffy otherwise." She turned to the bags of beans piled near the front of the shop while Mavis took off the knee-length puffy coat she'd had on over yoga pants and a tank top. Mavis walked over to where Martha stood next to one of the fifty pound bags, bent down and picked the whole thing up, her biceps flexing impressively as she hoisted it up onto to her shoulder.

"Wow!" Martha said, impressed. *Maybe I do need to take up yoga.*

"Where to?" Mavis asked.

"Right over here," answered Martha, gesturing to a spot on the floor under the large chute where she fed the beans into the machine.

As Martha cut open the bag with a pocketknife, Mavis said, "So, I suppose you'll be heading back to Boston soon?"

"Well, that's the million-dollar question," Martha responded, scooping the light colored beans into the machine, then wiping the back of her arm across her sweaty face. "I suppose I have to make some decisions soon."

"I guess I figured with all the money Lorna must have left you, you'd sell up and head home with your pockets bulging," Mavis said, laughingly. Martha felt surprised by the thoughtlessness of the question.

"It's not quite that simple, Mavis. Things are a lot more complicated here than I'd understood. Including the financial pieces."

Mavis snorted derisively. "I doubt you're exactly struggling. From what I've heard, Lorna was handing out money hand over fist before she died."

"*Excuse me?*" Martha stood facing Mavis, sure she'd either misheard or misunderstood the small woman as the noise of the roaster increased in pitch. "What are you talking about?"

"I knew Sentrich, and from what he told me, she'd been giving him cash for months. He said they'd stashed it around her house. It's too bad she wasn't as generous with *all* of her friends."

"Mavis, I'm not sure what you're talking about, but I'm thinking maybe I ought to finish this roasting myself. I appreciate your help, but..." Martha trailed off, hoping the other woman would get the message.

"Oh, you're going to be finished, all right. As soon as you tell me where to find that cash." Mavis had backed up to her bag and now reached behind her, drawing out the yoga strap Martha had glimpsed earlier. Flashes of images came together in her mind: the strap, Mavis's bulging biceps, and the O imprinted on Imbroglio's neck.

Martha put her hands out in front of her. "Mavis, I don't know a thing about Sentrich, his money, or anything else. Why don't we—"

"*Shut up!*" Mavis snapped. "I know what you're up to, so don't play dumb with me. You know all about Linc and you're planning to tell your cute little policeman boyfriend and everyone else in this stupid village, if you haven't already. I just want that money, and then I'll be on my way. Who knows? I may not even kill you. Now drop the knife and go up the stairs. Slowly." She held up the strap, tightening it between her two hands.

"You're going to kill me, like you killed Imbroglio? And Sentrich?" Martha said, surprised to hear the force behind her own voice. Perspiration was dripping down her sides and her heart pounded in her chest. She did as Mavis demanded and dropped the knife on the floor by the beans, doubting she was any match for Mavis's strength anyway.

They moved toward the stairs, Mavis staying within arm's reach of Martha's neck as she spoke. "Give me a break. I put Sentrich out of his misery, the sniveling little coward. He went soft once he started hanging around sweet little Lorna. Made me sick. I gave him the keys to the kingdom, but thanks to Lorna and that girlfriend of his, he lost his nerve." These last words, Mavis practically spat out. "He decided he didn't want to play anymore. So I kicked him out of the game. But then Imbroglio decided *he* was in charge and was going to get me to pay up. That didn't work out so well for him."

Now they were walking up the stairs, Martha going as slowly as she could while trying to figure out what to do. Then she heard Helen's voice calling from the shop.

"Hey, Martha, it's only me. Where are you? Just stopped in... handful of the laminated bird checklists... hike tomorrow." The roar of the roaster made some of Helen's words fade out.

Mavis had the strap around Martha's neck in a flash, pulling it tight, but not tight enough to cut off her air supply completely.

"Get rid of her. *NOW*," she hissed into Martha's ear.

Martha realized how easily Mavis could suffocate her. She cleared her throat as well as she could once Mavis eased up on the strap.

"I'm up here," she called, trying to be a combination of breezy and telepathic. *Help me!* her brain cried out. "Just finishing up. Oh, Helen, be sure to take Ethel Jean the scented candles she wanted for her place—one bluebird and two blue jays."

A pause, and then they heard Helen yell back, "Got it! See you tomorrow." As the backdoor slammed closed, Martha's heart sank.

"Get going," Mavis said, the strap still around Martha's neck as she coaxed her up the remaining steps. They reached the top and went into the room with the metal shelves holding extra supplies for the shop, where Mavis removed the strap from around Martha's neck. But Martha's relief was short-lived as the muscular woman shoved her into the room and stood between her and her only means of escape, the strap held firmly in her hands.

"Look, Mavis, I have no idea what this is all about. Just leave me alone and I'll head back to Boston, no questions asked." Martha hated the desperation in her voice, but she was… desperate.

Mavis rolled her eyes. "Don't play dumb with me. I was buying that stupid bird book for you when I heard Margaret say you were trying to get more information about Carville. You just had to nose around about Linc, didn't you?"

Martha was simultaneously confused and afraid. "Mavis, I have no idea about Linc, except that I think he was your brother—"

"You obviously *know* he was my brother. You know all about Carville, and you're going to spread it all around and ruin me. Who's going to come to a yoga studio run by someone with *that* in their family? Well, that's not going to happen. I've worked too hard."

Mavis raised the strap and stepped forward toward Martha.

"No more chit chat. It's time to tell me where Sentrich squirreled away that money. Or else you're going to decide life is just *a little too hard* and hang yourself from one of those." Mavis gestured up with her chin at the ancient copper pipes that ran in all directions along the exposed brick ceiling. Then she advanced quickly. Martha put her hands up in front of her face to fend off the strap.

One of the sets of metal shelves came tumbling down with a crash, scattering paper goods everywhere. Ethel Jean and Helen came charging through the door hidden behind it, red-faced and wild-eyed.

Helen aimed a can of bear spray at Mavis and screamed, "Martha, close your eyes!" Mavis pivoted smoothly on one foot and lunged toward Helen, dropping the strap and extending her strong arms. A short "PSSHHHTT" sounded and a cloud of red spray hit Mavis full in the face. She dropped as if she'd hit a wall and began screaming, fists wrenching her scalded eyes.

Then Ethel Jean looked at Martha with raised eyebrows.

"Scented candles? Really?"

Chapter Twenty-Seven

The late afternoon felt clear and crisp, the fading sun promising a bitterly cold night. Some eager shopkeepers had begun to string winter lights on their shopfronts. More cars than usual for this time of year were parked around the square, and a slow trickle of people headed excitedly toward A Toad in a Hole. The rickety old sandwich board that Martha had helped Mr. Bennett with all those weeks ago had been draped in wild grapevine.

Author signing today at five! it announced in trendy chalk lettering.

Martha finished wiping down a few tables, restocked the coffee stirrers at the to-go station, then took off her apron and popped it into the hamper. Checking the bird clock—*that blessed, blessed bird clock*, she thought—she saw that the titmouse was soon going to deliver its scolding five o'clock call.

Helen came out from behind the counter just as PJ descended from upstairs. Helen, predictably, was still in her birding attire with the addition of a parka, while PJ had changed into a black velvet pants suit and had applied a little more makeup than usual.

"Everyone ready?" he asked Helen and Martha.

Martha told them to go on. "Teddy is swinging by to walk over with me," she added.

"Teddy?" Helen had raised an eyebrow.

"Yes. You know, Detective Perry," Martha said. Helen and PJ exchanged a look, and then both nodded their heads, approving the escort.

A few minutes after they'd exited the shop door, the tall man came ambling along the sidewalk. Martha let him in as she gathered up her bag. As they stood just inside the door, Martha paused and looked out the large picture window toward Toad in a Hole.

"You OK?" Teddy asked, peering at her with concern in his dark eyes.

"It's just so odd, you know?" reflected Martha. "All the people in town who'd been blackmailed by Sentrich. Even after Aunt Lorna got involved with him and tried to put a stop to it all, no one came forward. Helen; Mr. Bennett and Margaret; other shopkeepers in the square. Carl, for heaven's sake. They'd even tried it on PJ! And no one told the police."

"Well, I guess everyone has secrets they're desperate to keep, even from their closest friends and loved ones."

Martha reflected on the friends and acquaintances who'd come forward in the wake of Imbroglio's death and the revelations about Mavis. Imbroglio had threatened to tell the whole village about Carl's prison time, so Carl had been paying him (through Sentrich) for months until the young man suddenly told him he didn't have to pay anymore. Mr. Bennett and Margaret had also admitted Sentrich had been blackmailing them—for reasons Martha now understood.

Others who had employed Cherry to help with light cleaning in their homes came forward to tell the police that Sentrich had successfully cashed in on their secrets as well. Some reported that he'd paid them back, Martha assumed with money provided by Lorna. Allison had surreptitiously shared some of their names with her, and all matched the names listed on the scrap of paper on Lorna's fridge.

Martha had been kept in the hospital for observation the night Mavis attacked her at the shop. A few weeks later, she'd been lying on the couch reading, watchful Penny curled up in her bed near the crackling fire, when there was a soft knock on the door. It was Delores and Jimmy. They'd sat together, drinking coffee.

"I've talked to Allison and the police have started to make sense of things," Martha had said. "Mavis is trying to position herself as a victim in hopes that it will cut down on her jail time. Apparently, Mavis was the first person Sentrich and Imbroglio tried to extort money from. They thought that because she'd started a yoga studio, she'd have piles of money sitting around. But, as she's now told the police, her whole story about living in India was a lie. Really, she'd been married to a small-time crook for years. When he was finally sent to prison, she was left high and dry and returned here to Riley Creek with just enough money to open the studio. But it was not doing well, so she needed money as badly as Sentrich and Imbroglio did. So much so that she saw the beauty in their extortion scheme and helped them to take the idea of blackmailing villagers even further. In exchange for a cut of the profits, of course."

Martha went on to explain how Mavis had come up with the idea for Sentrich to go through the homes Cherry was cleaning. Based on what he'd find, Mavis would then design a bespoke blackmail scheme. Hidden love letters? Blackmail the spouse to whom they were written. Articles of pornography? Easy. Find invoices from doctors about a hidden health condition? Old bankruptcy documents? Even easier. Mavis seemed to have a knack for using the documents Sentrich found in a way that exposed the victims' most carefully guarded secrets—secrets they would pay to keep hidden.

"Mavis and Imbroglio believed Sentrich had successfully been getting the victims to pay up. But right after Lorna's passing, Sentrich met with Mavis behind the cottage and said he was done with their scam. He said that it had been dead in the water for months anyway as Lorna had been the one making the payments, and that he was leaving town with his grandma soon. I guess he thought it was Imbroglio, not Mavis, he had to be careful with. He begged her not to tell Imbroglio, but as soon as he turned away, Mavis grabbed the scope and pounded him over the head with it. It was chilly out so she already had gloves on to cover up any fingerprints."

"But how did she just so happen to have the scope to hand?" Delores had asked.

"Realizing how valuable it was, Mavis had had no difficulty entering Lorna's cottage and helping herself to the scope. Suspecting Sentrich might be about to say something she didn't want to hear, she also recognized its potential as a weapon, took it with her and hid it in the bushes before her meeting with him. Who would suspect an elderly yoga practitioner of being a thief? Or a murderous blackmailer, for that matter. With her upper body strength, it was easy for her to dispatch her reformed 'business partner.' And just like that, Sentrich became forever silent."

Martha sipped her coffee before continuing. "When Imbroglio came in to Birds 'n' Beans and tried to continue the blackmail scheme they had been running against Aunt Lorna, Mavis was sitting right there. She must have realized he was going to try to take over the whole scam and cut her out. So, sometime during the evening of the owl prowl, she slipped into the used car lot, strangled him with a yoga strap, and disappeared. Easy peasy. No more partners to worry about and no one suspecting her of a thing."

Delores wrinkled her brow. "But what was she blackmailing Lorna about?"

"I'm not sure that will ever become totally clear," Martha responded. OK, she wasn't telling the whole truth, but she wasn't being totally dishonest in her response, either. "But I do know what made Mavis come after me. She overheard Margaret at the bookstore talking to me on the phone about Carville and assumed from the conversation that I knew about her brother. See, the police did some digging in old medical records and found out Lincoln had been diagnosed with leprosy—Hansen's disease—right after high school."

"Carville?"

"Yes. The location of the country's national leprosarium from the early 1900s, it was still the largest treatment center for the disease when Lincoln was diagnosed. As far as the police can tell, Mavis's whole family relocated there shortly after she graduated so they could be close to the very best facilities for his treatment. Mavis was desperately afraid of that news getting out and impacting her yoga studio. She was already having financial trouble, and then the money, which she now knew had been coming from Lorna, was ending. On top of that, she was sure that if locals found out she'd had a relative with such a horrible disease, they'd stop coming to the studio." Martha shook her head at the terrible sadness of it all.

"But why try to kill you?" Jimmy asked, his brow creased. "Hansen's disease is all but eradicated in this country, and it doesn't carry the social stigma that it would have back then. Why would Mavis have gone to such lengths to conceal it now?"

"I think I may know the answer to that, dear," said Delores. "At the time Lincoln was diagnosed, Hansen's disease *was* still misunderstood. I suspect Mavis and her family went to great lengths to conceal it, so she may never have quite grown out of that protective mindset."

"You know," Jimmy said reflectively, "Carville is just outside of New Orleans." The three took in his words quietly.

"I guess we all have skeletons in our closet," said Delores thoughtfully.

Truer words... thought Martha.

"Are you ready to head over?" Teddy asked. "I know you won't want to miss the big event."

"Yes, let's go. I wouldn't miss it for anything!" Martha flipped the sign to *CLOSED* just as the titmouse started its squawking and they made their way quickly across the square.

The inside of Toad in a Hole Bookshop had been transformed for the special occasion. Chairs had been arranged in rows in the center of the room, the tables that usually held books having been removed. A small area with a cash bar sat off to the side, with an hors d'oeuvres table next to it. Thirty or so people mingled, most of them recognizable to Martha.

"There's our secret weapon!" PJ yelled from across the room, making a bowling motion with his thick arm. Martha waved and parted from Teddy, who wandered over to the bar. Gathered in a small group were PJ, Ethel Jean, Mary Jane, Joanne and Helen. Leaning in, PJ said in a low voice, "My dears, I am so proud of our Margaret, but I hope this doesn't go on too long. We all have early practice tomorrow for the fall tournament."

"So it's true?" Joanne, who was decked out in enough purple to make an eggplant blush, looked expectantly at Martha. "You're staying?"

The group seemed to hold its collective breath.

"Well, yes. Yes, I am staying here in Riley Creek," Martha said, feeling something let go as she spoke the words aloud.

Just the day before, she'd sent her letter of resignation to the President of the college. So much had happened to make her change her mind about going back to her life in Boston. On one hand, her college was going to be all right without her. She'd definitely enjoyed her career there, but she was ready for something new. More importantly, after years and years of doing the *safe* thing, she felt she could step out of her comfort zone just a bit... and do it with the support of these new friends. And even though so many awful things had happened during her short time in Riley Creek, so many good things had happened, too. She'd picked up the operation of Birds 'n' Beans and had some ideas about ways to increase revenue. She'd cashed out her 401K and paid down some of the debt on the shop and most on the cottage, and she and Margaret had put together a plan to pay off the rest of it within five years. The bank had agreed.

Teddy walked up and handed her a glass of ginger ale with a cocktail napkin.

"They have some amazing scented candles in here," he said casually, glancing over at Ethel Jean. Martha and Helen both rolled their eyes.

"Ugh. I don't think I will ever feel the same about those two words," said Helen.

"Lucky for me you caught on fast," said Martha, shaking her head. They all knew the story by now of Martha's code to Helen, which only someone who knew Ethel Jean and Birds 'n' Beans could have deciphered. Not only would Ethel Jean scoff at the thought of owning scented candles, but on the shop's bird clock, one bluebird and two blue jays spelled out 9-1-1.

When Helen left the shop that fateful night, she headed right to Ethel Jean's apartment and told her Martha was in some kind of trouble. The two women ran right back to Silent Sisters, crept up the stairs and listened at the connecting door. Once they'd heard enough from Mavis to incriminate the woman, they burst in on the scene. The rest was *her*story.

An electrified puffing sounded at the front of the room. "Testing, testing," Mr. Bennett breathed into the microphone. Those assembled quickly took their seats. "Ladies and gentlemen, it is my pleasure to open our first—of many to come—Toad in a Hole author signing. This evening's guest author may not be new to our little shop, but she is quite new to the literary establishment. She wishes you to stay and enjoy your evening and the delicious treats supplied by our very own An Early Riser"—here everyone clapped, and Carl, sitting between Lewis and Cat, reddened up to his ears—"and she will be happy to sign copies of her new release *Love's Bitter Song.*"

He held up a hand in the direction of the table to the right of the podium where Margaret sat, dressed in black with a colorful corsage pinned to the breast of her jacket. Next to her were piles of her new book, which also filled the shop's display window. The book's cover, which featured an ample bosom and a chiseled jaw, left little to the imagination.

"That vixen!" hissed Ethel Jean. "All this time, our so-called mouse has been writing erotica."

"Stow it, sister," said Mary Jane, an uncharacteristic sharpness to her voice. "This is Margaret's day and we shall celebrate it with her."

Martha arrived home a few hours later, walking alone from the square to enjoy the cool breeze and give herself time to think over the perfect day. Detective Perry (*Teddy*, she corrected herself) had asked her to his place for dinner the next week, and the following day, after bowling practice, Helen was going to start teaching her about the many types of bulk bird food the shop carried. She had so much work ahead of her, but she also felt a lightness about her future that she hadn't experienced in a long time.

Penny greeted her eagerly and she popped into some comfortable jeans and a sweater. She opened the secretary and took out the curled envelope with her name on it that she'd found hidden in a wren house she'd been cleaning out a few days after Mavis's attack. A Ziploc bag, fat with cash, had accompanied the letter.

She stepped out to the front porch and sat down in the swing. The pages of the letter were just legible in the moonlight. The writing was clearly Lorna's, yet with a shaky edge that was uncharacteristic. It looked to have been written over multiple sittings, different pens used throughout. Martha had practically memorized it, but read it one more.

My dearest Martha,

If you are reading this letter, I suppose I have run into trouble. I don't write as well as I once did, but I'm going to work on this letter so that it's there if you need to find it.

I've met a young man named Curtis, ironically through his blackmailing of Riley Creek citizens, including myself. His business partners are two nasty characters, Mavis Settler and Cenzo Imbroglio. More about them momentarily.

Curtis has a poor reputation in Riley Creek, some of it earned and some of it not. His teachers and everyone else put him in a particular box and gave up on him. And he lived up to their low expectations. I know others struggle to believe it—some days I wonder if I totally believe it myself—but he wants something more for himself and his grandmother, and I am trying to help him. He reminds me in some small way of you, so determined to go it alone. Yet little by little, he has agreed to accept my help.

For some time, our little arrangement has worked. You might say I've been on a payment plan—just like Sears! I make two payments to Curtis each month: one to pay Mavis and Imbroglio to keep their silence and leave me and other Riley Creek folks alone, and the other to Curtis to reward his hard work and honesty and to help him save for a new future. He is keeping that money here in a plastic bag and has allowed me to place it with this letter for safekeeping.

The idea was that he'd save up enough money, then leave town to start anew, taking his grandmother with him. I would then go to the police and tell them everything: the scam, our counter-scam. And I'd tell you my secret that they've held over my head. Everything would be tied up with a bow and Curtis would be on his way. But things aren't working out as we'd planned.

You see, I've begun to lose track. I suppose this is part of what my doctor has told me is dementia. I know you'll find out about it sooner or later; PJ and Helen have begun to suspect something, I'm sure. The bank is telling me that I'm running low on money, so I can't keep this up much longer. Thank goodness PJ and Helen are running most everything at the shop, but soon I'll have to tell them what I've done.

The plan is now for Curtis to tell Mavis the whole thing: that we have been running a scam against her and Imbroglio these many months, but that it is over. He'll tell her that we aren't going to pay any more money, but neither will we go to the police, as long as she buys Curtis enough time to leave town. He's also going to tell her that the secret she's held over me has no more value; I'm going to tell you and all the girls about it. Curtis is convinced that Mavis will keep everything from Imbroglio long enough for him to leave with his grandmother. After all, she won't want Imbroglio to do anything that might draw attention from the police.

Just as it's time for Curtis to turn over a new leaf, so is it time for me to "come clean" as they say. Mavis and Imbroglio have been blackmailing me about something I did not want you or anyone else to discover. But Curtis has helped me see that there is no shame in one's life journey.

You see, Mavis's brother Lincoln and I had a relationship right after high school—long before your Uncle Tommy and I married and before Lincoln became ill and he and his family left for Louisiana. It was short but... meaningful. I became pregnant with a little girl, whom we allowed to be adopted. Given Lincoln's health matters and our young age, it was really the only decision we felt we could make. Suffice to say that I've been committed to this secret for so long, I lost perspective on the secret itself. But I am no longer ashamed and won't continue to let Mavis hold it over my head.

For a time, after your Uncle Tommy's passing, I even thought about trying to find Linc. I sent money to the foundation that used to run the clinic where he received treatment, and even traveled to the area several times to see if I might run into him. I just wanted to see him, to find out how he was. And perhaps ask him if we should try to find our little girl. But I never did run into him. Then, when your parents died, it's as if my decision was made for me. I knew it was time to stop living in the past. I focused all of my energy on providing for you.

But now that you have grown into such a sturdy and self-sufficient young woman, I know it's time for me to face my own secrets, to find Linc and our child. I just want to know that she, too, is well.

If you find this letter before I can tell you everything myself, it likely means something did not go as Curtis and I planned. If that happens, I know you'll see that this money gets to Curtis's grandma, and that you'll do as your heart tells you with the rest of what I've shared.

Love,

Aunt Lorna

Martha looked up from the letter and concentrated on the sounds of the night. *So many secrets*, she thought. She would get the money to Donna tomorrow. And she would continue trying to understand what this revelation meant for her life. But tonight, she would just sit here on Aunt Lorna's porch, like a Cooper's Hawk perched on a familiar branch, and keep on keepin' on.

About the Author

Mary Lucal is happy to be putting her English and Women's Studies double major to use, creating flawed yet brave female sleuths who get a little help from Mother Nature to solve mysteries. A university administrator by day, Mary resides in Tennessee and spends her free time birding, hiking, camping, biking, or gardening.

Please visit Mary at marylucal.com